Mankiller

Mankiller

Collin Wilcox

Random House: New York

Library of Congress Cataloging in Publication Data
Wilcox, Collin.
    Mankiller.
    I. Title.
PZ4.W665Man   [PS3573.I395]   813'.54   79–5548
ISBN 0–394–50550–6

Manufactured in the United States of America
9 8 7 6 5 4 3 2
First Edition

Remembering all those
good years, this book
is dedicated to Addie Gilbert

Mankiller

One

"In my whole life," Canelli said, "I never been inside the Stanford Court. Not once." He pulled our cruiser into the Stanford Court's curbside passenger zone, and watched a uniformed doorman ceremoniously approaching a Rolls that preceded us. Canelli's eyes were round and somber, staring first at the doorman, then at the high-fashion occupants of the Rolls and finally at the hotel's impressively understated entryway. At age twenty-seven, with a full, swarthy moon face, a hulking, suety body and a perpetually bemused manner, Canelli existed in a state of permanently perplexed innocence. For Canelli, every new experience was a source of wonder, and usually the subject of a long, rambling commentary. When I'd chosen him for my squad, taking him out of uniform, some of my superiors thought I'd made a mistake. They'd been wrong. Precisely because he didn't look like a cop, or act like a cop or think like a cop, Canelli often succeeded where other detectives failed.

"Have you ever, Lieutenant?" Canelli asked. "Been inside, I mean."

"Once or twice," I answered, at the same time swinging

my door open. I'd decided to spare the doorman the pain of attending a police vehicle, even though it was unmarked. "Thanks, Canelli. I'll check with you in the morning. Take the car home, why don't you?"

"Well, Jeeze, thanks, Lieutenant. I'm a whole lot closer to home than to the Hall. So maybe I will, then. Take the car home, I mean. Thanks."

I said goodnight, and walked quickly beside the long, reflecting pool that led to the Stanford Court's lobby. Behind the lobby's floor-to-ceiling glass walls, I saw Ann and her father sitting side by side on a tufted velvet love seat. As the glass door slid smoothly open before me, I saw Ann's father glance impatiently at his watch. The time was seven-thirty. I was a half hour late.

As I saw Ann get to her feet, smiling, I suddenly realized how much I'd been dreading the next few hours. Wearing a gold brocade dress and a single strand of pearls, holding a small embroidered evening bag, she looked like a beautifully poised stranger. During the year we'd been together, I'd never seen the brocade gown, or the evening bag, or the pearls.

I'd never seen her father, either. He was a small, wiry-looking man in his vigorous middle sixties. His body was slim, but his face was improbably round and ruddy, with rosy cheeks, lively eyes and a fringe of impeccably trimmed gray beard. Except for a pair of stylish silver-and-Lucite glasses, the face somehow recalled one of Disney's seven dwarfs. His suit was a conservative pin stripe, but a paisley-printed red silk tie struck an independent note. Except for tufts of gray hair over the ears, his head was totally bald.

"Sorry I'm late," I said, speaking to Ann. "I just couldn't get away. Something—came up." I stopped a single step short of Ann, momentarily uncertain whether this was the time or the place to kiss her. Solving my problem, she took the last step and kissed me on the lips. It was a brief, businesslike kiss, exactly right.

4

"Dad," she said, turning to her father with her arm linked through mine, "this is Frank Hastings. Frank, this is my father, Clyde Briscoe."

His small hand was muscular, his grip firm but not aggressive. "The name is Clyde," he said. "Just plain Clyde. Come on. I've got a table reserved." He turned and led the way through the lobby to a door marked The West Room. He walked with a sprightly, bouncy stride that didn't quite conceal a slight limp. As we walked behind him, I put my arm around Ann's waist, hugged her quickly, then self-consciously released her as a maitre d' stepped forward, bowing over the three menus he held ceremoniously before him.

"It's been some time, Mr. Briscoe," the maitre d' murmured, speaking with an accent that could have been French. "It's a pleasure, sir."

"Thank you," Clyde Briscoe said briskly, exchanging nods with the maitre d'. "Paul, isn't it?"

"Pierre."

"Oh. Sorry." Clyde glanced pointedly toward the dining room, signifying that the pleasantries were over. Instantly picking up the cue, Pierre turned and led us toward a window table set for three. Beyond the window, the lights of San Francisco's skyline looked like countless multicolored jewels scattered across the black velvet of the night sky.

"What're we drinking?" Clyde asked, settling himself across the table from me, with Ann between us. Ann asked for a martini and Clyde decided on a bourbon-and-water. When I ordered plain tonic water, Clyde's quick glance appraised me as he asked:

"You're not a drinking man, Frank?"

"Not any more," I answered. Then, meeting his eyes, I decided to add: "I used to drink—too much. So I had to quit."

He studied me for a long, shrewd moment before he said, "You're a person with willpower, then."

I shrugged. "That depends on what you mean by willpower. For years, I drank too much. It finally got to the point where I had to choose between working and drinking." As I said it, I watched him covertly, looking for a reaction. I saw only a momentary flicker in his shrewd gray eyes. He would think about what I'd said, then pick his time to probe deeper. Meanwhile, speaking crisply, he began the inevitable questions:

"Ann tells me you're a detective."

I nodded. "That's right."

"What division?"

"Homicide. I'm a lieutenant." Watching him nod, I realized that he'd been anticipating the answer. Ann, of course, had told him about me.

"You played professional football, too."

"I played three seasons for the Lions."

"I don't follow football. Is that Detroit?"

"Yes, it is."

He waited while a blonde waitress brought our drinks, smiled politely all around and left us with a pleasant nod and a graceful switch of hip and thigh. Admiringly, Clyde watched the waitress walk away from us, his gaze fixed frankly on the provocative movement of her buttocks. Then, raising his glass, he toasted: "Here's to the two of you. You're a good-looking couple. A better-looking couple, I suspect, than you might realize."

Over her glass, Ann smiled at him before she turned to me, playfully explaining, "Dad's a philosopher—or so he thinks. Except that he's very cryptic about it."

To keep the conversation in balance, I asked, "What do you do, Clyde?"

"I'm a self-made millionaire," he said, speaking with bright, straightforward self-satisfaction. "In fact, what with inflation, I'm a multimillionaire. Most of my life, though, I didn't amount to a damn thing. Or, at least, so most people thought—including my wife." As he said it, he glanced quickly at Ann, measuring her reaction. Except for an almost

6

imperceptible tightening of her mouth, warning her father not to press his luck, she didn't respond. To myself, I smiled. I knew that look of subtle, stubborn warning.

"I started out thinking I was an artist," he continued. "And I was pretty good, too. I was a good draftsman, and I guess I would've made a passable illustrator. But, of course, I was an idealist. I was going to do something significant. And eventually I did. Or, to be more precise, I had a few showings at a few good galleries—and one showing at the Museum of Modern Art in New York. By then I'd turned into a sculptor. I worked in metal, and also in plastic, which was an innovation at that time. As it turned out, though, it was the high point of my career. I got good reviews, but not much else—not many sales, and therefore not much money. The taste-makers agreed that I was an innovator. But then they found an innovator they liked better.

"By that time"—he glanced again at Ann—"by that time, I was married—to one of the taste-makers, in fact. And we had a child. And suddenly I wasn't selling anything. I'd gone out of vogue, you see. To make ends meet, I started making things out of plastic—which I knew something about. I eventually started making small boats. But, unfortunately, the plastics available weren't up to the job. They couldn't be laminated in large enough pieces, because the cure was too quick. So the business folded—and so did I."

For a moment he paused, briefly looking off across the opulent candlelit dining room. A shadow of sadness appeared in his eyes; his voice dropped to a lower, more somber note as he continued: "As the years went by, I became accustomed to thinking of myself as a failure, I'm afraid. My wife, meanwhile, met a stockbroker, and decided to make a change for the better." Once more he looked at Ann, mutely challenging her to contest the bitterness of his memories. This time, her eyes fell before his. I couldn't hear her sigh, but I felt it.

With the hardest part of his story behind him, Clyde's eyes

brightened again. His voice quickened as he said, "We were divorced in 1956, when Ann started college. I drifted around the world for a while after that. I'd decided to go back to painting, which was just another way of feeling sorry for myself. But then"—he was smiling now, remembering— "then I got my million-dollar idea. I was back in the plastic business, working for wages—and still feeling pretty sorry for myself. I got together with a chemist, and we figured out how to make a catalyst that would make fiberglass behave on long-radius laminates. We formed our own company, to make the catalyst. The first year, we grossed a million dollars. Five years later, a conglomerate bought us out, after accepting a very generous licensing agreement. So—" He spread his hands cheerfully. "I was rich. Filthily, wonderfully rich." He drank half his bourbon-and-water, his shrewd gray eyes looking at me over the rim of the glass.

"That's my story," he said, setting the glass down decisively on the table and shifting in his chair to face me squarely. "What's yours, Frank?"

Deliberately, I matched his bit of business, drinking from my own glass and setting it down firmly, all the while holding his eyes. If he knew a few tricks, so did I.

"My story isn't as long as yours," I began. "And, so far at least, it doesn't have the—" I hesitated, searching for the phrase. "It doesn't have the spectacular ending. I grew up here, in San Francisco. I played football in high school, and when I graduated I got a football scholarship to Stanford. I studied just enough to get a degree, no more. I don't think I learned much. But when I graduated, I got drafted by the Lions. So I went to Detroit, and played three seasons as a second-string halfback. I had three knee operations, and the third one finished me. At the end of the first season, I met a woman named Carolyn Bates. She was good-looking, and her father was rich. We made a beautiful couple, according to the society columns. So we decided to get married. But then my knees gave out, and I found myself living in a fancy house with no money coming in. My wife didn't worry about it, because she had her own money. But I worried—a lot. So I made the mistake of going to work for my father-in-law. I was supposed to do PR. Which, translated, meant entertaining VIPs. Before I knew it—before I realized how unhappy I'd become—I was drinking too much. At first, I drank in the line of duty, entertaining the customers. Then I started drinking on my own time. Once in a while—" I paused, stole a look at Ann. "Once in a while, I was given to understand that a VIP wanted a girl for the night, and that I was expected to arrange it. Which translated, I finally figured out, to pimping. So, after a few years, it all blew up. Everything. First it was my marriage. Then, naturally, it was my job. Finally, I—I just left town. I came back to San Francisco with my tail between my legs. An old friend got me into the police academy. I was the oldest rookie in the class, and without my athletic background I wouldn't've survived the training. But I did survive, after a fashion. I quit drinking—eventually. I got my shield and I started climbing the ladder. So here I am." I forced a smile, raising my glass to him. "Here I am, having dinner with a self-made millionaire."

"What about children?" he asked quietly, holding my gaze.

"I have two. The girl is seventeen. The boy is almost fifteen. They live in Detroit. I see them once a year." As I said it, I dropped my voice to a hard note of finality. About the children, I wouldn't say any more. Catching the cue, he said:

"That's your past. What's the future?" Asking the question, he moved his eyes toward Ann, then back to me. To each of us, his meaning was clear. He was a father inquiring after my intentions concerning his daughter.

I finished my tonic water, and took a moment to study the impression left by the glass on the gleaming white damask tablecloth. Finally I drew a long, deliberate breath, raised my eyes to meet his squarely, and said, "Frankly, I've just about now come to terms with the past, after being divorced for twelve years. I don't know whether—" I hesitated, searching for the right phrase. "I don't know whether I'm ready to face up to the future, if you want the truth."

As I said it, the wine steward appeared, followed a discreet moment later by our waiter. The break couldn't have been better timed, and during the rest of the meal we talked about Clyde's adventures, beginning with his first million and ending with his recent marriage to an astrologist half his age.

Two

Ann pulled into my driveway, turned off the engine and switched off the headlights. For a moment she sat staring straight ahead, both hands gripping the steering wheel. Her hands were small, her fingers short. I'd always thought her hands expressed her perfectly: small but capable, moving with no pretense or affectation.

Except for an exchange of brief, anecdotal remarks about her father, we'd said very little during the drive from the Stanford Court. Drawing closer to my apartment, our silences had lengthened uncomfortably until, now, I felt almost awkward as I asked, "Why don't you come in? It's still early."

For a moment she didn't reply, still staring straight ahead. I saw her hand tighten on the wheel. Then, lifting her chin, she cleared her throat.

I knew that mannerism. I recognized the hardening around her mouth, and the purposeful narrowing of her eyes.

She was angry with me. Hurt and angry. I should have sensed it earlier—should have realized that her long aloof silences during dinner meant more than merely polite boredom, listening to her father's stories.

"When are you going to face the future, Frank?" She spoke softly—regretfully, almost. But, still, purposefully.

Hearing her say it, I felt a sudden sense of foreboding mixed with a kind of dull, dogged sense of betrayal. Without ever having expressed it in words, we'd mutually agreed that the present was all we could handle. If the present was right, we'd once said, pillow-talking, then the future would take care of itself. It was as close as we'd ever come to discussing our future—about living together, or getting married. Ann had been divorced for two years. She had two sons, one eleven, the other seventeen. Her ex-husband was a society psychiatrist named Victor Haywood, who affected Gucci accessories, a turbo Porsche and a luxuriant hair transplant. During their marriage, Haywood had been hard on her, systematically slashing away at her sense of self-esteem. After their divorce, his attacks had become more sadistic, more lethal. Using his head-doctor's tricks, he'd flayed her at will, mercilessly.

So Ann wasn't ready to make another commitment. She was still too vulnerable—too scarred, too unsure of herself.

And so was I.

I let the silence lengthen before I replied. Matching the soft-spoken, somber note in her voice I said, "It's not just 'me.' It's 'we,' really."

She didn't reply. After a moment, I decided to try a lighter note: "Your father's a nice guy. I like him. But I think he was doing a little matchmaking tonight. Without really knowing the situation."

She released her grip on the steering wheel and twisted in the seat to face me fully. Her mouth was still set, her eyes still uncompromising as she said, "What situation is that?"

I sighed—more sharply and impatiently than I'd intended. "You know what I mean."

"Tell me." Her voice could have been a stranger's. And her eyes, too. "Tell me what you mean, Frank."

"Oh, Jesus—" I lifted my hand in a gesture of sharp, futile

protest. "Come on—lighten up, as the kids say." I reached across her, unlatching the driver's door. "Let's go inside. What's the point of talking about it in the car, anyhow?" With the door unlatched, I rested my hand on her upper thigh, drawing her subtly toward me. It wasn't a time for words. It was a time for holding her, stroking her, kissing her. It was a time for me to be tender, and for her to come close.

But, instead, she moved against the pressure of my hand.

"Listen, Ann." I took my hand away. "I've had a hard day, to use a cliché. I'm tired, and it's late. And what's more, you're tired, too. So let's go inside and—"

"That's the trouble with us, you know? Instead of talking about things when we're together—*really* talking about things—we just get into bed and start making love. And pretty soon, everything seems all right. Except that, really, nothing's changed. We feel better, but nothing's solved. Or rather, we feel—" She paused, groping. "We feel released."

Aware of my rising anger, I let a long, deliberate beat pass before I said, "Is that a complaint, or what?"

"No," she answered, too quickly, "it's not a complaint. And it's not meant as a slur on your masculinity, either. It's just that—" She suddenly broke off as her voice caught. Was she going to cry? I'd only seen her cry once, when her favorite aunt died.

Her father was the cause of her sudden, irrational pique. If she didn't know it, I did. Her father, and his millions and his brand-new wife—he was the one responsible. Trying to tinker with Ann's life, he'd upset her. She was angry with him. And I was the target of opportunity.

I knew it, but I never should have said it:

"If I were you, Ann, I'd do my own thinking about your life. I'd make my own decisions. I like your father. He's a hell of a guy—one of a kind. But he's a different person from you. What works for him won't work for you. Or for me, either. So when you—"

"You're trying to—" She broke off, blinking against sudden tears. Seeing her eyes shine in the darkened car, I realized that I was shaking my head sharply, suddenly angry. Tears for a lost aunt were one thing. Tears used as a weapon were something else.

"You're trying to blame my father for your own problems," she said hotly. "All he was doing was . . . was showing *interest* in you. He likes you. I could *tell* that he likes you. But instead of accepting that—instead of simply liking him in return—you've got to start double-thinking, looking at it from the underside. It—it's typical of what you do, all the time."

"Maybe it's an occupational hazard," I said. "Looking at things from the underside, I mean. Take tonight, for instance. I was a half hour late because I had to investigate a very messy, very smelly murder, down in the Tenderloin. Maybe that's the real problem, Ann. Maybe there's just no way to go from the Tenderloin to the Stanford Court." Hearing myself say it, I realized that my voice had sunk to an icy, dangerous note. And suddenly the past rushed back to smother me. The last time I'd spoken with that same cold, measured malice, I'd been speaking to my wife. The next day, she'd gone to see her lawyer.

I wanted to keep myself from going on. But I was helpless to stop what came next:

"Maybe the real problem is that you're tired of having a cop around. Is that it?" As I said it, I stared directly into her eyes, bullying her. It's a squad room cliché that a cop's most efficient weapon is a long, cold stare.

It was the first time I'd turned the weapon against her.

I saw her blink, heard her sigh, felt her falter. The next moment, I knew, could bring us together, lovers repentant. I knew that I shouldn't say any more. I knew that I should wait for her to speak.

And I knew that, most of all, I should give her some sign that I was sorry. A look would have been enough. Or a gesture.

14

But I couldn't do it—couldn't send the signal that I sensed she needed. Something inside me had been hit too hard. Some almost-forgotten scar tissue had been ripped away, revealing a wound cut too deeply to ever heal.

So, instead, I said goodnight, and opened the car door, and walked down the areaway to my apartment. I didn't look back.

Three

I'd once heard a pundit say that television was a refuge for the lonely. As I walked into my apartment and automatically switched on the set, sound off, I remembered the nameless pundit's remark. Standing in the empty living room, lit only by a single lamp that I kept on a timer, I felt loneliness strike with sudden, numbing force. It was a quick, cruel blow, and it caught me squarely in the solar plexus.

I flung my topcoat on the sofa, and tossed my jacket beside it. I'd bought a fifteen-dollar silk tie, especially for dinner at the Stanford Court. I unknotted the tie, pulled it free and stood for a moment with it dangling irresolutely from my fingers. Then, savagely, I crumpled the tie into a tight silken ball and hurled it into the fireplace.

Exactly a week ago, Ann and I had cooked steaks in the fireplace. Afterwards, we'd made love in front of the fire. In the soft light from the dying flames, her body had never excited me more.

Thinking bitterly of the symbolism so plain in the image of the tie lying dust-covered and twisted in the ashes of last week's fire, I realized that my gaze had wandered aimlessly

16

to the silent TV, my newest symbol of emptiness and defeat. The eleven o'clock news program was almost over; the TV's integral clock read 11:22.

In fifteen minutes, Ann would be home.

I would call her—talk to her—tell her I was sorry. Tomorrow was Saturday, and I had the weekend off. On Sunday, I'd arranged to take Ann and Billy on a tour of Alcatraz. In the evening, Ann's oldest son, Dan, would join us for dinner at Fisherman's Wharf.

It would be a family-style day, and with Ann's father gone, tonight's wounds would heal. The thought began to ease the empty ache of my loneliness.

I'd been standing in the center of my living room, mindlessly watching the images flickering across the TV screen. The camera was panning spasmodically from a surging, out-of-control crowd to kaleidoscopic close-ups of anguished young faces, to three black-and-white patrol cars arriving at a parking lot, red lights flashing. As each car braked to a jolting stop, four patrolmen hit the pavement, running.

Even before the camera lingered on a huge "Cow Palace" sign, I'd guessed what was happening. There'd been a rock concert at the Cow Palace. A rock star had failed to make a scheduled appearance, or a hot new group had refused to play one last encore. A disturbance had started, igniting into a riot. It was a familiar, predictable scenario. The police response was equally predictable. At the Hall of Justice, downtown, the riot squad was assembling, running to muster like firemen answering the bell. They would be getting into their flack jackets, their thigh protectors, their helmets with the plastic visors. For this job, they'd be issued three-foot batons, weighted at the business end.

I glanced again at the clock. Ten minutes more, and Ann might be home.

I had just picked up my jacket and topcoat from the sofa and was taking them to the closet when the phone rang.

Had she gotten home so soon? No, it wasn't possible. She

must have stopped at an outdoor phone booth, or a tavern. As I lifted the phone, I frowned at the thought. Ann should know better than to use outdoor phone booths at night. And stopping at a tavern could be almost as bad.

"Hello?" I tried to make it sound warm—eager—loving.

"Lieutenant Hastings?"

As I bit back an obscenity, I recognized the background clatter on the other end of the line. Police Communications was calling.

"What is it?"

"I've got Lieutenant Friedman for you, Lieutenant. Can you hold?"

"I can hold," I answered shortly. "But not for long."

"Yessir. Just one moment." The line clicked dead, and for a full thirty seconds I heard nothing but static. Waiting, I took the phone over to the fireplace, knelt on the hearth and used one hand to fish out my new silk tie from the ashes. Tomorrow, I would take it to the cleaners.

Suddenly Friedman's voice grated hard in my ear. "Frank?"

"It's eleven-thirty," I said stolidly, "and I'm half undressed for bed."

"Then I hope you're alone," he answered promptly, "because I've got a real production number going down here, for God's sake. I need help. Have you been watching the news?"

"No."

"Well, I'm at the Cow Palace. And let me tell you, it's a mess."

"That part of the news I watched. So it's a riot. What's it got to do with us?"

"Ever heard of Rebecca Carlton?"

"The rock singer?"

"Right," Friedman answered heavily. "The rock singer. She's dead. Shot. And it's causing lots of very, very big problems."

"Have you got anyone in custody?"

"If I had anyone in custody," he answered acidly, "I wouldn't be calling you. Right?"

I sighed. "Right."

Savagely, the sergeant punched a siren switch, then clamped his hand down on the horn ring. In front of our car, caught in the headlight glare, contorted faces did a manic dance, defying us. We were inching our way through a thousand wildly writhing figures, taunting us with screaming obscenities and stiffened middle fingers.

"These goddamn sonofabitching hippies," the sergeant said, raising his voice against the wail of the siren. "Had my way, I'd line them up against a wall, I swear to God."

"It's not much further, is it?"

"Christ almighty, we're only making about a foot a minute. Want me to fire a couple over their heads, Lieutenant?"

As he said it, I saw a police helicopter suddenly swoop down out of the night sky to hover directly over the entrance to the Cow Palace. Momentarily its searchlight beam fell on an enormous sign reading "Rebecca Carlton and Pure Power." I cut the siren, reached for the car's microphone and called Communications.

"This is Lieutenant Hastings," I said. "We've got a helicopter over the Cow Palace. It's number Charlie-seven-two-three-Juliet. Patch me through to him, please. Quick."

Thirty seconds later, I heard a static-sizzled voice acknowledge my call. The voice was shouting over the high, whining whirl of helicopter blades.

"This is Lieutenant Frank Hastings," I said into the microphone. "We're in black-and-white car"—I glanced at the dashboard plaque—"we're in car Alpha 243, trying to make the rear entrance to the Cow Palace. Have you got us in sight?"

"Yessir, we have you in sight."

"Then come over here, and give us a hand. See if you can move this crowd."

"Yessir."

I saw the helicopter suddenly dip, then swing in a wide, screaming circle, coming up on us from behind. As it drew closer, the helicopter dropped down until it was hovering barely ten feet above the milling mob, its blades churning up a whirlwind of dust and debris. Now it was directly overhead, lashing us with the sound of rolling thunder gone wild. Slowly, the copter moved to a position just ahead of our car, and dropped another few feet. The figures caught in our headlights began flailing their arms against the whirlwind. Now they were beginning to scatter, falling away from each other.

"All right," I yelled to the sergeant. "*Go.* Bump a few, if you have to do it. Gently."

"Damn right," he yelled, throwing me a quick look of leering pleasure.

I felt the car move forward, felt a thud. From the radio came a call I couldn't hear, even with the volume at full blast. Then, from the sky, I saw some small round shapes falling —one, two, three. Looking up at the helicopter, I saw its open side door sliding shut. It dipped, veered, recovered. Suddenly it was flying back toward the building. At the same moment, a yellow cloud erupted before us.

Tear gas. They'd dropped tear gas canisters. They'd tried to warn us over the radio.

"Jesus Christ." I twisted in the seat, checking our windows for cracks. "Go," I shouted above the shuddering, whirling rush of sound left behind by the copter. *"Go."*

One last bump, and we broke free. Moments later, we were pulling to a stop beside a police barricade.

I thanked the sergeant, got out of the patrol car and stood for a moment looking back on the scene we'd just left behind. It looked like something out of Dante's *Inferno.* Clouds of yellow gas hung above the crowd like sulphurous vapors hovering over the writhing hosts of hell. A searchlight beam moved toward the cloud, adding another bizarre touch: the

20

world premiere of some strange, unearthly new Hollywood production.

Turning back toward the building, I came face to face with another uniformed sergeant. It was Neal Cassiday, from Mission station. Years ago, we'd gone through the Academy together.

"Hello, Neal. How've you been?"

"Fine, Frank. You?"

Wryly, I thought about my lover's quarrel with Ann. Cassiday was the father of four boys. His oldest son was just beginning to walk a beat. Neal had been married for thirty years.

"No complaints," I answered. "What's happening here, anyhow?"

Cassiday's broad, beefy face broke into a cheerful grin. "Damned if I know. This is like the war, for God's sake. All you can see is what's dropping around your foxhole. A deputy chief told me to secure this entrance, and pass the big shots through." He grinned again. "That's you, I guess, isn't it? A big shot?"

Answering his smile, I shrugged. "If you say so, Neal. Where's the body?"

"Come on. I'll show you."

I followed him through a sliding metal fire door and down a long, bare, windowless corridor. Its sidewalls and ceiling were rough-cast concrete, painted a pale institutional green. I'd been in this same stark, squared-off tunnel years ago, when the Republican party had held its national convention at the Cow Palace. I'd been in uniform then, detailed to guard Nelson Rockefeller, who'd tried for the nomination and lost. After Goldwater's acceptance speech, Rockefeller had come down this tunnel to his waiting limousine. He'd been accompanied by his wife, his son, his police bodyguard and a mere handful of sober-faced supporters. I'd held the car door for him, and as he thanked me, politely, I saw tears in his eyes.

Except for a single patrolman lounging with his back propped against the green concrete wall, the corridor was deserted. Our footsteps echoed and re-echoed as we walked, each of us nodding once to the patrolman as we passed. The patrolman was a stranger to me. Wearing a modified handlebar mustache and hair trimmed as long as departmental regulations allowed, the young patrolman nodded amiably in return. He didn't bother to push himself away from the wall.

"The new breed," Cassiday muttered heavily, resigned.

I smiled, then asked, "How's your family?"

"Fine. Just fine. Peter, you know, graduated. He's walking a beat down in the Tenderloin."

"I know. How's he doing?"

"So far, so good. How're your kids?"

"Claudia is just starting college, back in Michigan. She'll be eighteen next month. Darrell just turned fifteen. He was out here to visit me, a few months ago."

"I know. I saw him at the pistol range. He looks like you, Frank. The spitting image."

Caught by surprise at the sudden flush of pleasure I felt, I nodded. "That's what everyone says."

I'd always liked Cassiday. He was a man who cared what happened to his friends.

At the end of the corridor, Cassiday pointed to the left, down a narrower hallway. Its sidewalls were wood-paneled, decorated with huge photomurals of San Francisco, taken from the air. At the end of the hallway, smiling amiably at me and lifting a hand in a gesture of awkward greeting, I saw the large, lumpy figure of Canelli, my driver.

"There you go, Frank." Cassiday clapped me lightly on the shoulder. "Good luck. I better get back to my foxhole."

"Thanks. Give my best to Peter, will you?"

"Sure will, Frank. See you." He turned back the way he'd come, walking briskly down the pale-green corridor. As I went toward Canelli, I took my shield case from my pocket and pinned my badge on the lapel of my corduroy sports jacket.

"Hello, Lieutenant," Canelli said affably. "Jeeze, this sure is something. I'm glad to see you." He was standing with his back to a crowd-control door, one with no handle or lock on the outside. As he spoke, he rapped sharply on the door, which immediately swung open.

Stepping through the doorway with Canelli following close behind, I found myself facing the controlled confusion typical of backstage theater. A ganglia of serpentine power cables covered the floor. Lighting scaffolds towered fifty feet high. Three large motor homes and a half dozen smaller vehicles were arranged in a rough semicircle facing the back of a stage raised ten feet above the floor.

But the scene was strangely frozen. Sounds were muted; movements were hushed and hesitant. Costumed performers sat, or stood, or walked slowly among the cables. Some of them carried musical instruments, some were empty-handed. A group of blue-jeaned stagehands stood apart, clustered at the base of one of the light towers. A half dozen big, tough-looking black men wearing red nylon windbreakers with "Security" stitched across their backs mingled aimlessly with the crowd, deprived of their purpose by dozens of policemen, in and out of uniform. Most of the uniformed policemen stood guard at a rope barricade that divided the Cow Palace amphitheater from the backstage area. The division was defined by multicolored fabric falls and skims hanging from a track suspended from the huge domed ceiling that arched a hundred feet above the floor. Some of the fabric falls were opaque, some semitransparent. Through their gauzy folds I could see the huge oval of the Cow Palace arena. The building could seat seventy-five thousand, rising tier on tier from floor level to the network of enormous curving girders that supported the dome of the ceiling.

From beyond the flimsy fabric falls and skims I heard a low, rhythmic pulsing, primitive enough to have come from the veldt. I recognized that sound. It was the voice of the mob, indecisively muttering. Any moment, though, the sound could erupt into a howl of sudden rage—followed by mayhem.

Beyond the footlights, a beast was growling.

"Over there, Lieutenant." Canelli gestured to a large aluminum motor home. As he spoke, I heard a woman's voice blaring through the massive speakers that hung fifteen feet from the amphitheater's floor, aimed out toward the crowd:

"Here he is. He's just come over from Oakland—just this minute. So let's have quiet, please."

But, when she paused, the beast still muttered and rumbled.

She tried again. "Here he is. He'll be with us in a second, now. Just as soon as it's quiet out there. He's come to talk to you—David Behr, everyone. So let's, please, hold it down. Let's listen to David, everyone. What'd you say? How about it, now? He's right here, backstage. He's waiting. You can believe it. This is Pam telling you. Pam Cornelison. You know me. You know I don't jive you. And I'm telling you that David's here, waiting for a little quiet, so he can talk to you about what's happened. So let's have it quiet, now. For David."

David Behr—a name almost as well known as Rebecca Carlton. David Behr—rock impresario. David Behr—multimultimillionaire. An immigrant Lebanese, penniless not so long ago. Now a national figure.

And then I saw him: a short, stocky man dressed in wrinkled cords and a fisherman's sweater. With his neck bowed, with his dark, snapping eyes glowering from under black, beetling brows, he looked a little like Napoleon out of uniform. He was standing between two of the hulking security men at the top of a flight of rough wooden stairs that led up to the stage.

Could he quiet the beast?

At the moment, nothing was more important. Dead bodies

can wait. But out in the amphitheater, disaster was boiling.

The woman tried again—and again. She was crooning to the crowd as a mother might croon to a distraught child. Her technique was flawless. Slowly, soothingly, she dropped her voice—and the crowd lowered its voice to hear her.

Finally, Behr took a single quick, decisive step through the parted curtains.

Instantly, the crowd's voice changed to a note of excitement and anticipation. Through a semitransparent skim, I could see Behr standing at a microphone placed at center stage. He didn't speak, didn't gesture. He simply stood perfectly still, imperiously waiting for quiet.

And slowly, the crowd noise dropped. Finally, speaking softly, conversationally, the impresario's voice came out over the mammoth speakers, amplified thousands of times:

"I felt just like all of you did, when I heard about it. I was driving on the Bay Bridge. I was heading for here, in fact, when I heard. I was hoping to catch Rebecca's last set. I planned to watch her glow, when she came offstage. I did that for a lot of years, you know—watched her glow, coming offstage."

He paused. As I listened to the crowd's voice sink, I saw a beautiful young woman appear from between the parted curtains. It was Pam Cornelison, leaving the stage. She was tall and blonde, dressed in a blue silk jump suit. She descended the short flight of backstage stairs with her back straight and her head held high. She carried herself like a princess, with a hint of royal disdain for the rabble.

Behr was speaking again, confessing to the crowd:

"I suppose," he said quietly, "that most of you know Rebecca and I were married." Another pause. And this time, a murmuring note of sympathy came from the crowd. The beast was no longer dangerous. To myself, I nodded. David Behr had a light, sure touch, quieting a crowd. It was a rare, subtle talent.

"We aren't married any more," he was saying. "Or,

rather—" The voice caught. Was it an actor's trick? "Or,
rather, we *weren't* married any more, I should say. But,
anyhow, we were always friends—always partners. We
worked together on this concert, just like we worked together
on all her other concerts—before, during and after we were
married."

Still another short, deft pause. Then, speaking through the
powerful sound system in a hushed voice that rolled out
across the arena in a rich, throbbing tremulo, Behr said,
"And now, Rebecca is dead."

He paused again, letting it sink in. Whether he knew it or
not, he was probing the beast's wound, testing its lingering
potential for violence.

"She finished the best concert she ever gave," he said. "It
was a concert dedicated to her father, who died just three
weeks ago. She sang the concert, and she gave four encores.
And then someone killed her—shot her. You all heard about
it. That's why you're still here." He let a beat pass before he
added quietly: "And that's why the police are here."

At the word "police," a ripple of anger swept the crowd.
But Behr quickly raised his hand, saying sharply, *"Wait.
Just *wait.* Quiet down a minute." It was a command, not a
request. And, momentarily at least, they obeyed him.

"Wait now," he repeated. "Don't blow your cool, just
because you hear a word you don't like. That's silly. Just
plain silly. Sure, some of us have been hassled by the police.
Most of us, maybe, at one time or another. But don't let's
forget that the police have their problems, too. And, right
now, their problem is that they've got to get things cooled
down here, so they can do what they have to do, to find out
who killed Rebecca."

A dubious murmur greeted the statement. Behr let the
rumbling continue, then raised his hand. Obedient now, the
crowd quieted.

"You've got to help them," Behr said flatly. "You've got
to go home. You've got to leave here, quietly. You've got to

get in your cars, and go home. That's what you've got to do, if you want to help find Rebecca's murderer. And that's what I'm here to ask you to do—go home. And I'm asking you please. *Please.*" The last words were spoken in a low, half-broken voice. I wondered whether the emotion was real, or contrived.

He stood motionless for a moment, head slightly bowed over the microphone. Then, slowly and deliberately, completely in control of his audience, he turned and walked offstage. It had been a masterful performance. And, out beyond the footlights, I could sense that the crowd was moving sluggishly toward the exits, obeying him.

I turned again toward the huge aluminum mobile home, following Canelli as he led the way. I stepped over a tangled skein of electrical cables, rounded the far corner of the aluminum monster and found myself facing a grimly familiar scene: a dead body, surrounded by a solemn semicircle of policemen.

Four

She'd fallen backward, down a temporary flight of three low wooden steps and a small landing that had been built against the door of the mobile home. The door was standing open. She was sprawled face up, with her legs on the landing, her torso slanted down the three steps and her head jammed at a cruel angle on the concrete floor of the arena. Her left arm was flung wide, fingers crooked in death's final agony. Her right arm was crossed over her waist. Her eyes were open wide, staring toward the stage. Her blouse was a flaming red, and almost concealed the small bloodstain centered on her heart.

Beneath the body, blood was puddled on two of the three wooden steps. A small rivulet of blood ran across the concrete floor toward the trailer.

Raising my eyes from the body, I saw Pete Friedman, my senior co-lieutenant in Homicide, talking to Albert Farley, San Francisco's coroner. The two men were standing slightly apart from the semicircle of men surrounding the victim. Seeing me, Friedman lifted one beefy hand, waved, and gestured for me to join them.

After Farley and I exchanged perfunctory pleasantries, Friedman turned to me. "We're about to move the body." As he spoke, two ambulance stewards carrying a gurney began edging their way toward the body.

"What's it look like?" I asked Friedman. Farley excused himself, moving off toward the two stewards. He was observing protocol. Policemen had full access to the coroner's information, but the opposite wasn't true.

"It seems pretty open and shut," Friedman said. He turned, pointing a pudgy forefinger to the gap in the backstage curtains that both Pam Cornelison and David Behr had used going on and offstage. "She finished her fourth encore, which apparently was some kind of a track record. She came through the curtains and down the stairs. She started walking directly from the bottom of the stairs to her trailer. The distance, as you can see, is about fifty feet. Along the route, she collected about a dozen well-wishers and hangers-on. They were congratulating her, and walking with her toward the motor home, here." As he spoke, Friedman turned back to face the body. "The door to the motor home was closed. Rebecca, by all accounts, was ecstatic. Everyone was telling her she was a smash. Did you hear what David Behr said, just now?"

"Yes."

"Well, it was all true, I guess. Anyhow, with the faithful crowded around the stairs, there—" He pointed. "She went up to the landing, and opened the door to her mobile home. But then, with the door open, she turned back to take one last bow. Which probably gave the murderer a beautiful chance to take careful aim."

Now he turned to face the stage, once more pointing. "Everyone seems to agree that the shot came from there— from the direction of the stage, or maybe from that light tower." He gestured to one of the four tall, narrow rectangles built of tubular metal scaffolding.

"Whichever it was," Friedman continued, "the murderer

was either very well briefed, or else very lucky. Because, at the time the shot was fired, the entire backstage area was blacked out—except for one spotlight that followed Rebecca to her trailer." Wryly, Friedman smiled. "Rebecca, it seems, had a pretty good sense of the dramatic, even offstage."

"Was that her usual MO—going to her dressing room with the backstage area blacked out and a spotlight following her?"

"Yes. Always."

"Then it sounds like good planning, not good luck."

Friedman shrugged. Until all the facts were in, he never liked to theorize.

"What about a weapon?"

He pointed to the base of a light tower, guarded by two uniformed patrolmen. For the first time I saw the crime lab's white tape arranged in a rectangle around the base of the tower. A small circle was chalked inside the taped perimeter.

"It was probably a .38 Smith and Wesson," Friedman said. "Five shells were in the cylinder, one shot was fired. It was ditched there, in the circle. It's on the way down to the Hall."

I took a long, deliberate moment to survey the backstage area, slowly pivoting in a full circle as I tried to fix the scene firmly in mind. The Cow Palace was essentially a huge oval arena surrounded by an amphitheater of seats and bleachers. It got its offbeat name because, originally, it had housed the biggest annual indoor rodeo and livestock exhibition west of the Mississippi. In later years, as the complex was expanded, almost every kind of indoor amusement came to the Cow Palace, including basketball games, circuses, political conventions and countless exhibitions of everything from hot rods to orchids.

The interior of the main building was laid out with spectator entrances around three sides, and a huge rectangular entrance on the fourth side that was large enough to accommodate a dozen horses galloping abreast into the arena. Tonight, the fabric falls and curtains that separated the audience from the backstage area had been strung on a track that extended across the entire width of the arena at a distance of about two hundred feet from the big rectangular entrance. The cable on which the curtains were hung was suspended about thirty feet from the floor, with the four scaffold towers rising another twenty feet above the curtain.

After he fired the shot and ditched the gun, the murderer would have had his choice of escape routes: either slip through the curtains to mingle with the departing spectators, or else melt into the group of fifty-odd performers, stagehands and technicians that had doubtless been backstage at the time of the murder.

"Security is pretty tight at these rock concerts," I said.

"True," Friedman answered. "But it's all aimed at gate-crashers. Someone wants to get out, they let him out."

"Still, there were probably guards posted there and there—" I pointed to the line of curtains, then at the performers' entrance to the arena. "They would've been guarding against anyone getting backstage after the performance."

Friedman nodded. "You're right. I've got Culligan and Marsten talking to them, one at a time." Following his pointing finger, I saw Culligan and Marsten, each interrogating a red-jacketed security man. Four other security men were standing close by, obviously waiting their turns.

"It's possible," I said thoughtfully, "that the murderer is still right here backstage. He might not've wanted to go past the guards, even though he knew he wouldn't be challenged. He might not've wanted to be noticed."

Again, Friedman nodded. "I'm aware of that. In fact, it's my offhand opinion that it's something like fifty-fifty that, literally, we could throw a rock and hit the murderer." As he said it, he let his shrewd, dark eyes wander around the oddly assorted group of people scattered backstage. As always, Friedman's jowly, swarthy face was as smooth and unrevealing as a Buddha's. "The problem is, though," he said, "that we can't detain this many people for questioning. Not for more than another hour, anyhow. Already, some of them are beginning to squawk. Loudly."

As he'd been speaking, I looked toward the far end of the stage, in the opposite direction from the taped-off light tower. David Behr and Deputy Chief Lawrence Pomeroy were surrounded by a half dozen reporters and TV cameramen. Smiling genially for the cameras, Pomeroy was gracefully gesturing with his hands as he talked.

Following my gaze, Friedman snorted. "When a wino gets murdered for what's left in his bottle, Pomeroy is playing bridge at his club, sure as hell. But whenever a camera's around, he's always there. The asshole."

I sighed. For as long as I'd known him, Friedman had been engaged in a grueling guerrilla struggle with almost all the departmental brass, including William Dwyer, the Chief of Police. In fact, Dwyer was Friedman's favorite target.

"Come on." I nudged him and pointed to Farley, who was projecting ill-concealed impatience as he stood beside the body. "Farley's waiting for us."

"Big deal," Friedman muttered sourly. But, obediently, he followed me to the body. Farley nodded to us, then ordered the two stewards to lift the woman.

Friedman pointed to the floor beside the makeshift wooden stairs. "Put her there, face up."

The two stewards obeyed, then stepped back. Friedman and I moved to either side of the body, both of us staring down at the remains of Rebecca Carlton.

She'd been in her middle to late twenties, perhaps her early thirties. Her chestnut hair was long and straight. Her face was oval. Her eyes were brown, slightly almond-shaped. Her nose was small and straight, her mouth wide and generously formed. She was heavily made up for the stage, with long false eyelashes, fluorescent blue-green eye shadow, bright orange lips. From throat to forehead, her skin was covered with a thick, shiny substance, tan-tinted. Decorating the dead face, the effect of the exaggerated stage makeup was grotesque. Trying to imagine the face without its makeup, I decided that it was probably an ordinary face, neither pretty or ugly.

She was about five foot seven inches tall, and probably weighed close to a hundred fifty, twenty or thirty pounds overweight for her height. Beneath the flame-red silk blouse her breasts were round and full. The straight-cut blouse was worn outside her slacks, falling to her upper thigh. The gleaming white silk slacks were tight at the thigh and flared at the ankle. Her slippers were silver, decorated with red and gold sequins. The ambulance stewards had arranged her so that the blouse covered her crotch. It was a thoughtful gesture. Rich or poor, famous or infamous, most homicide victims lose their bodily wastes when they die. Rebecca Carlton was no exception.

Slowly, knees cracking, Friedman knelt beside the body and began unbuttoning her blouse at the neck. His fingers moved deliberately, dispassionately. As the blouse fell away, I saw that she'd worn a full body stocking cut in a deep "V" between her breasts. The bullet had struck her just below the lower heart.

Was it a lucky shot?

Or an expert shot?

Friedman looked up, questioning me with a glance. I nodded. He took a firm hold of her blouse and slacks. Bracing himself, he grunted as he tried to heave her over on her stomach. At first the lifeless, inert body seemed consciously to resist him. But then, balanced at midpoint on shoulder and thigh, the body suddenly seemed to move of its own volition, flopping face down on the dirty concrete. The body settled itself like a bag of viscous liquid, obscenely flattened on the underside.

Once more, the steward stepped forward, this time moving the victim's face to one side, making it more comfortable.

Glancing at him, I wondered whether he was one of her fans.

Her back was blood-soaked, as we'd expected.

Friedman straightened, his knees cracking again. "No surprises," he grunted.

"No."

"Are we done with her?"

I nodded. With Farley's agreement, I gestured for the stewards to load her on their gurney and wheel her away. They did their job quickly and efficiently. Less than a minute later the coroner's van was driving through the performers' entrance. I borrowed a walkie-talkie from a patrolman, and ordered two fully loaded patrol cars to escort the van downtown. Remembering the frenzied fans outside, I could imagine them tearing the van open for one last look at their dead idol.

Five

"Jesus," Friedman said, shaking his head as he stared at the backstage scene, "this thing is turning into a real media circus. Honest to God, I've never seen anything like it. Everyone's in the act. We've got—" He moved his head, chin bobbing, counting. "We've got five TV cameramen here. And there's a couple of freelancers outside, trying to talk their way in."

"Have you had your picture taken?" I asked.

"No. Have you?"

"Yes," I admitted.

Friedman didn't comment, but his grumpy, shoulder-shrugging silence was eloquent. For Friedman, there were only two kinds of cops: the "politicians" and the "pros." Politicians schemed to get their pictures in the papers. Pros didn't.

"How the hell are we going to sort this out?" As I spoke, I glanced at my watch. The time was a little after one A.M. During the hour I'd been on the premises, we hadn't developed any new information beyond the few facts that Friedman had gathered when he first arrived at the Cow Palace.

All we had was a puddle of blood, a crime lab seal on the door of Rebecca Carlton's mobile home and a chalked circle at the base of the light tower. The technicians had made their measurements and dusted for fingerprints and labeled a dozen plastic bags full of floor sweepings. Now they were packing up their equipment, finished for the night. The police photographers were already gone. The uniformed men were yawning at their posts, guarding the exits and wearily explaining to impatient bystanders that, for now, no one could leave the premises. Some of the bystanders took it good-naturedly, some angrily.

I wondered whether they realized that a murderer might be among them.

"I'm going to see what Culligan and Marsten found out," Friedman said. "That's the key—backstage security." But his voice lacked its usual note of flat, complacent confidence. I thought I knew why. The hoopla had thrown him off stride.

I was looking at David Behr, who was surrounded by a group of costumed performers, stagehands and two men dressed in three-piece suits. Two of the performers were women. One of them was dressed in calico and homespun. She was crying, her cheeks streaked with makeup. The other woman was Pam Cornelison. Standing half a head taller than Behr, beautiful in her shimmering blue silk jump suit, Cornelison's eyes were dry, her expression cool and calm.

"Have you talked with Behr?" I asked.

"No."

"Then I'll talk to him."

"Good idea."

I walked over to the group surrounding Behr, and saw them fall silent as I approached. Some of them avoided my eyes; others looked at me with a mixture of cynicism and skepticism. The crying woman dabbed futilely at her eyes, making the runny makeup worse. Pam Cornelison transferred her calm, speculative stare from Behr to me.

"I'm Lieutenant Frank Hastings, Mr. Behr. Can we talk for a few minutes?"

Behr studied me for a long, deliberate moment before he asked, "Are you in charge of the investigation? Is that it?" His voice was brisk and clipped, accustomed to command. Beneath their dark, uncompromising brows, his small black eyes were as hard and unrevealing as two pieces of round, smooth obsidian. Even though he was a small man, Behr's muscle-bunched shoulders and his thick neck gave the impression of power. With his coarse hair falling in unruly curls across a broad, low forehead, Behr seemed more like a rough-and-tumble stevedore than a man who'd made a million before he turned forty.

I nodded, looking him straight in the eye. "That's it."

Apparently satisfied that I was important enough to claim some of his time, Behr turned abruptly away from the group, leading the way around the closest corner of the stage. Standing in an angle formed by the stage and an orange nylon curtain that fell to the floor, we could talk without interruption.

Turning to face me, Behr thrust his hands deep into his pockets, rocked forward on the balls of his feet and demanded, "Well? What's it look like?"

I studied him for a moment, then decided to say, "The truth is, it doesn't look like much. All we've got is the gun, and not much else. I'm hoping you can help me."

"Help you? How?"

"First, by telling me who would have wanted to kill her."

Behr's thick lips twisted in a tight, grim smile. The smile didn't warm his eyes. And it didn't change the hard, aggressive line of his bulldog jaw.

"If you're asking whether Rebecca had enemies," Behr said, "the answer is 'yes.' Lots of them. But if you're asking who could've killed her—" Still with his hands thrust deep in his pockets, he shrugged, once more rising on his toes. "That's something else. And it's not something I care to speculate about."

"You say she had enemies. Are any of them here?"

"You mean *right* here? Backstage?"

I nodded. "That's what I mean. Right here."

I saw his dark eyes shrewdly narrow. Then, abruptly, he moved two bandy-legged paces away from the stage and stood with his back to me, surveying the backstage scene. Again, he looked like Napoleon out of uniform, this time reviewing his troops. Finally he turned to face me.

"Remember, now," he said truculently, "I'm not talking about terms like 'enemies.' And, sure as hell, I'm not going to speculate about motives for murder. However, I'm willing to supply some input. The conclusions are up to you."

I nodded. "Fair enough."

"In other words," he pressed, "it's off the record."

"All I need are names, Mr. Behr. As for what's off the record, there's no witness to what we're saying. So, automatically, it's off the record."

"Okay—" He pointed toward the group he'd just left. "Rebecca's biggest current non-fan is probably Pam Cornelison. She introduced me, on stage just now."

"I know. What's her story?"

Her story is that she's *Pure Power*'s number two singer, after Rebecca. And Pam's coming up fast, some say. Myself included. I was telling the truth when I said that Rebecca never sang better than she sang tonight. But that was tonight. The last year, though, she's been going downhill. Fast."

"And Pam Cornelison was her competition. Is that right?"

He nodded. "That's right. You've got it."

"Why did Rebecca start to slide? Was there a reason?"

"Some would say she was just plain burned out. This is a full-throttle business, you know. Either you give it everything, or you're out on your ass. It's that simple. And she'd been going full throttle almost nine years. Full throttle, and then some." He paused, then said, "But I don't think that was it. Or, anyhow, it wasn't the whole story. Her personal life was a mess. She started drinking too much, and doping too much. Which is always the beginning of the end, guaranteed."

"What was wrong with her personal life?"

"The usual," he answered. "Men. Sex. Love." Indifferently, he shrugged. "Take your pick."

"It's all the same."

"Right. It's the same merry-go-round. The faster you go, the harder it is to get off."

"You said you were married to her."

He didn't reply, but only nodded. His black eyes revealed nothing.

Matching his silent stare, I let the silence lengthen. Then, quietly, I said: "Can you give me a rundown on her, Mr. Behr—a thumbnail sketch of her life, maybe? It would be very helpful."

With his brooding, uncompromising eyes boring into mine, he took a moment to consider. Then, again, he shrugged his chunky shoulders. The shrug was apparently a trademark.

"Did you ever hear of Bernard Carlton?" he asked brusquely.

"The writer? Sure. You mean—?"

He nodded. "Rebecca's father. And if you want to understand how Rebecca got the way she was, you've got to start with her father. He was a goddamn monster. He had neuroses that rock musicians never heard of. And that's saying something."

"But he was talented."

"Right. Talented. And so was Rebecca. We started in this business about the same time, Rebecca and I. Literally, we made each other. She was nineteen years old when I first heard her sing. I was thirty-four. I was just scratching out a living, trying to find someone I could make explode. She was the one. She signed with me and I got a group together behind her. The timing was perfect. San Francisco was where it was just starting to happen, and Rebecca jumped way out in front. Me, too. A year later, when she got her first gold record, we celebrated by getting married.

"It only lasted two years—two roller-coaster years. We were both of us off on our own separate highs. Looking back—" He shrugged. "Looking back, I can see that, among other things, we made the mistake of believing what we paid people to write about us. She was the 'reigning queen of rock,' and I was the 'rock impresario,' a 'genius.'" He snorted bitterly, shaking his head. "Big deal."

"But it was true, it seems."

Once more, he snorted. "Sure it was true, if you went by the sales figures. The problem was, though, that we were destroying ourselves, and our marriage, and a half dozen people around us in the process. Neither of us had the faintest idea who we were, or where we were really going. All we knew was that we wanted more of everything—more money, more fame, more success. But the more we got, the more we wanted. And by the time we realized what was happening, it was too late. Or, at least, it was too late for Rebecca. She started running wild. She was on the road most of the time, and I was here. Inevitably, she started screwing around. And—" Again, the shoulder-bunched shrug. "And I did, too. It was all part of the life. The more sensations you had—the more men or women you screwed—the more you wanted.

"So finally, two years later, we got divorced. But, as you heard me say earlier, we were still business partners. I—" He paused, and for the first time his voice sank to a softer, more reflective note. "I always tried to look after her, financially, at least. And in—other ways, too, whenever I could." He blinked, and cleared his throat. He was staring at Rebecca's motor home, with "Pure Power" painted on the side in huge block letters.

"Did she get married again?"

"Oh, sure. Immediately. She married Sam Wright, the singer." He glanced at me. "Ever hear of him?"

"No. I don't know much about music, I'm afraid. I just

know the famous names, that's all—Dylan, Ronstadt, Carlton."

"Yeah. Well, the point is that Sam might've been one of them, if he hadn't married Rebecca. He had it all—he was on his way. He could write the songs, and he could sing them, too. With management, he could've done it all, no question."

"Were you his manager?"

"No, I wasn't. But I knew him, and tried to help him. I always liked Sam. I warned him not to marry her. But, of course, he thought I was jealous. And, looking back, I can't blame him. It was only natural."

"I take it they're not still married."

"As a matter of fact, they are. Or rather—" He winced. "They were. But it hasn't been a marriage for years. Not really. Or, at least, not for Sam. I gather that, once in a while, when Rebecca was playing San Francisco, she'd drop by Sam's place for a quick screw and maybe some scrambled eggs in the morning. But that was the end of it. She married him, and she sucked him dry. And then she left him. I always thought of her like you think of the female praying mantis. She finds a mate, and copulates with him—and then she eats him. That's what happened to Sam. She destroyed him. She made it a contest, him or her. But there was never any question who would win. She was strong, and Sam was weak. Or, at least, he was weaker than Rebecca."

"You make her sound almost vicious," I said.

Once more, he shrugged impassively. "Rebecca was a mankiller. In this business, you see a lot of them. Maybe it goes with the territory. Sometimes I think it does."

"She didn't kill you," I prompted.

Slowly, he shook his head. "No, she didn't. So we got a divorce. It was a little like a peace treaty, I guess—a negotiated peace. Neither one of us could win, so we called it a draw."

"Is Sam Wright here tonight?"

"No."

"Let's get back to Pam Cornelison—" As I spoke, I looked at Cornelison, so tall and blonde and beautiful in the blue silk jump suit. "What about her?"

"I already told you that she's been closing in on Rebecca. Both of them knew what was happening. They hated each other."

"Why did they both sing with *Pure Power*? I'm surprised Rebecca stood for it."

"She didn't have a choice," he answered shortly. "It was my decision. They're both first-class talents, and *Pure Power* is a first-class group. They're all under contract to me. If I say 'play,' they play. Period."

I smiled wryly. "You're tough."

"This is a tough business, Lieutenant. You're either way up, or you're way down." He stared at me for a long, defiant moment before he said flatly: "And I intend to be up. Always."

"Who's the leader of *Pure Power*? Rebecca?"

"No. She was the lead singer—the front person. It was her show, and she was the one they came to see. She chose the music, and set the style. But she didn't know a thing about writing music, or arranging, or playing the instruments. She just knew what she liked to sing. I knew what the people liked. And that was it."

"I gather, though, that you made her let Pam sing, too."

"That's right. I was taking out insurance. Rebecca was on her way down. It was obvious. It didn't matter whether her problems were self-induced or not. Facts are facts. So I'd be pretty stupid not to be bringing someone else along. It's only good business. And also, as I said, they're all under contract to me—Rebecca, Pam, Richard." He spoke in the same flat, defiant voice.

"Who's Richard?"

"Richard Gee—" He turned away again, scanned the backstage crowd and pointed to a group of two men and a woman sitting together on the makeshift steps of a motor home parked adjacent to Rebecca's. "He's the leader of *Pure Power*—that Chinese kid. He's only twenty-one, but he's a genius. He's one of the best guitarists in the country. Plus he writes, and arranges. He's amazing. He never smiles, and he doesn't talk, unless he's got something to say. But, Jesus, he can play. And write, too. He's got seven gold records. *Seven.* "

As he spoke, I watched Pam Cornelison leave her own group and walk toward Richard Gee. Seeing her approaching, Gee rose to his feet and stepped to the end of the motor home, where she joined him. Gee wore blue jeans, short boots and a faded khaki safari jacket open down the front. The deep "V" of the safari jacket revealed a smoothly muscled torso. His straight black hair hung almost to his shoulders. His features were classically Oriental: calm, impassive, remote. He moved gracefully and deliberately, projecting a kind of aloof disdain for those around him. If he'd been dressed in embroidered silks instead of denims, he could have been an ancient Chinese prince.

Gee and Cornelison spoke briefly, their faces revealing nothing. Now they turned their backs to the throng and moved closer together, thigh touching thigh. It was a quick, instinctive movement, revealing an unmistakable physical intimacy. I saw him raise his hand to the small of her back, where it lingered a moment before it fell to the swell of her buttocks. In response, her blonde head inclined toward his shoulder. But then, quickly, they stepped away from each other.

"They're friends," I said. "Good friends. Right?"

"You noticed, then." Behr spoke noncommittally.

"I noticed."

For the first time he smiled. His small, shrewd eyes mocked me as he said, "A sensitive cop. The new breed, eh?"

I didn't reply. I didn't like cop jokes.

The smile lingered for another sardonic moment. I had the unmistakable feeling that, while he eyed me with obvious condescension, he was wondering how many times he could divide my salary into his income. Finally he said, "You're bound to hear the rest of it, so you may as well hear it now—" He gestured to Gee and Cornelison. "Yes, they've got something going. You're right. But the rest of it is, Rebecca and Gee had something going, too. Or, to be more precise, she had a thing for him. It's an open question how much he responded."

"He's responding to Pam."

He snorted. "Most men respond to Pam. It's called animal magnetism. And she's got it. Lots of it. Rebecca, on the other hand, was getting a little pudgy from all the booze she drank. As you may have noticed."

"So maybe we've got a triangle," I mused aloud. "Except that the loser is dead, not the winner. Usually it's the other way around."

"No comment."

"Who else should I know about?"

"The enemies list, you mean? Or the lovers list?"

"You choose. Just give me some names." ·

"All right—" He turned again, facing the group he'd left when he'd joined me. "Do you see that tall, dark, good-looking man who was standing beside me—the one who's dressed like a stockbroker?"

"Yes."

"Well, that's Ron Massey. He's been Rebecca's manager for about a year. Which, in this business, means different things to different people."

"What'd it mean to Rebecca?"

This time, Behr's shoulder-bunched shrug was contemptuous. "It meant," he said, "that he did everything Rebecca told him. Everything, and anything. The old-fashioned word was toady, I think. And that describes him. Perfectly. He's a tall, handsome toady—a goddamn gigolo. But he's rich. Thanks to Rebecca."

"Were they sleeping together? Is that what you mean by 'gigolo'?"

"Whenever she felt like it they did," he answered coldly. "She used him like a bottle, or a needle. And, all the while, he was getting his ten percent."

"What's ten percent of Rebecca Carlton worth?"

"I'd just be guessing, if I named a figure. And I don't like to guess."

"Try," I pressed him. "Off the record."

"Well," he answered, "in a bad year, which this year has been, Rebecca would easily gross a million dollars on record royalties alone. Probably more."

"Jesus."

He nodded. "Right. This is big business, Lieutenant. I've been trying to tell you."

"Massey would want to keep her alive, then," I mused.

"Not necessarily. The rumor is that she wasn't going to renew his contract, which didn't have long to run—again, according to rumor. If that's true, and if their contract insured him against her loss, then he'd have a gilt-edged reason to kill her." He spoke flatly, without inflection. All business.

"Are agents' contracts usually written like that?"

He nodded decisively. "Definitely. It's almost universal. In fact—" The smile returned, quietly mocking me now. "In fact, I'm insured against her loss." He looked me straight in the eye, amused at my inevitable next question:

"How much will you get?"

"A half million dollars," he answered. "Tax free." The mocking smile widened as his eyes still held steadily on mine. He was enjoying my awed reaction:

"Jesus."

"Exactly."

"Will Massey get that much, too?"

"You'll have to ask Massey."

"I will. Who else was a beneficiary?"

He shrugged. "I have no idea. I imagine, though, that Sam Wright was. Or, even if he wasn't named in an insurance policy, he's still probably a rich man. I doubt very much if Rebecca left a will. I'm almost positive she didn't, in fact."

As he spoke, I heard a familiar voice calling my name. It was Canelli, from somewhere behind me. As I turned, I heard Behr mutter:

"Christ, it's the idiot brother. Now the goddamn cast is complete."

Canelli was walking beside a tall, gangling young man who looked to be in his middle twenties. He was dressed in sandals and dirty chino trousers. A roughly woven, peasant-style Mexican serape covered his upper body, falling to mid-thigh. A huge pagan sun-symbol hung around his neck, supported by a thick chain. His shoulder-length blond hair was dirty and tangled. His beard, a darker blond, was thin and ragged. Because his face was pale and gaunt, his colorless eyes seemed abnormally large beneath sparse, unformed brows. The eyes were fixed and fervent—locked inexorably on me as he advanced with long, uneven strides. There was something potentially violent about him—something wild and unpredictable. He could have been part of a fanatic foreign mob, rioting in support of some strange, avenging holy man.

"This," Behr muttered, "is where I fade into the scenery. Meet Justin Wade, the victim's stepbrother. Lots of luck. You'll need it."

As he turned away, I put my hand on his arm. "Where can I find you tomorrow?"

"Call my office. David Behr Productions. I'll leave word at the switchboard, so they'll either put you through or else tell you where I am." He nodded, glanced once more at Justin Wade, then walked off quickly.

Even before I turned to face Justin Wade, I heard him saying, "Is this the man—the one in charge?" His voice was high and sharp: a thin, ragged falsetto.

"That's him," Canelli said. "Lieutenant Hastings."

Wade stood an inch taller than me, but beneath the serape his body was scarecrow sharp. He looked underfed, or ill— or both. His complexion was sallow. His throat was scrawny, his hands and wrists bony. His sandaled feet were long and narrow.

"Where is she?" Wade demanded. He stood barely a foot from me, with his face thrust close to mine. His lips were drawn back over his teeth, as if he were in pain. His voice was trembling now, almost breaking. His breath was bad. Seen close up, his enormous eyes shone with a strange, unhealthy luster. I wondered whether he was running a fever.

"She—" I hesitated. "She's gone. Taken away."

"And she's dead? *Dead?*" Now the feverish eyes came closer, accusing me. I realized that I'd stepped back before him, disconcerted by the sheer force of his emotion. Was it grief? Anger? Something else? I couldn't decide.

I gestured to the angle of the stage and the curtains, where Behr had taken me earlier. "Let's step over here, Mr. Wade." I took his arm, guiding him. Canelli questioned me with a look, and I gestured for him to come along. With Wade's back to him, Canelli caught my eye, inclined his head toward Wade, and rolled his eyes elaborately upward, shaking his head. The message: Canelli voted with Behr. Wade was a weirdo.

Wade strode quickly to the orange curtain, then wheeled to face us. With his lips still drawn back from his teeth, he opened his mouth and lifted his chin. He could have been struggling for breath—or hyperventilating. Both his bony, long-fingered hands clutched hard at the rough woolen material covering his chest. With his wild eyes, his tortured mouth and his desperate hands, he looked as if he might rip his clothing, parodying a paroxysm of Old Testament grief.

He held me for a moment with his luminous eyes locked into mine before his voice dropped to a hoarse whisper: "I knew it would happen. I felt it happening. It came like a pain —a terrible, mortal pain. And I knew. *Knew.*"

As Canelli's eyes again rolled upward, I asked quietly, "How do you mean, you knew it would happen?"

"I told you," he breathed. "I felt it. That's why I came.

I felt the pain, and I knew. So I came. To help."

"If you knew it would happen," I said, "then you must have some idea why she was murdered—and who murdered her. Is that right?"

Slowly, disparagingly, he shook his head. "No. You've got it wrong. All wrong."

"Then tell me how it was." I folded my arms, prepared to wait. For a long moment we stood facing each other, silently staring. Finally, with his eyes fixed just above my head, he began speaking in a kind of hollow, eerie monotone:

"You are a policeman, Lieutenant Hastings. That's your profession. Your calling. Is that right?"

I nodded, but he took no notice. So, as if I were forced to join in a responsive reading, I answered, "Yes, that's right."

Satisfied, he continued in the same strangely disembodied voice: "My calling is different, though—different from yours, different from anyone else's." With his eyes still raised, he paused. Then, softly: "We are all unique, each one of us. And my uniqueness—my gift—is that I am a seer." Another long, somber pause followed, plainly calculated for its effect. As he'd spoken, his hands had unknotted themselves from the woolen serape, and now hung loosely at his sides. He stood with his chin raised, eyes elevated. But now the tension was gone. The painfully corded muscles of his neck were smooth. The harsh, haggard contours of his face had been transformed into an expression of almost beautific calm.

"I was at Aztecca, with my people, when I first felt it," he said softly. "It tore at me like a murderer's knife, here—" He raised one hand, to touch his heart. "And, instantly, I knew she was dead. I knew that she'd been murdered."

Self-consciously, Canelli cleared his throat. "How'd you know it was murder? I mean, couldn't it have been an accident? Or a heart attack, maybe?"

Wade shook his head. "No. I knew it was murder. I could feel the tearing of flesh. And I could feel the terror, too. And then I knew. *Knew.*"

48

"What you're telling us," I said, "is that you have ESP. Is that it?"

He didn't answer, but instead turned toward Rebecca's trailer, raising his serape-draped arm to point.

"Is that where it happened? There?"

"Yes."

Still staring at the trailer, he nodded. His eyes were blank, as if he'd gone into a self-willed trance. Slowly, dreamily, the outstretched arm dropped to his side.

I tried another tack: "You said you were at Aztecca when you—" I hesitated. "When you felt she was killed."

Again, his head inclined gravely. "Yes."

"Where is Aztecca? How far away?"

He shook his head. "I don't know. I don't think in terms of space and distance. Or time, either."

I decided to join in the game: "You think in terms of the spirit, then." I tried to make it sound hushed, respectful.

He turned toward me, searched my face for a moment, then intoned: "That's right, Lieutenant. The spirit. Exactly."

Canelli cleared his throat again. "What's Aztecca, anyhow?"

Wade's empty eyes moved to Canelli. "It's a place of refuge, Inspector. A retreat."

"For you and your people, I gather."

"Yes."

Frowning thoughtfully, Canelli nodded. "How many of you are there?" he asked.

Wade's pale lips moved in a small, indulgent smile. "It's not a numbers game, Inspector. Others count. Not us."

Shaking his head, Canelli murmured something inaudible.

Still trying to play the game, I asked, "What did you do, when you felt your stepsister die?"

"She was my sister. Don't say stepsister. Not now."

"All right. Sorry. Sister, then. Tell me what you did. What action did you take?"

For a moment he didn't reply, but simply stared off toward

Rebecca's trailer, at the same time stroking his scraggly beard. Then, very softly, he said, "I began the process of willing my entrance into a different dimension. I knew she was gone, you see, and I knew I must go with her, as far as I could. So I withdrew to a dimension we could share, together."

"What the lieutenant is after," Canelli said, "is something a little more—" He cleared his throat. "A little more down-to-earth. Like, how you got here, for instance. Did you drive, or what?"

"Yes," he answered. "I drove."

"How long did it take you?" Canelli pressed.

"I don't know. I left after midnight."

"Was that immediately after you felt her die?" I asked.

"No. I meditated first. I've already told you."

"Did anyone come with you?"

"No. I wanted to be alone. It was probably a mistake—probably a dangerous mistake, because I slipped from one dimension to the other as I drove. I shouldn't have done it. I shouldn't have driven. But I knew I must be alone, so that I could keep in contact."

"With your sister, you mean."

"Yes."

I nodded, at the same time glancing at my watch. Already, I'd spent too long with him.

"Would you mind waiting here for a moment, Mr. Wade?" I asked, at the same time gesturing for Canelli to follow me as I stepped toward the corner of the stage. "We've got a little business to take care of."

Again the dreamy smile touched his lips as he raised his hand in a kind of parting benediction. As we walked around the corner of the stage, I saw Wade's eyes return to his stepsister's trailer.

"Whew—ee," Canelli breathed. "He is something else. What'd you make of him, Lieutenant?"

"I'm not sure. But I *am* sure that I don't have any more time for him. He's yours, Canelli."

"Oh, Jesus." He shook his head. "I could feel it coming."

"Get his whole story," I ordered. "He's part of the victim's family. He should have something for us. Clear?"

"But, Jeeze, the way he rambles, Lieutenant, it could take me all night."

"Just get his whole story, no matter how long it takes. Go back to Aztecca with him, if he's going."

"But what if Aztecca isn't even in San Francisco?"

"Canelli—" Wearily, I dropped my hand on his shoulder. "Improvise. Use initiative. Already, this is a big case, and by tomorrow it'll be a lot bigger. Whatever help you need, get it. On my authority. But I want his story. Clear?"

He sighed heavily. "That's clear, Lieutenant. I guess I'll see you tomorrow, then? At the Hall?"

"Right. At the Hall. Good luck."

"Yeah," he answered ruefully. "Thanks."

Six

I watched the murder scene replayed on the TV news while eating breakfast the next morning. Driving to the Hall, I heard the story repeated on news-talk radio. When I parked in the Hall's underground garage, three local newspaper reporters were waiting for me at the elevator. When I got out of the elevator on the third floor, two TV crews followed me down the hallway to my office. Inside the office, my phone was ringing.

The caller was Friedman. "I hope you wore a clean shirt," he said.

"Where are you?"

"In my office, hiding. It turns out I didn't have a clean shirt."

"What time did you leave the Cow Palace?"

"About a half hour after you did. Two o'clock."

Rubbing my burning eyes, I sighed. Even when I'd gotten home, I hadn't slept well. I couldn't forget the quarrel with Ann.

"What now?" I asked.

"Now we compare notes, and then put the pieces together.

I'll see you in a few minutes, just as soon as I hear from a couple of computers."

Friedman knocked once on my office door and came in without being invited. He made for my visitor's chair, and sank into it with his customary grateful sigh. It was Friedman's contention that, in the entire department, my visitor's chair was the only one that could comfortably accommodate his two hundred forty pounds.

He settled himself, took a cigar from his vest pocket, and began thoughtfully stripping off the cellophane wrapper as he said, "Lately, it seems that we've had more than our share of homicides that turned into media events. But this one, I predict, will be a record-breaker."

He balled up the wrapper, tossed it casually at my wastepaper basket, then began searching his pockets for a match, grunting as he shifted from one big ham to another. Beginning with the balled-up cigar wrapper, which had missed the wastebasket, it was all part of an inevitable early-morning ritual. Eventually he would find a match, light his cigar and toss the match toward the basket. If the wrapper always missed, the smoking match invariably sailed straight and true.

"Rebecca Carlton was a big star," I said. "One of the biggest, apparently."

Friedman lit the cigar and tossed the match into the basket. As I watched the basket for smoke, he got the cigar going to his satisfaction before he said, "Did you hear the rumor that she's going to lie in state on the stage of the Cow Palace while millions of fans come from all over the world, to file past the bier?"

"Jesus, no."

"That's just one scenario. There's also a rumor that her ashes are going to be scattered over the Pacific from an airplane that'll be leading a formation of a thousand other planes. God—" He shook his head, awed by his own speculations. "Just imagine what the *Rebecca Carlton Lives* T-shirt concession will be worth, to name just one skam."

"Has Canelli come in yet?"

"I haven't seen him," Friedman answered. "By the way—" He shifted his cigar from one fat hand to the other, and drew a computer printout from his inside pocket—in the process dislodging an inch-long cigar ash, which fell unheeded on his vest. Tossing the printout on my desk, he said, "The ownership of the gun just came in from Sacramento. Sam Wright. Who's he, anyhow?"

"He's the victim's husband."

Friedman's eyebrows shifted slightly higher. Except in extremities, it was the only sign of surprise that ever registered on his smooth, swarthy face. Friedman's style was to startle others, not be startled himself.

"Are you sure?" he asked.

I shrugged. "I haven't seen the marriage certificate. But David Behr said they were married several years ago. It hasn't been a marriage for a long time, Behr says. But it's apparently still legal."

"Well, then, I guess we should talk to him," Friedman said thoughtfully. "How about you doing it? I'll stay here and try to keep the strings together."

"All right. What does ballistics say? Is it the gun that killed her?"

Friedman nodded. "It's the gun, all right. One shot was fired. The lab identified four sets of latent prints on the gun itself, and two on the cartridge cases. One set belongs to the victim. The other three are up for grabs."

I lifted my telephone and ordered Culligan, in the squad room, to locate Sam Wright and have his premises staked out, front and back. When he'd done it, Culligan would notify me. I broke the connection, then called the lab, ordering them to get a three-man crew ready, with a paraffin-test kit added to the usual fingerprinting and specimen-collecting equipment. And, finally, I phoned for a search warrant.

As soon as I replaced the phone in its cradle, it rang.

"It's Canelli, Lieutenant. Jesus, what a time I had last night. You want me to come in?"

"Come on in, Canelli."

Gently, Friedman smiled. "Do I understand that we're about to be treated to one of Canelli's suspense-filled reports from the field?"

Staring at the computer printout, I didn't reply. The gun was a .357 magnum, Smith and Wesson, purchased three years ago, new.

According to Behr, Sam Wright hadn't been backstage at the Cow Palace last night. But he could have been in the audience. After the encores, he could have slipped through the curtains and killed his wife. Then he could have gone back through the curtains and left with the departing crowd, one face among thousands. Fifteen minutes later, he could have been at the airport. By now, he could be in New York, or Mexico.

Or Europe, or South America.

Or else at his home, waiting for us—ready with a plausible reason why the murder weapon bore the victim's finger-prints.

I heard Canelli's soft, tentative knock at the door. Even though Canelli had been my driver for almost a year, he still approached my office as if he were a schoolboy sent to the principal for misconduct.

Canelli edged into the office, greeted Friedman with a hesitant nod and slid uneasily into a chair. Physically, the two men were almost identical. Each of them weighed well over two hundred, not all of it muscle. Each of them managed to look perpetually disheveled, no matter what he was wearing, or how recently he'd been to the barber. Each man's face was round and swarthy, with full lips, a large nose, at least one double chin and brown eyes beneath thick, dark eyebrows. Their dark-brown hair grew low across the forehead, and was never quite combed.

But their personalities were almost exact opposites. At age fifty-four, a homicide lieutenant for almost twenty years, Friedman knew exactly who he was, and precisely what he thought of almost everything. His mind was quick and subtle, his humor ironic and whimsical. As long as I'd known him, Friedman had always kept at least one jump ahead of everyone, the good guys as well as the bad guys. To Friedman, police work was a long-running, good-humored game.

Canelli, at age twenty-seven, was always playing catch-up ball. He was the squad room's resident innocent. He was the only policeman I'd ever known who got his feelings hurt, and admitted it. He didn't think like a cop, or look like a cop, or act like a cop. But, precisely for those reasons, Canelli could do things that left his colleagues gasping. On stakeouts, or trailing a suspect, Canelli was the last one to be made. No one, it seemed, took him seriously. He was a consistent loser in a constant succession of minor skirmishes with machines, especially cars. Yet, in hot pursuit, Canelli seemed to drive with an angel on his shoulder.

Now, as he balanced his outsize body precariously on the edge of his chair, Canelli was nervously clearing his throat, ready with his report on Justin Wade.

It was Friedman, lolling belly-up in his own chair, who asked Canelli how it went last night.

"Well," Canelli said fervently, "I want to tell you, Lieutenant, that guy is really something else. I mean, he's either crazy, or else he's some kind of a genius. Or maybe both, for all I know. I mean, it's like he's on one level, or something, while everyone else is on another level. Which, when I think about it, is what he keeps talking about. Like, different levels of existence, and experience, and everything, with him on some kind of a plane all his own."

"Maybe that's where you got the idea," Friedman murmured. "From him."

"Maybe so," Canelli said amiably, oblivious to Friedman's good-humored gibe. "Well, anyhow, taking it from the top, you might say, I spent the first hour or so just following him around, backstage at the Cow Palace—and out in front, too. He kept asking me where we thought the murderer stood, and how we thought he got away, and how many shots were fired, and everything. Which, of course, I didn't tell him. I mean, even if I'd known, which I didn't, I wouldn't've told him. So anyhow—" He paused for breath.

"So anyhow," he continued, "after an hour of that, when he seemed to be kind of sniffing everything out, sort of, he finally said that he was ready to go back home. So, remembering that he'd said he really should't've driven to the Cow Palace by himself, I asked him if he wanted me to drive him. He said okay. So we got in his car, which is a big old Cadillac that's about ten years old, and all dented up, and sounds like a threshing machine, and we started out. By that time, it was almost two o'clock. He was exhausted, he said, and he kind of laid his head back on the seat beside me. And then he started to ramble. You know—just saying whatever came into his head, you might say."

Canelli paused, took out his notebook, thumbed the dog-eared pages back and forth, read busily for a moment with his lips laboriously moving, then continued: "He said that his mother and Bernard Carlton—Rebecca's father—were married when he was twelve years old, and Rebecca was sixteen. His mother, I gather, is just about as high-powered as Bernard Carlton was, which is pretty high-powered. I mean, it sounds like they were both pretty high livers, but also pretty mixed up, and pretty hard on each other. They were always breaking up, Justin says, and then getting back together, and like that. And also, there was a lot of drinking. Or, at least, Bernard Carlton did a lot of drinking—and, according to Justin, a lot of everything else, including screwing around."

"It sounds like he and Rebecca had a pretty tough life," Friedman observed.

Canelli nodded. "Right. It sounds like they were—you know—the typical poor little rich kids, with all the money, and cars, and servants, and everything that they wanted, but no love."

"How did Bernard Carlton die?" I asked. "Cirrhosis of the liver?"

Canelli shook his head. "Nope. It was an airplane crash. His own airplane, for God's sake."

Friedman sat up straighter. During the Second World War, he'd been a bomber pilot. "How'd it happen?" he asked.

"He didn't say," Canelli answered. "It was about three weeks ago. At the time, Rebecca was going to give a concert, down in L.A. Which, of course, she canceled, when she heard her father had been killed. So, last night, she was giving a make-up concert, you might say. I mean, the promoters of the L.A. concert lost a bundle, when she canceled."

Remembering Behr's comments, I said, "They were probably insured."

Canelli shrugged. "Maybe. I don't know about that."

"What about Justin?" Friedman asked. "What's his story?"

"Justin's story," Canelli said, "is that he's the kooky head of one of those kooky religious cults. At least, that's my opinion."

Wryly, Friedman shook his head, at the same time leaning laboriously forward to deposit his cigar butt in the ashtray. "Life in California," Friedman grunted, settling back in his chair. "In the East, you know, they say that someone tilted the country, and all the nuts rolled out here, to California."

Canelli smiled. "Hey, Lieutenant, that's a pretty good one. I never heard that before." He nodded appreciatively, repeating, "That's pretty good. I like that."

"What about this cult?" I said. "How's it operate?"

"Simple," Canelli answered. "It operates around Justin. He's the messiah, I guess you'd say. He's got the faithful convinced that he sees visions. Which, of course, is what the hocus-pocus is all about. His visions. They apparently do a kind of a pagan thing, the way it looks to me. You know— primitive rites, and everything."

"What's Aztecca?" I asked. "Is that their headquarters?" Canelli nodded. "That's right, Lieutenant. It's an old, tumbled-down mansion down near the Daly City line, out by the ocean. And, honest to God, it looks like a haunted house. I mean, you'd have to see it, to know what I'm talking about. It's like—" Canelli frowned. "Who's that guy that does those weird cartoons, and they made that Munsters TV series about them, once?" Canelli chewed at his lip, searching for the name.

"Charles Addams," Friedman said.

Brightening, Canelli nodded. "Yeah. Right. Well, this house looks like one of those Charles Addams houses, and that's no fooling."

"How many are in this cult?" I asked.

"Justin said about forty."

"Do they all live in the house?" Friedman asked.

Canelli shrugged. "I guess so. I mean, at that hour, I didn't see any of them. But Justin said they were there. So I guess they were, all right."

"Were you able to get independent confirmation that Justin used ESP to learn about Rebecca's death?" I asked.

"Not last night I couldn't. I mean, they were all asleep, naturally, when we got there. But, first thing this morning, I went back. And I talked to a good-looking black woman. Her name is Anya. That's not her real name. It's the name she took, when she joined up. They all have those kinds of names, I guess. So, anyhow, Anya said that, about midnight last night, when mostly they were all asleep, Justin suddenly came tearing out of his room, which is right next to hers. I gathered that she was kind of the manager, out there, sort of. So, anyhow, she said that Justin came busting out, carrying a kerosene lamp. Did I say that they don't have electricity?"

"No."

"Well, they don't. But, anyhow, Justin suddenly starts wailing, she said, and carrying on, and saying that he's got to get to his sister, who just died."

"Were those his exact words?" I asked.

"That's right, Lieutenant. Exact. At least, according to Anya."

"You didn't happen to toss his room, did you?" Friedman asked, "to see whether he had a transistor radio?"

"No," Canelli admitted. "I thought about it, naturally. I mean, I was *curious,* you know? But I didn't have a warrant, or anything. And I could tell, by the way those characters were acting, that they weren't about to let me poke around. But, naturally, I asked Anya whether he had a radio, being as subtle about it as I could."

"What'd she say?"

"She said that there wasn't a radio, or a record player, or anything electronic in the whole place. Except for flashlights, for emergencies. It's part of their pagan, back-to-nature thing, the way I get it."

"Did you believe her?" I asked.

Again, Canelli shrugged his beefy shoulders. "I didn't see anything electronic. Nothing at all."

"Are you saying," Friedman said, "that you think this so-called vision of Justin's was the straight goods?"

"Jeeze, Lieutenant—" Canelli turned his soft brown eyes plaintively on Friedman, at the same time spreading his hands. "Jeeze, I don't know *what* to think, if you want to know the truth. I mean, I—"

My phone rang.

"It's Culligan, Lieutenant. I just wanted to tell you that Sam Wright's at home, and the place is staked out."

"Is it staked out tight?"

"Tight. Guaranteed. I'm at the scene now."

"All right. Good. Canelli and I will be out in about a half hour. I want to pick up a warrant first."

"You want me to try and soften him up a little?"

"No. Let me. Just make sure he stays put."

Seven

"That's the one." Culligan pointed to a one-story house situated on the slope of a Mission district hill. It was a Victorian-style house, one of thousands built row upon row at the turn of the century. For decades, the Mission had been a workingman's neighborhood, but in the fifties and sixties, San Francisco began evolving into the Manhattan of the Bay Area. It was a carefully calculated evolution. First, the city began exporting its slums across the bay, to Oakland. Second, places like Fisherman's Wharf and the Barbary Coast were given a coat of gilt and handed over to the tourists. Corporations were offered tax incentives to build downtown skyscrapers. Convention centers were erected. And finally, a debt-plagued, disaster-prone rapid-transit system was built to connect San Francisco to the surrounding suburbs.

In the process, neighborhoods like the Mission district changed from blue-collar to a kind of radical chic. Victorian houses that sold for twenty thousand dollars ten years ago had been repainted to accent the gingerbread trim, and sold for fifty thousand dollars five years later. In San Francisco's current go-go real estate market, the same house, repainted again, with a remodeled kitchen and bath, could bring a hundred fifty thousand.

Standing with Canelli and Culligan, I studied the house. With its three-color façade, its plate-glass picture window and its newly built used-brick wall and walkway, it was a textbook example of a restored-for-profit Victorian. But, on close examination, both the house and its grounds were beginning to show signs of neglect. A drape had come loose from its track on the window. One of the beveled glass panes in the elaborately carved turn-of-the-century door had been cracked and then repaired with aluminized tape. The small front garden was a thicket of weeds. The big Mercedes convertible parked in the driveway was dirty and dented, with one of its taillights broken out.

Was it lack of money? Lack of interest? Something else?

"Is there a back alley?" I asked Culligan.

The tall, bony, stoop-shouldered detective shook his head. His expression was doleful, almost dejected—as if the absence of a rear alley might jeopardize the whole operation. If Canelli was the squad room innocent, Culligan was our crepe-hanger. Culligan had a peptic ulcer, a nagging wife and a son who grew organic marijuana in a Colorado commune. In all my twelve years in Homicide, I'd never seen Culligan smile. His expression always remained as I saw it now: face folded into long, morose lines, with sunken cheeks and a mouth drawn down at the corners, permanently discouraged. From everyone, Culligan expected the worst. He was never disappointed.

"There's no alley," Culligan said. "But I got a man in an adjoining yard, back there."

"Is Wright inside, do you know?"

"Yeah. When I got a man for the front, I went around the corner and called the house, pretending that I was selling aluminum siding. He's in there, all right. Or, at least, someone's in there—some guy."

"Where's our man in front?"

Culligan pointed to a battered van parked a few doors down the hill. I frowned. The percentage play was to park up the hill, in case a pursuit developed.

"I've been up the hill in my car," Culligan said, anticipating.

"Oh. Good." I realized that I'd never really doubted it. Culligan was thorough. Steady, and dependable, and thorough. And brave, too. I'd never seen him flinch.

"You stay here," I ordered. "Canelli and I will go in."

"There's a shotgun in the van," Culligan suggested. "If you want me to, I could park it in front, and cover you."

I shook my head. "I don't think so. Thanks anyhow." I looked at Canelli, who nodded in return. He was ready. Walking briskly, side by side, we crossed the street and mounted the three steps to Sam Wright's small front porch. I hoped we looked like two salesmen, or city inspectors.

A dirty curtain was hung across the three glass panes set into the door. Again I questioned Canelli with a glance, at the same time unbuttoning my jacket and loosening my revolver in its spring holster. With his hand on his own revolver, Canelli nodded, then moved to his right, out of line with the door's three panes. I pressed the bell-button, then stepped to the left.

For the first two rings of the doorbell, nothing stirred inside. I felt my stomach slowly, uncontrollably tightening. Entering suspect premises, an officer could count on a kind of grim predictability: the longer the suspect took to answer the door, the tougher it could get for the man ringing the doorbell.

But on the third ring, I heard footsteps approaching down the hallway. A moment later, the door swung open. A tall, slim, sandy-haired man stood slouched in the doorway. He wore blue jeans and a gray sweatshirt that had been haphazardly cut off at the elbows. Both the jeans and the sweatshirt were slightly soiled. His sparse hair was uncombed, earlobe-long. His face was covered with a dark, two-day stubble of beard. His bloodshot eyes were dull, and looked defeated. His face was pale, puffed beneath the eyes, painfully drawn around the mouth. His feet were bare.

Even from three feet away, I could smell liquor on his breath. As if to confirm it, he lurched slightly, touching the wall for support. His outstretched fingers trembled.

"Mr. Wright? Sam Wright?" As I spoke, I took my shield case from my pocket, flipped it open, and showed him the badge.

He looked down at the badge, frowned, then looked up at me, squinting into the Saturday morning sunlight.

"I'm Lieutenant Frank Hastings," I said. "This is Inspector Canelli. We're here about your wife, Rebecca Carlton. Can we come in?" Asking the question, I stepped expectantly forward. Without protest, he gave way. A moment later, with the door closed behind us, we stood crowded awkwardly into the small entry hall. I stepped to my left, and glanced through an archway into a cluttered living room. "May we sit down?" I asked.

He drew a deep, unsteady breath, pushed himself heavily away from the wall and lurched into the living room.

"Whew," Canelli breathed, wrinkling his nose as he whispered to me: "Smells like hundred proof, at least."

With Sam Wright sprawled on a leather sofa, Canelli and I found separate chairs that faced the sofa across a huge tile-topped coffee table. As I settled myself, I looked quickly around the room. Obviously, the furnishings had been chosen with no thought of expense. My chair was made of zebra skin stretched over oiled walnut. The sofa was glove leather. Across the room, one wall was covered with elaborate sound equipment. Original paintings hung everywhere. Oriental rugs were scattered on a floor already carpeted with beige wool. The lamp beside my chair had been made from a huge Oriental brass urn that looked like a museum piece.

But, like the outside of the house, the interior showed signs of neglect. Polished wooden side tables were marked with rings. Not one of the paintings hung straight. Some of the Oriental rugs had been cigarette-burned, and the leather sofa was ripped across one arm. Although the furniture was dusted and the windows clean, the room smelled of dirt. Magazines, discarded newspapers, records and tapes were scattered everywhere. Dirty dishes and empty wine bottles covered the top of an ornately carved Spanish sideboard.

Sam Wright was sitting motionless, with legs spread wide, arms slack at his sides. His chin was sunk on his chest. His breath was coming hard, rattling loose and wet in his throat.

Now, suddenly, he raised his head. With his mouth slack, eyes blinking blearily, he looked first at Canelli, then at me. Then, with his washed-out eyes fixed on mine, he raised his right hand in a gesture of wan futility. He lifted his chin, cleared his throat and said, "She's dead. Just like her father. Murdered, for God's sake."

I nodded. "That's why we're here, Mr. Wright."

"Oh, Jesus—" The hand rotated, palm turned up, then fell heavily to the sofa beside him. "Call me Sam. Anybody calls me Mr. Wright, I automatically know they're after something."

I watched him until I caught his wandering eye and held it. Then, softly, I said, "You're right. I'm after something."

His lips twitched into a drunk's slow, crafty leer. "You're one of the clever ones, then. You admit it up front, so I'll put my guard down. Is th—" He burped: a sudden explosive exhalation. "Is that it?"

Still holding his eyes with mine, I nodded slowly. "That's it."

He braced his bare feet on the floor, pushed with his hands on both sides of his body and finally succeeded in levering himself to a more erect position on the leather sofa. He raised his chin and frowned, making an obvious effort to focus his bleary stare on me.

"You've got kind eyes," he said suddenly. "They can be cold, but they're kind." He continued to stare at me for a

66

moment. Then, suddenly: "How do you feel, when you kill someone? How does it make you feel, afterwards?"

"How do you know I've killed anyone?"

"It's in your eyes," he said softly. "It's all there, in your eyes."

Beside me, I heard Canelli sigh.

"Are you interested in killing, Mr. Wright?" I asked.

"I'm a singer," he answered. "And a songwriter. And there was a time when people told me I was a poet, too. They saw poetry in my lyrics, they said. And poets, you know, are interested in everything. That's what makes them poets." As if the thought suddenly overwhelmed him, he stopped talking. His eyes wandered off toward the sound equipment. Following his gaze, I saw a gold record, framed and hung on the wall above the equipment.

"They called me a balladeer," he said softly, still staring at the gold record. "A poet of the people. *Time* did a piece on me once. It was a page and a half. And that was the headline."

"What was the headline?" Canelli asked.

Wright frowned and looked at Canelli, puzzled. Finally he said, *"Sam Wright, a Poet of the People."*

"Oh." Canelli nodded. "Sorry."

Indifferently, Wright shrugged, waving away the apology. I watched him sink into his previous slack, boneless posture. He'd lost interest in his story.

"Were you at the concert last night, Mr. Wright?" I asked quietly.

He shook his head. "No. I haven't been to one of her concerts for years. Two, three years. Maybe longer."

"Where were you, last night?"

I saw a small, uncertain spark of defiance stir deep in his washed-out eyes. "Why?"

"Just answer the question."

For a long, resentful moment he didn't reply. Then, frowning, he said, "I was here. Right here."

"Alone?"

"Yes."

"All night?"

He nodded. "All night."

"Did you talk to anyone on the phone?"

He blinked, frowned again and finally shook his head, sighing deeply. "Last night wasn't any different from most other nights, Lieutenant. I stayed here, and listened to tapes. And, if you want the whole sordid story, I drank wine. Lots of wine. Then, finally, I went to bed. It was—" He burped —quietly, this time. "It was what you might call a typical evening, around here." He spoke in a low, mumbling monotone. He didn't raise his eyes.

"Don't you have any friends?" Canelli asked.

I glanced at Canelli, slightly frowning. It was the wrong question—a question that could put the suspect on the defensive. As he often did, Canelli had acted impulsively.

Wright turned to Canelli, studied him for a moment, then slowly shook his head. "No, Inspector," he said softly, "I don't have any friends. I have a few fans left, here and there. And, every once in a while, someone calls to ask me for a favor, or maybe for a loan. But I don't have any friends. I used to think I had friends—lots of friends. When I was giving concerts, and seeing my picture on posters, and reading about myself in *Time,* I used to think I had friends. But it turned out I was wrong."

I waited a second before I said, "You have a gun registered to you, Mr. Wright. A Smith and Wesson revolver. Is that right?"

He looked at me, frowning at the question. Then, slowly, his eyes incredulously widened. "You're saying that you think I killed her," he whispered. "That's why you asked where I was last night."

Not replying, I let him search my face for the answer.

"Jesus," he said, shaking his head in a dull, defeated arc.

"Jesus Christ. What'd she do—leave a note saying I wanted to kill her?"

"It wasn't a note," I answered. "It was the gun. Your gun. And it was found backstage last night, about thirty feet from your wife's body."

He blinked. "My gun?"

I nodded.

"But I didn't have the gun." As he spoke, his voice rose a single thin, plaintive octave. "I haven't had it for years."

"Can you prove it?" Canelli asked.

"Prove it?" As if he were puzzled, Wright squinted at Canelli with forehead furrowed, mouth puckered. His eyes were frightened.

"The gun is registered to you, Sam," I said. "It's your gun. And it killed her. There's no doubt about it."

"But—Jesus—that's impossible."

"Why?"

"Because Rebecca had the gun. She kept it in her motor home. All the time."

"Can you prove that?"

Still puzzled, he scanned my face. Then, as realization dawned, he shook his head, suddenly resigned. His body went slack. Once more, his head fell until his chin rested on his chest. "I can't prove that I didn't have the gun, and I can't prove that I wasn't there, last night. So you think I killed her. Jesus."

I decided not to reply.

He heaved a deep, self-pitying sigh. "Are you here to arrest me? Is that it?"

Again, I didn't answer. If he was sinking into a drunken, maudlin bout of self-pity, I could learn more by listening than I could by talking.

For more than a minute, the silence held. Then I saw his shoulders shaking, and I heard him chuckling. "God," he said, "it's the final bit of irony, you know that?"

"How do you mean, irony?" I said it softly, careful not to intrude on his mood.

"I mean," he answered, "that even when she's dead, she's still screwing me over. She's—Christ—she's never going to let go. Never. Not until she's got me dead, like her. It—" Once more, he began laughing, this time tittering on the edge of a kind of exhausted, defeated hysteria. "It's so typical—so goddamn typical. It—Christ—it's my goddamn destiny. My karma. I might just as well—" He broke off, then began slowly, sadly shaking his head. At the same time he stretched out his hand toward a side table, and groped blindly behind a table lamp until he found a half-filled glass of white wine. As if he were meditating, he stared deep into the wine. Then, quickly, he drained the glass.

"I might as well face it," he mumbled.

"Face what?" I asked.

"Face the fact that I'm never going to get rid of her. I had—" He gulped, then grimaced. "I had about one minute—just one—after I heard about it, when I thought, Christ, I'm free. *Free.* But then—" Once more he helplessly, hopelessly shook his head. "Then it all came back. Everything. Right from the beginning—right from the first time I ever saw her. I—I knew she was trouble, even then. It was in her eyes, and in her gestures, and in the way she carried herself. There was a special kind of arrogance about her. I can still see her sitting on a musician's stool, watching me. We were about even, then—both of us coming up, fast. So, of course, we'd heard of each other. We were both cutting demos. She was scheduled right after me. She was listening to me sing, and she was keeping time with her hand, tapping her thigh. She was smiling, too. It was kind of a bold, knowing smile. I had the feeling she knew something about me that I didn't know myself, and she was deciding whether or not she'd let me in on the secret." He drew a long, shaky breath, sighing sadly. "It's incredible," he said, "but the whole thing between us started then. The pattern was set, from that first moment. It was set, and it didn't change. It was like she was drawing something out of me, just looking at me like that. Because I couldn't concentrate on what I was singing, for watching her. I knew I was fluffing it. And, sure enough, when I heard the tape, everything was off. Not off by much—but off enough.

"But when it was Rebecca's turn, she did it just right. And, in fact, that was the first time she ever recorded "Nightingale Morning," her first big hit. But the tune I was recording never got off the ground. And that's the way it was, for both of us. That's the way it started. And that's the way it ended, too."

"How did you hear that she'd been killed?" I asked.

"I heard it on the TV, just like anyone else. Just—" Bitterly, he snorted. "Just like the rest of her fans. Millions and millions of them."

"Do you know where she kept the gun?" Canelli asked.

He waved a wan hand. "I already told you. In her mobile home."

"But where in her mobile home?"

He shook his head. "I don't know. How should I know?"

"When was the last time you were in her mobile home?"

"Ab—" He cleared his throat. "About six months ago, I guess. Or maybe it was longer. Maybe it was more like a year. Christ, who knows? Who remembers dates?"

"Is that the last time you saw your wife?"

"No. I saw her at her father's funeral. And then, that night, she stayed here. That's the last time I saw her."

"That was about three weeks ago?" Canelli said.

Wright's head bobbed loosely, nodding. "Right. Three weeks ago."

"When you say—" I hesitated. Then: "When you say she stayed here, do you mean that you—slept together?"

Again, the disheveled head bobbed loosely. "Yes," he answered, almost inaudibly. "Yes, we slept together. Because, you see, that's the problem."

For a moment, I looked at the bowed head before I said, "You loved her, you mean. That's the problem?"

Silently, he nodded. Then, softly, he began to cry.

Eight

"What'd you think, Canelli?" I asked, bracing myself as he took the cruiser around a corner too fast. "Was he telling the truth?"

Canelli frowned. "To me, Lieutenant, it looked like he was. Plus I don't see him killing her. I mean, what we got here is premeditated murder, probably. And that takes balls, as they say. And Sam Wright, he just doesn't have them."

"I agree. But, still, he had a motive. She was driving him crazy. And Behr says that he'll inherit her money. Millions, probably."

"It seems to me," Canelli said, "that he was driving himself crazy, and blaming her for it."

"If we get independent confirmation that she kept the gun in her motor home," I said, "then Wright's probably off the hook."

"He could've gotten backstage, though, to get the gun. For him, it would've been easy."

"Agreed. But, backstage, he would've been spotted, sure as hell."

"Yeah, that's right, Lieutenant. I see what you mean. But,

on the other hand, if he's lying about her having the gun, then he could've been out in the audience, with the gun on him. The rest would've been easy. He'd just wait for the concert to end, and then slip through the curtains, and pull the trigger—and then go back through the curtains. No sweat."

"Except for one thing," I said.

"What's that?"

"Everyone who goes to a rock concert gets searched at the door."

"What?" Disbelieving, Canelli looked at me with round, astonished eyes.

I nodded. "Everyone," I repeated. "Mostly, they're looking for liquor. But they search for weapons, too."

"Well, I'll be damned." He considered for a moment, then said, "Still, with his knowledge of the layout, he could've stashed the gun."

Nodding agreement, I said, "I think you should pin that gun down. Try to find someone who spent a lot of time in the mobile home with Rebecca, and see whether they actually saw the gun."

"A maid, maybe?"

"A maid, or a lover. Try Richard Gee. He's the leader of *Pure Power.* David Behr says they were lovers. Try Ron Massey, too. Her manager."

"What about you, Lieutenant? What're you going to do while I'm doing that?"

"I'm going to talk to Rebecca's stepmother. She's at 3670 Pacific Avenue. Drop me there, and then start working on the gun. I'll see you back at the Hall."

"Yessir."

"If you'll wait just one moment," the maid said, "Ms. Dangerfield will be with you." She gestured me to a small damask armchair, nodded politely, and was about to leave the room when I said:

"I wanted Mrs. Carlton."

Again, she nodded politely. She was a young, attractive Chicano woman with the smooth, impassive face of a Mayan madonna. "Yes." To reassure me, she smiled gravely. "Yes. Mrs. Carlton."

Ms. Dangerfield—Mrs. Carlton. Referring, apparently, to the same person.

I sighed. The deeper I dug into Rebecca's life, the more complex the investigation of her death became.

I looked around the small study. The room was furnished entirely with delicately scaled antique furniture, obviously to a woman's taste. The walls were covered with watered silk; the drapes were a rich brocade. The desk was French provincial, exquisitely carved. An old-fashioned French phone rested on the desk, along with a small picture framed in filigreed silver. Looking at the picture, I recognized a head-and-shoulders likeness of Bernard Carlton. Dressed in a tweed sports jacket and soft shirt worn open at the throat, he stared straight into the camera, unsmiling. He appeared to be in his early forties when the picture had been taken. His face was narrow, with a wide, firm mouth and aquiline nose and intense, remorseless eyes beneath generously arching brows. It was an arresting face: handsome, intelligent, obviously well-bred. But, perhaps, a little overbred. As I looked at the picture, I remembered F. Scott Fitzgerald, and his lost generation.

I glanced at the phone, then at my watch. The time was almost noon. Since eight o'clock, when I'd stumbled out of bed, I'd been trying to find a free moment to call Ann. I wanted to tell her that, because of the Carlton homicide, I might not be able to spend tomorrow with her and her sons, as we'd planned.

And I wanted to tell her that I hadn't slept well last night, because of the things we'd said to each other—and the things that had gone unsaid. I wanted to tell her that, all day, I'd felt empty and alone. I wanted to make her understand that

I couldn't face the possibility of not seeing her—of not spending time with the three of them: Ann, and Billy, and Dan. I couldn't imagine not making love to her, holding her naked body warm against mine, with her head tucked into the hollow of my shoulder while we whispered together in the bedroom darkness.

But I wanted to tell her, too, that I needed more time with her—and with myself—before I could answer the questions that she'd asked last night.

I'd risen to my feet, and had my hand outstretched to the phone when the door suddenly opened.

Guiltily, I turned to face a strikingly beautiful woman who stood with one hand on the doorknob, the other hand propped on one slim, exciting hip. She was dressed in a light gray woolen turtleneck sweater and beautifully cut wool slacks. Her dark eyes came provocatively alive as she smiled at me.

"Reaching for something, Lieutenant Hastings?"

"I—ah—wanted to call my office."

She swept her arm gracefully toward the desk. "Go ahead. Please."

"No—" My own gesture of denial felt stiff and awkward. "That's all right. But thanks, anyhow."

Still smiling, she moved to sit behind the desk, at the same time gesturing me to the damask armchair. As I sat down, I realized that my chair was lower than hers, and that I must look up at her.

Sitting as erect as I could, I said, "I've come about your stepdaughter, Mrs. Carlton. If it's convenient, I'd like to ask you some questions."

"It's Ms. Dangerfield," she said. "Cass Dangerfield. I'm a writer, like my husband was. A novelist. And I've always used my own name."

"Sorry." As I said it, I considered the progression: Dangerfield, then a probable marriage to Wade, the father of Justin. And then, finally, marriage to Bernard Carlton.

And, in between, there could have been other marriages, other names.

"What're the questions?" As she spoke, she picked up a slim, jewel-handled dagger, balancing it idly in her hand. She was looking out through French doors that opened on a small formal garden, and I took the opportunity to study her. Even though the close-fitting sweater and slacks suggested the body of a much younger woman, the coarsening texture of her face and neck put her age in the early forties. Her brown hair was thick and curly, cropped close to her head. Gray hairs mingled with the brown asserted her independence without diminishing her vitality, or her beauty. Her face was small, but its features were strong, decisively drawn. She held herself with a calm dignity that was, I suspected, often taken for arrogance. Her dark eyes were both bold and quick, yet unrevealing. Watching her eyes, and remembering her opening gambit, I decided that Cass Dangerfield's natural instinct was to take the initiative—and keep it. Whatever the game, she would play to win.

"The first question," I said, "is the most obvious. Do you have any idea who would have wanted to kill Rebecca?"

"None whatever," she answered briskly. "But I've always assumed that, in the rock-and-roll milieu, life is cheap. Either they OD on drugs and kill themselves, or else they hallucinate and kill someone they think is the devil—or, maybe, an angel, depending on the drugs they take."

"That's a pretty harsh assessment, Ms. Dangerfield."

"It's a pretty harsh life," she countered coolly. "No one should know that better than you, I'd think. And, therefore, I make the assumption that you want the truth as I see it, unvarnished. If I'm wrong—if you'd rather have homilies, and protestations of grief, and a few pious platitudes about how sweet and wonderful I found Rebecca and her friends—then I'm afraid you've come to the wrong place, Lieutenant. Because I don't have time for all that. I've got funeral arrangements to make." As she

77

spoke, she idly tested the dagger's edge with her thumb. "It's your second funeral in three weeks."

She nodded, staring straight into my eyes. "That's correct." There was no sign of sorrow, either in her face, or in her gestures, or in her voice.

"As I understand it, then, you think that someone who was associated with your stepdaughter's profession got high on drugs, and killed her. Is that right?"

She shrugged. "Yes and no. I don't have anyone specific in mind. I'm speaking generally."

"You don't know of any enemy she might have had?"

"No."

"I wonder whether you could give me some background on Rebecca."

"What kind of background?"

"Anything that occurs to you. What kind of a person was she? How did she get along in the family? What about her friends and associates? Did she dislike anyone? Hate anyone? Love anyone?"

Her mouth stirred in a small, cynical smile. "Hate, yes. Love, no. At least, not if you subtract sex." She paused, letting her gaze wander out to the garden. Then, speaking slowly and deliberately, with what seemed like carefully calculated malice, she said, "Rebecca wasn't capable of love. Neither was her father. They were, however, capable of lust —a neurotic, insatiable lust. Both of them."

Watching her, I wondered whether she was capable of love either. I remembered Justin Wade, with his strange visions, and his wild, blazing eyes. Was the son capable of love? I doubted it.

"It sounds like—" I hesitated, searching for the phrase. "It sounds like you might've had a difficult time together, the four of you."

The cynical smile returned. It was broader now, more ironic. "It wasn't exactly an average, middle-class American life, if that's what you mean. We didn't say grace at the table,

78

or roast chestnuts over an open fire." Now the smile was condescending, subtly taunting me. The meaning of the smile was plain. She doubted whether I could comprehend the kind of life she led. To Cass Dangerfield, policemen were plebes: proletarians whose only function was to make life easier for the Carltons and the Dangerfields of the world. People like me read about people like her in the newspapers and the magazines.

Briefly—peevishly—I wondered whether she'd ever noticed my name in the newspapers.

To try and disconcert her—shake her infuriating poise— I decided on another tactic: "I met Justin last night. When he heard about the murder he came to the Cow Palace."

Unperturbed, she nodded. "Yes. Justin would do that. Did he come looking for emanations? Or was it publicity? Or both?"

"Does he actually see visions? Are they real?"

She shrugged. "They're real to Justin. They've always been real to him."

"And to his followers, too, I gather."

She looked at me narrowly for a moment before she said, "It's easy to sell Justin short, Lieutenant. He's always been a little—odd. All his life, people laughed at him. But he might have the last laugh."

"How do you mean?"

"I mean," she said, "that Justin can make people catch fire. Most of them, admittedly, are neurotic, if not downright unbalanced. But, still, they do what Justin tells them to do. And that's power."

"To me, it sounds a little frightening."

Again, she shrugged. "The early Christians frightened a lot of people, too."

"Are you comparing Justin to Christ?"

The question amused her. "If I compare Justin to Christ," she said, "it's only because I'm a card-carrying atheist."

I thought about it for a moment while I watched her toy

79

with the small jeweled dagger. Then, mostly out of curiosity, I asked, "How long were you and Mr. Carlton married?"

"Eleven years."

"So—" I calculated. "So Rebecca would have been about sixteen years old, when you were married."

"That's right. And Justin was twelve. If you want the other numbers, I was thirty-one and Bernard was forty-eight. And, if you're trying to decide what kind of a marriage it was, I can tell you that the first few years were pure hell. Bernard and I always had an up-and-down relationship, even before we were married. And it's no secret that both the children were discipline problems, to say the least. By the time she was seventeen, Rebecca had already spent six months in Juvenile Hall."

"What was the offence?"

"She was a runaway."

"That's not usually cause for arrest."

"It's cause for arrest if the runaway was caught trying to steal a drunk's wallet in Los Angeles." She smiled as she said it. Obviously, the memory gave her a perverse pleasure.

"Was it her first felony offence?"

"Yes."

"Then, normally, she still wouldn't've served time. She would've been paroled to your custody. There must've been something else."

"There was something else," she answered calmly. "Her father refused to take her back."

Grimly, I smiled. "He thought six months would shape her up. Is that it?"

Examining the tip of the dagger, she nodded.

"But it didn't work," I said. "Did it?"

"Why do you say that?" It was a quiet, offhand question. She wasn't defensive. She was simply curious about my reaction.

"Because," I answered, "it never works."

"What does work, Lieutenant?"

"Parental love," I answered. "And parental time, too. Lots of both."

Her smile mocked me as she said, "You're a real do-gooder, aren't you? A bleeding heart. Somehow you don't look the type."

"I'm a professional policeman, Ms. Dangerfield. And any policeman will tell you that, in ninety percent of the cases, adult criminals were juvenile delinquents. It's a simple matter of statistics."

"Well," she said, "Rebecca was one of the ten percent. Every time she opened her mouth, she made a million dollars. She was a success."

"That's a matter of opinion. To me, her life sounds pretty grim."

"We were talking about criminal behavior, Lieutenant. Not happiness. Remember?"

"Someone killed her," I said. "That's criminal behavior."

"Some sickie killed her."

"Are you sure?"

"No," she retorted. "But you aren't either, are you?" There was an unpleasant edge to her voice. In that instant, I thought I understood the nature of Cass Dangerfield's relationship to men. It was an antagonist relationship: a constant, grueling contest.

I decided not to play the game with her. Instead, changing the subject, I said, "I understand that she was very upset by her father's death."

"Why do you say that?" Her voice was still edged. Her eyes were cold. She was still looking for a fight.

"Because, for one thing, she canceled a concert when he died."

She snorted. "Anything else would've been bad PR. The truth was, she and her father hated each other. Or, at best, they had a love-hate relationship."

"How do you mean, 'love-hate'?"

"I mean," she said, "that it was almost a textbook example

of a totally guilt-ridden relationship—on both sides. Bernard was incapable of sharing any of himself with her. So, to compensate, he spent money on her. Which, of course, she rejected. Or rather, she rejected the things that money could buy. If it was a car, she smashed it up—and herself, too, sometimes. If it was clothes, she either ruined them or gave them away. If it was money, she lost or squandered it. And, all the while, she punished herself—because she felt guilty for punishing him. It was a process that gathered a momentum of its own—like a steam engine running wild, with the governor broken. She even intended to give away her inheritance, when she got it—more than a million dollars."

"*A million dollars?*"

She nodded.

"How much was his estate worth?"

"About five million," she answered calmly.

"Did he leave more than a million to you, too?"

"I'm not sure that's any of your business, Lieutenant."

I held her eye for a moment before I said, "In a homicide investigation, Ms. Dangerfield, everything is my business."

Her smile mocked me as she said, "The answer, then, is yes. We were to get equal shares—Rebecca, Justin and me."

"But Justin wasn't even his natural son."

For a moment she didn't reply. Then, as her eyes strayed again out toward the impeccably landscaped garden, she said, "Bernard didn't care about money. He made lots of it, and he inherited lots more. He also spent lots of it. But, except for its value as a weapon, or as a means of mocking people, he never cared about money."

"What did Bernard care about?"

Her gaze returned to me, and now the mockingly ironic smile teased the corners of her mouth again as she said quietly, "It wasn't me, if that's the question. We had a love-hate relationship, too. True, it was a little more complicated than his relationship with Rebecca. But, basically, it was the same. Except that we were more equally matched. Rebecca could only hurt him by hurting herself. I could give him a better fight. Which is what he wanted, of course. A fight."

"You make your husband sound like a monster, Mrs.—Ms. Dangerfield."

"He was a monster. But he was also talented. And, at another level, he was dangerous. Living with him was an adventure. You know—like climbing mountains, or keeping lions for pets."

"Are you saying that he threatened you?"

"No," she answered, "not physically. Bernard was more complex than that. His arena was the mind—the soul. He was an absolute virtuoso. I've seen him reduce people to tears with a single sentence—one short, cruel thrust. It was an art form with him—like a matador, killing with exquisite grace and economy. But, ultimately, he was self-destructive. He was killing himself, both physically and psychologically. And, of course, that's what happened. He killed himself."

"Suicide, you mean?"

"That wasn't the coroner's verdict," she answered calmly. "But, sooner or later, he was bound to kill himself, flying. Everyone knew it. No one would fly with him. He was almost always drunk when he flew. The miracle was that it didn't happen sooner." She paused a moment, staring thoughtfully down at the dagger. Then she said: "It was the perfect end for him, actually—Götterdämmerung. A grand, fiery finish for a godlike figure. That's the way he saw himself, and that's the way he died. He orchestrated it. Just like he orchestrated everything else in his life. In a way, it was magnificent. Sick, but magnificent."

As she said it, the French phone rang. *Newsweek* was calling, asking for an interview. It seemed like a good point to end the interrogation. I left her in her elegant study, talking to *Newsweek*.

Nine

Riding to the Hall in a sector car, I switched the radio to a civilian band, and learned from a local news program that David Behr had just offered a $25,000 reward for information leading to the conviction of Rebecca's murderer. I smiled to myself. Someone less cunning—and more serious about the offer—would have paid the reward when the suspect was arrested, not when he was convicted. As the offer stood, Behr could easily get $25,000 worth of free publicity before the trial even started.

At the Hall, I used a back stairway to avoid reporters, then went through Chief Dwyer's anteroom and down a short hallway that served Dwyer's office, the Bureau of Inspectors and Homicide. Except for a single bored-looking sergeant taking calls that the switchboard couldn't—or wouldn't— handle, both the chief's office and the inspector's bureau were deserted. Even the white-hot publicity furor surrounding the Carlton homicide hadn't been enough to bring the departmental brass and their plainclothes subordinates into their offices on an unseasonably warm Saturday afternoon in March.

If the rest of the bureau was deserted, a peek around an aluminum-and-glass partition revealed that Homicide's small reception room was packed. Against one wall, Richard Gee and Pam Cornelison stood side by side before a window that offered a view of San Francisco's downtown skyline, with Treasure Island and the Bay Bridge for background. An NBC cameraman was focusing on the pair, while a man-and-woman reporter team conducted the interview, on camera. All four of the principals—Pam, Richard and the two reporters—were dressed in the rock tradition: fashion-faded blue jeans, expensive shirts opened to the third button and elegant boots. Behind the cameraman, obviously acting as stage manager, Ron Massey was in earnest conversation with Howard Rappaport, NBC's San Francisco manager. Massey was dressed in an impeccable maroon blazer, gray flannel slacks, silver-buckled loafers and a striped tie. With his finely chiseled profile and his elegantly styled hair, he looked as if he might be on his way to a Hillsborough garden party.

Across the room, I saw Justin Wade. Today, he wore a one-piece white woolen robe that fell to his ankles. The robe was circled at the waist by a narrow beaded belt that was secured by a knotted cord. With his long hair combed and his face composed, fingering the massive Aztec sun medallion hanging on its heavy chain around his neck, Justin looked convincing in the role of a pop messiah. The illusion was enhanced by four of his youthful followers who stood two on either side of him. Dressed in robes identical to Justin's—but with smaller medallions around their necks— they stood silently, impassively staring straight ahead. I wondered whether they'd been interviewed by NBC. Somehow I doubted it.

The remaining chairs in the reception room were taken up by an oddly assorted group of people who, at first glance, seemed to have nothing in common. Adam Farwell, the newest member of Homicide, sat at the reception desk. Catching my eye, he raised his eyebrows and

85

surreptitiously lifted his shoulders. Then he pointed to the phone, and nodded to me. I had a call—or an important message. Or both.

I backed away from the glass partition and walked down the inside corridor to my office. When I lifted my phone, Farwell was already on the line.

"Inspector Canelli is back from the field, Lieutenant," he said, speaking softly. "And Lieutenant Friedman would like to talk to you."

"All right. Ask them both to come into my office. What about Justin Wade?"

"He's—ah—" Discreetly, Farwell coughed. "He's waiting to see you, Lieutenant."

"Does he know I'm here?"

"No, I don't think he saw you."

"Then don't tell him. But don't let him leave without notifying me. I'll get to him as soon as I can. Clear?"

"Yessir, that's clear."

"Who else have you got out there, anyhow? The place looks like a zoo."

"That's about it, Lieutenant," he answered laconically. "They're the confessors."

"Christ, there must be ten or fifteen of them."

"Yessir. Lieutenant Friedman says it's a record."

"I can believe it."

"Jeeze," Canelli said, marveling as he shook his head. "I can't get over it. Fourteen of them. And it hasn't even been twenty-four hours since she was killed."

"That's only the ones who applied in person," Friedman said drily. "I took three confessions over the phone."

"But why do they *do* it?" Canelli asked plaintively. "I've never understood why."

"Everyone wants to be a big shot," Friedman grunted. "And the more important the victim, the more important the murderer. It's simply mathematics."

"But, Jeeze, they're admitting to *murder.*"

"If it gets them some attention, they're willing to take their chances," Friedman answered. "Next to being loved, that's what people crave most—attention."

"Who's taking their statements?" I asked Friedman.

"Culligan and Marsten," he answered. Then: "How'd it go with Sam Wright and Mrs. Carlton?"

As concisely as I could, I described the two interrogations, beginning with Sam Wright. When I finished my account of the Dangerfield interview, Canelli was once more shaking his head. "That," he said, "sounds like a very, very sick marriage."

"Apparently that's what sells books," Friedman said. "And records, too." He paused a moment, then said thoughtfully: "I wonder what'll happen to Rebecca's share of Carlton's estate, now that she's dead."

"That's a good question," I admitted. "I should have asked."

"Has the will been probated?"

"I don't know. But he's been dead for three weeks. I imagine it's been probated."

"I'll check on it," Friedman said, taking out his notebook and jotting a reminder to himself.

"Good." I turned to Canelli. "What about the gun?" I asked. "Did she keep it in her motor home?"

Canelli waved toward the reception room. "I talked to them all, Lieutenant—Cornelison, and Richard Gee, and Massey. I questioned them all separately, plus I talked to David Behr on the phone. And I found Rebecca's maid, too. And I talked to her fitter, or whatever you call him—the one that made all her clothes, and her costumes, and everything. And they all said the same thing."

As Canelli paused, Friedman murmured, "He's doing it again—building the suspense."

"They all said," Canelli continued, "that they'd never seen her with a gun, and they'd never seen a gun in her motor home, either. And, what's more, they never even heard her *talk* about having a gun."

"Which would seem to put the ball in Sam Wright's court," Friedman said.

"Not necessarily," I said. "Don't forget—Rebecca's fingerprints were on the gun."

"That's true," Friedman admitted, frowning.

"Maybe Sam Wright gave her the gun, and she put it away and didn't take it out again," Canelli offered. "Then the murderer could've stolen it, and used it to kill her. He could've stolen it weeks ago. Months ago, even—and then waited for the right time."

"All of which doesn't let Sam Wright off the hook," Friedman said. "If he was planning ahead, he could've let her handle the gun, to get her prints on it, and then taken it home." He turned to me. "Have you got him under surveillance?"

I nodded. "Two men. Around the clock."

"Is there any way we can prove he wasn't home last night?" Friedman asked.

I turned to Canelli. "Why don't you check out his neighbors? If that Mercedes in the driveway is his, it's a car that people remember. We might find someone who saw it leave, last night."

"Yessir." Plainly glad of the chance to escape from my office, Canelli bobbed his head goodbye and quickly left.

"I get the feeling," Friedman observed, "that you don't think much of Sam Wright as a suspect."

"I can see him getting drunk, and killing her in a rage. But I can't see him planning to do it. And any of the scenarios that we've been discussing involve planning. Lots of planning."

"I don't agree. He might not've planned it. He might've simply taken the gun to the concert, and sat in the audience. He could've been drunk, or stoned, or both. It's the accepted thing at rock concerts, I understand. Then, after the encores, he could have gone through the curtains and done the job."

"Don't forget that he would've been searched at the door."

"Big deal. He could've put the gun down the front of his pants."

"Maybe," I answered doubtfully.

Pressing the point, Friedman said, "To me, it sounds like he probably blamed her for all his troubles. It also sounds like he was brooding about it—more than he realized, maybe. And brooding, plus booze, or drugs, can be a very powerful combination. And that's not even counting his profit motive."

"Why don't you talk to him?"

"Perhaps I will. Incidentally, do you know that Justin Wade is waiting for you?"

"Yes. What's he want?"

"I don't know. However, I get the feeling that he's taken quite a fancy to you."

"To me?"

Friedman nodded, smiling owlishly as he said, "He seems to think that, for a cop, you're a sensitive, feeling human being. And, obviously, he considers himself an authority."

I snorted.

"So," Friedman said, grunting as he hoisted his bulk out of my visitor's chair, "I'll leave you with Justin, while I have a talk with Sam Wright."

"What about the other ones—Cornelison, and Gee? And, especially, Ron Massey. One of us should talk to them, as long as they're here."

"You're right. Why don't I take the beautiful Pam, and the talented Richard. Then, on my way home—if I should be so lucky, tonight—I'll interrogate Sam Wright."

"Fair enough." I nodded goodbye to Friedman, at the same time lifting my phone. I told the officer on duty to ask Ron Massey to wait for another fifteen minutes. Then I ordered Justin Wade sent in—without his disciples.

Standing behind my desk, I gestured Justin to my visitor's chair. But he shook his head, and instead stood midway between my desk and the door. I hesitated, then decided to resume my seat. It was the wrong decision. Looking up at him, I felt as if my authority were shriveling. With his arms calmly folded, chin lifted, dressed in his early-Christian robe, he was obviously at ease—in control. Last night, distraught and disheveled, he'd seemed a farcical figure. Today, he was convincing.

He spoke in a thin, clear, concise voice: "I've been waiting for you, Lieutenant. It's been more than an hour."

"I've been in the field," I answered. "I've been interrogating suspects." And, immediately, I regretted saying it. To myself, I sounded like someone trying unsuccessfully to explain away some unspecified shortcoming.

He seemed not to have heard. Instead, with his eyes fixed just above my head, he said, "This morning, during meditation, I was able to see how it happened, last night. And, of course, I wanted to tell you about it. Immediately." He spoke in the same precisely measured voice. But now, as if he were speaking from a trance, the cadence had fallen into a slightly singsong monotone.

"Good," I said. And—again—I felt faintly foolish, having said it.

"It came to me during my morning meditation," he repeated. "All night, you see, while I slept, I'd willed my unconscious self to return to the murder scene. I realized, of course, that the pain would be acute. But, nevertheless, I understood that, before I could find peace, I must return, with Rebecca. I must *know.*"

This time, when he paused, I decided to say nothing. Instead, I watched his face. Still fixed above my head, his pale, nondescript eyes had become strangely luminous, focused on some distant unearthly void. Whatever vision he'd seen this morning, it was returning now. Following where it led, he was wandering off into another world.

"And—suddenly—it all came clear," he said. "It happened without conscious warning—as it often does. First I was with her, on stage, singing her last song. And then, while she was still singing, I was leaving her. I could still hear her, but I'd gone. I was backstage, behind the curtain. My vision had become remote—as impersonal as a camera's eye, seeing everything, feeling nothing, judging nothing. I saw faces, all of them turned toward her. Some of the faces were familiar, others were strange to me. And then—" His voice trailed off. His empty eyes narrowed, as if he were straining to see his vision more clearly. "And then, I saw the man's figure. I saw it go behind her van, and disappear. Even though I tried to exert my will, I couldn't follow him behind the van. So I had to wait until he emerged. By that time she'd finished her song and was approaching the van. She was surrounded by people —friends, and enemies, too. As she came toward the van, he began moving away from her. And, now, I could see the gun he carried. Or, rather, I could *feel* the gun, because he was concealing it.

"It was as if I was focused on both of them," he went on. "It was as if I'd moved back, so I could see everything. I saw her walk up the stairs to her van. Then I saw him step behind the scaffolding, to the left of the stage. And then, for the first time, I saw the gun quite clearly. And then—" Suddenly he shuddered. As if he were a marionette with its strings cut, his knees buckled, his body sagged. He braced his hand against my desk, then slumped into the visitor's chair. His face was pale. His eyes were hollow, haunted by what he'd seen.

"Then came the shot," he whispered. "Just one shot. I saw flame exploding from the gun's barrel, like a huge flower of fire. For a moment it was suspended in the darkness, as if time and motion had frozen around it."

In spite of myself, I was excited by the story. Leaning toward him, I asked, "Did you see his face?"

Slowly, infinitely weary now, he shook his head. "No. The light was too dim. But I could see that it was a man. A rather tall man, with hair about like mine." He gestured to the hair hanging almost to his shoulders.

"Was he thin? Stocky?"

Once more, he wearily shook his head. "I'm sorry. I can't tell you, Lieutenant."

"Let's go back. You say that when you first saw him, before the shooting, he disappeared behind her motor home."

"Yes."

"Is it possible that he went inside, through a small door in the rear of the van—a door you couldn't see?"

Once more, he dully shook his head. "I don't know. He was out of my sight, as I said. I couldn't follow him. I had to remain fixed. Like a camera, you see." As if he were puzzled, he frowned. "I couldn't follow him," he repeated tonelessly. "I was helpless. Totally helpless." Uncertainly, he raised his hand to stroke his scraggly beard.

"You say you were aware of him having the gun when he reappeared. Is that right?"

"Yes," he answered. "Yes, that's right."

"But you weren't aware that he had the gun when he first approached the trailer."

"I—I—" Helplessly, he raised one hand. "I don't know. I can't be sure. All I know is that, when he reappeared, I realized that he had the gun, even though I didn't actually see it."

"But you did see the gun when he fired it?"

"Yes."

I opened my desk drawer, found a Stoeger's gun catalog and rifled through the pages until I found a Smith and Wesson .357 magnum with a four-inch barrel, identical to the murder weapon. Next I found a picture of a Colt .45 automatic, and finally a Walther PPK. Holding the catalog so he could see it, I said, "I'm going to show you three handguns, Mr. Wade. Tell me which one is similar to the one he held."

With great effort, as if he were totally exhausted, he sat up straighter in the chair and looked at the three illustrations.

Then, without hesitation, he said, "It's the first one."

I turned to the .357. "This one?"

He nodded.

"You're sure? You're absolutely positive?"

"I saw it," he answered simply. "I couldn't be mistaken."

"What did he do after the shot was fired?"

He shook his head. "I don't know. When the shot came, everything disappeared. It was like a—a mirror that shattered."

As he spoke, my phone rang. It was Farwell, in the reception room, apologetically saying that Ron Massey must leave soon.

"All right," I answered sharply, impatient at the interruption. "Tell him I'll be with him shortly." And to Justin Wade, I said: "Is there anything more you can tell me, Mr. Wade? Anything that could help us?"

Fingering his massive sun symbol, he shook his head. His eyes were clearer now, his expression more composed. For a moment I sat silently, watching him. Was he telling the truth? Was his vision genuine—something I should take seriously? Other police departments, both in the United States and Europe, routinely used clairvoyants to help solve crimes. And his mother, whose appraisal of her son was totally realistic, had volunteered that his visions were real—to Justin, at least.

But were they true?

He'd "seen" the murderer disappear behind the van, and "seen" him appear with the murder weapon, concealed.

If the vision was true, it could mean that the murderer first stole the .357 and then concealed himself behind the light standard, waiting for Rebecca. Therefore, the vision could confirm Sam Wright's contention that the murder weapon was in Rebecca's van.

But, on the other hand, Justin's description of the murderer fitted Sam Wright.

Deciding to shift ground, and test his responses to something other than the murder, I said, "I talked to your mother this morning."

He looked at me for a long, inscrutable moment before he said, "I haven't seen my mother for over a year." He let another moment pass before he added: "She's—alien to the life I've chosen. She probably told you that." As he spoke, his voice dropped to a harsh, uncompromising note. His eyes hardened. His fingers tightened around the medallion.

"No," I answered, "she didn't say anything like that. But I got the feeling that there was—" I hesitated. Then: "There was considerable tension in your family."

His pale, thin lips stretched in a mirthless smile. "You're a diplomat, Lieutenant."

I answered his smile. "In my business, it goes with the territory." I paused, then probed deeper: "Your stepsister was acutely unhappy, I gather. She was even a runaway, your mother said."

"I ran away, too. Did my mother tell you that?"

"No, she didn't."

Grimly, he nodded. "I ran away from home three times between age fifteen and age twenty-two. Then I left for good."

"How old are you now?"

"Twenty-three."

"How old was Rebecca?"

"Twenty-seven."

"Were you fond of each other?"

"For most of my life, I thought I hated her," he answered. "And I suppose I did. She was—" He grimaced. "She was always selfish. And sometimes she could be frightening, too—unpredictable and vicious. And so was my stepfather. He could be a tyrant, especially when he was drinking—which was all the time. And—" He shook his head sharply, as if he were flinching at the memory.

94

"And my mother was frightening to live with, too. She's ice-cold, completely self-controlled, utterly self-centered. But, underneath, she's a hedonist. She's seething with—" He broke off, searching for the phrase: "She's seething with depravity," he finished.

"I'm afraid I don't understand this," I said. "You tell me that you hated Rebecca—that she was terrible to live with. And, from everything I hear about her, I believe you. Yet, last night, you were totally distraught. When I called her your 'stepsister,' you corrected me, and called her your 'sister.' And today—now—you're trying to help us find her murderer. But apparently you didn't really feel close to her."

He looked at me silently for a moment. Then, speaking in a slow, measured voice, he said solemnly: "I respond to my feelings, Lieutenant. I never analyze why I do anything. I simply do it. Because that's the only truth—and the only real freedom. Descartes said, 'I think; therefore I am.' I say that I feel; therefore I am."

"You haven't answered the question." I paused to get his attention. Then: "What was the nature of your relationship with Rebecca during the last year?"

"During the last year," he answered slowly, "we saw each other frequently. Rebecca was—" He hesitated. "She was interested in my work."

"How do you mean, 'interested'?"

"I mean," he answered, "that she contributed to my work."

"Money, you mean."

"Yes."

"Much money?"

He waved away the question. "I don't recall the numbers. I never remember the amounts—only that people give and help. That's all that matters."

I decided to shift ground: "In your family," I said, "it sounds like you were the odd man out."

He frowned. "What do you mean?"

"I mean that the three of them sound like they were pretty self-indulgent. Sensualists, I guess you'd call them. But you're—different."

"Sensualists—" He nodded. "Yes, they were that. And more. Both of them—my mother and Rebecca—they were corrupted by Bernard. He was—" He let it go eloquently unfinished.

"You said he could be a tyrant. Yet he left you a third of his estate."

Contemptuously, he shrugged. "I don't care about money, Lieutenant. I've already told you that. It's one of the things I've forsworn. Money—the urge of the flesh—drink—they all corrupt."

"Will you take your inheritance, though?" I pressed.

"Probably. But I'll take it for Aztecca."

"That's your—your sect."

"That's the community I live in. At Aztecca, everyone is equal." He made the correction gently. Whenever he spoke of his "calling," his voice was quiet and serene. But whenever he spoke of his family, a harsh, uncompromising note edged his voice. His manner changed, too, and his whole body stiffened.

"You're the leader at Aztecca, though?"

He didn't reply, but made a sign of impatient denial.

Thinking of Friedman's question, I asked, "Do you know what will happen to Rebecca's share of Bernard Carlton's estate?"

"It will be divided between me and my mother. If either Rebecca or I died before age thirty, the share would be divided between the two survivors. The same holds true for my mother's share, if she dies before we do."

"So you and your mother will split Rebecca's share of the estate."

"Yes," he answered readily. "We'll both be rich." He was obviously indifferent to the prospect.

My phone buzzed. It was Farwell again.

"I'm really sorry, Lieutenant," he said earnestly. "But Mr. Massey says that, if you can't see him immediately, he'll have to leave. I need instructions."

I sighed. "Tell him to come in."

Ten

"I'm sorry, Mr. Massey," I said, gesturing him to a chair. "This has been one of those days, I'm afraid."

"For me, too, Lieutenant," he said. Then, peevishly, he added: "I'd think that would be obvious."

I decided not to respond. Instead, I watched as he adjusted his trouser creases, touched his tie and hunched his shoulders, settling his jacket. Finally, he smoothed down his small, silky mustache before he said, "I don't quite understand why it was necessary for Inspector Canelli to put me to the trouble of coming down here. As I understand it, he wanted to know whether Rebecca kept a gun in her van. For that, he could have phoned me." He looked at me accusingly for a moment before he added, "I don't know whether you're aware of it, Lieutenant, but Rebecca Carlton was practically an institution, not only in this country, but in Europe, too. Alive or dead, she's significant. And it's my responsibility to see that her memory is preserved and protected."

He spoke as if it were a speech that had been carefully prepared and rehearsed. I decided that my job would be easier if I could shake some of his bland self-confidence.

98

"The gun is only part of it, Mr. Massey." I spoke in a flat, official voice. "There's more." I decided to let him guess what I meant. As I sat silently, watching him frown as he thought about it, I tried to imagine how this humorless, pompously dressed man could have risen to the top in the free-wheeling, free-loving, far-out world of rock music. Everything about him suggested a fast-rising young executive yes man, destined to find his niche somewhere in the executive suite of a large corporation.

"You say there's more," he said, looking at his watch. "What is it?"

"We're interrogating everyone who profited by her death." I spoke in the same flat, hard voice, locking my gaze with his. "That, I believe includes you."

"Me?" His handsomely arched eyebrows rose over eyes round with surprise. "Christ, how do you figure I profited?" As he returned my stare his eyes narrowed angrily. His mouth tightened; a muscle alongside his jaw bunched theatrically as he said, "Do you have any idea how much I make —made—as her manager?"

I dropped my eyes to my desk, pretending to consult some notes. "According to my information," I said quietly, "your contract with Rebecca was about to be terminated."

I saw him start. "How—?" He caught himself. "Where did you hear that, for Christ's sake?"

I'd learned long ago never to answer a suspect's question. Instead, I said, "I also understand that you were insured against her death. Is that right?"

"Well—Christ—yes. But that's a part of the standard contract. It certainly doesn't mean that—"

"How much will the policy pay you, Mr. Massey?" I tried to make my voice sound slightly bored, as if I already knew the answer.

"Well, it—" He stroked his small, foppish mustache again. But this time, the gesture lacked assurance. "Well, it's about two hundred fifty thousand, I think. But—"

"So, assuming that you were about to be fired," I said quietly, "then the fact is that since she died while your contract was still in effect, you—"

"*Wait* a minute, goddamnit." He jumped to his feet, breathing hard. "Do I understand that you—" Momentarily his mouth worked impotently. *"Wait a minute."* He was breathing hard now, staring at me with outraged eyes. "Do I understand that you—you're accusing me of *murdering* her? Is that what you're doing?"

"In my business, Mr. Massey, we deal in facts. And the facts are that—"

"The facts are, Lieutenant, that—" His voice broke on a high, half-hysterical note. Eyes hot and accusing, both fists clenched hard at his sides, he struggled for self-control. Finally, managing an unconvincing bluster, he said, "The facts are that I was standing five feet from her when she was killed. I was the first one to reach her, after she fell. I—I got her blood on my hands. And on my jacket, too." As he said it, I had the fleeting impression that, to Massey, a bloodstained jacket was unthinkable. "And now you—Christ—you have the goddamn unmitigated gall to accuse me of—of—" For a last long, baleful moment he stood staring at me, unable to speak. Then he wheeled, blindly knocking over a chair as he lurched toward the door.

Carrying a plastic-wrapped sandwich in one hand and a Styrofoam container of coffee in the other, I was approaching my office from the vending machines at the end of the hallway when I heard my phone ring. Remembering that I'd left strict orders that no calls were to be put through unless they came from officers assigned to the Carlton case, I hastily gripped the sandwich in my teeth while I unlocked my office door on the phone's third ring. One more ring, and I lifted the receiver.

"It's Culligan, Lieutenant. Are you busy?"

Taking the sandwich from my mouth, I said, "It's all right. What've you got?"

"I have a woman named Carole on the line. She said she's got something for us. But she says that she wants a piece of Behr's reward now—up front."

I sighed, at the same time prying the lid off my coffee container. "Is this the first one we've got looking for the reward?"

"As far as I know, yes."

"What's her story, anyhow?"

"No story," he answered laconically. "But I get the feeling that she really knows something. So I thought I'd see if I could get you. If you'd rather not talk to her—" He let it go indifferently unfinished. Typically, Culligan wasn't pushing it any farther. He'd given me his opinion. The decision was up to me. He was doing his job, earning his inspector's salary —no more.

But, after almost twenty years in Homicide, Culligan's opinion was worth considering.

"All right." I replaced the lid—in the process spilling coffee on the lab's report of the S&W .357. "Put her on."

I heard a click as Culligan completed the connection, then silence. On the other end of the line, someone was breathing.

"This is Lieutenant Hastings," I said. "Who'm I talking to, please?"

"This is Carole," she said, speaking in a low, hoarse voice, obviously disguised. "And I'm not going to hang on much longer, either, while you're pushing buttons down there, or whatever you're doing."

"Sorry. What can I do for you?"

"I think I know who killed that singer. Rebecca Carlton. If you want to hear about it, fine. Otherwise, forget it."

"I want to hear about it. How do you want to handle it?"

"We gotta meet."

"All right. Where? When?"

In the brief silence that followed, I heard music in the background, and the confused sounds of voices laughing and talking. She was probably talking from a pay phone in a bar.

"I'll meet you on the sidewalk in front of the Hilton. How'll I know you?"

"I'm six feet tall, and about two hundred pounds. I'm forty-four years old. Brown hair, brown eyes. I'll be wearing a gray tweed sports jacket, an open-neck beige sport shirt and brown slacks." I hesitated, looking around my office. The lab report had come in a large envelope, letterhead size. "I'll be carrying a ten-by-twelve-inch brown envelope in my left hand. What about you?"

"Never mind about me. I'll be there at two-thirty. I'll find you."

"That's only ten minutes from now. I can't get there so soon. Let's say three o'clock."

"All right, three. Wait. Don't hang up."

"What's the problem?"

"The problem is the goddamn money. Behr says he's paying when someone's convicted. That's bullshit."

"It's his money, not mine."

"But it's your problem. If you want the one that killed her, I can give him to you. But not for any goddamn twenty-five-thousand dollars' worth of promises."

"You say you want more than promises. I've got the same problem. The conviction, we can talk about. But I'm not paying a cent unless I get something for it."

Another silence. I heard a woman laugh. A song from the forties was playing on the jukebox. Finally: "Then we haven't got a deal," Carole said. "Because, for sure, I want something up front. I'm taking a risk, just talking to you. And I want something for it."

"But not the whole twenty-five."

She didn't reply.

I let the silence continue for a moment before I said,

"Listen, there's no point in arguing about money over the phone. It's not my money. I've got no control over it. Give me an extra half hour. I'll talk to David Behr. I'll see what I can do about something up front."

"What'd you say your name was, anyhow?"

"Lieutenant Frank Hastings. I'm the co-lieutenant in charge of the homicide squad. You can trust me."

"Sure I can," she said derisively.

"Listen, Carole—I assume that you've got friends that've been busted once or twice. Am I right?"

No response.

"If you do know some people," I said, "then you can ask them about me. Ask them if you can trust me. They'll tell you."

Still no response. Now someone was swearing loudly in the background. Momentarily Carole muffled the phone, and I heard the indistinct sound of her shouting for silence. Then: "Are you the same lieutenant from Homicide that was on TV a little while ago, when someone killed that reporter named Murdock? The one from Washington?"

"Yes."

"You're kind of good-looking. That one?"

I smiled at the phone. "If you say so, Carole."

Another silence. Then, wearily reluctant, she said, "All right. At least we can talk. You'll be alone. Right?"

"Right."

"And remember, tell David Behr no money, no name. For sure."

"I'll see what he says. That's all I can do."

At the other end, the line clicked dead.

I called Culligan, ordering a three-man surveillance team under his command to follow Carole after our meeting. Then I put in an urgent call for David Behr.

On the sidewalk in front of the Hilton, in the warm Saturday afternoon sunshine, the Powell Street Jazz Band was playing hot-lick Dixieland for a semicircle of smiling, foot-tapping, head-bobbing tourists. Across the street, two saffron-robed Hare Krishna novitiates were trying to trade ten-cent flowers for dollar bills. At the Powell Street corner, a drunk wearing a red Shriner's fez was staggering after a cable car, shouting for the gripman to stop. On the cable car, the passengers were laughing and yelling, urging the drunk to run faster.

As I shifted the brown paper envelope to my left hand, I glanced down toward Mason Street, where Culligan and Marsten were parked in a nondescript Datsun 510. Across the street, a detective recruited from General Works was sitting in the lobby of a small residential hotel, watching me over a copy of *Playboy*.

A woman in her early thirties was walking toward me. She was dressed in a tightly belted wet-look brown vinyl jacket, black velour slacks and high-heeled red plastic boots, also wet-look. Her hair was a bleached orange-blonde piled on top of her head in lopsided, untidy coils. Her face was pale and thin, prematurely etched with deep, bitter lines around the mouth and eyes. Plastered over the pallor of her skin, iridescent green-black eye shadow, bright red lipstick and heavy pancake makeup all contrived to create an imperfect mask carelessly drawn to conceal the disillusionment so plain in her face. Despite the lipstick, her mouth was small, pursed and petulant. Centered in their iridescent shadowing, her street-wise eyes were as quick and furtive as a cat's, constantly on the prowl.

In the past five minutes, she'd already caught my eye twice, but had made no sign of recognition. Now, as she came abreast of me, she broke stride, muttering, "Are you Lieutenant Hastings?"

"Yes."

"I'll keep walking. There's a Chinese restaurant around the corner. And a booth, in back."

I turned to watch the Powell Street Jazz Band, now playing "When the Saints Come Marching In." I dropped a dollar in the open banjo case lying on the sidewalk, answered the clarinet-playing leader's cheerful smile of thanks, and turned to follow the woman. As I passed Culligan, I nodded.

Eleven

She slid a slatted bamboo curtain across the booth's doorway and pushed a chair into position across the table from me. The table was covered in red Formica, worn thin along the edges and at the center.

"Nobody'll bother us," Carole said. "It's all set. I know them here."

"Good." I nodded, but said nothing more. I'd decided to play a waiting game, letting her come to me. In my inside pocket, I had the game's prize: a packet of fifty-dollar bills.

It had taken me almost fifteen minutes—and some heavy-handed cajolery—to get through to David Behr. But as soon as I told him about Carole's call, and about her demand for front money, he'd immediately seen the problem. A half hour later, a young man dressed in a three-piece pin-striped suit delivered the fifty-dollar bills to me in the Hilton's main-floor men's room.

"What about the money?" She spoke in a low, tight voice.

I glanced at the curtained-off doorway, then took the fifty-dollar bills from my pocket. The bills were secured by a thick rubber band. As if I were riffling a pack of cards, I thumbed the bills for her to see, then returned the packet to my pocket.

"That's a thousand dollars. You get four thousand more when we decide your information is good enough for us to get an arrest warrant, and another five thousand when we get an indictment. That's ten thousand dollars. You get the other fifteen when the D.A. gets a conviction."

"It's still nothing but a thousand dollars in cash and fourteen thousand in promises." Coldly, defiantly, her eyes challenged mine. Whatever she'd done, wherever she'd been, she'd fought for what she'd gotten. She knew how the game was played.

I stared at her until her eyes fell. Then, quietly, I said, "You mind if I ask you something, Carole?"

She shrugged a loose, indifferent shoulder. "Go ahead. Ask. I've got the booth for an hour."

"Have you ever done anything like this before—ever turned anyone, for money?"

"What's that got to do with anything?"

"I'll get to that. *Have* you?"

"Well—no."

"That's what I thought. You know why?"

"No." Her red-painted lip curled. "Why?"

"Because," I answered, "you're acting like an amateur."

Still with her lip curled, patronizing me, she said, "I guess I'm supposed to ask how you know. Is that it?"

"If you'd ever turned anyone before," I said, "or ever made any deals with the cops, you'd know that you've simply got to trust me to do what I say I'm going to do." I tried to put a weary, patient note in my voice, playing the part of a teacher instructing a backward pupil.

"You'd also know," I continued, "that police work isn't like you see it in the movies. We don't do clues. We don't sit around and try to put pieces of a puzzle together. We make deals. Trades. That's what police work is all about. It's the barter system, pure and simple. Mostly we trade freedom for evidence. We catch someone way down the ladder who's

107

dirty, and we offer him a deal if he'll turn someone at the top. That's the game—that's what makes it all go around. Sometimes, instead of trading jail time for information, we trade goods—part of a heroin bust, for instance. Or, in very rare cases—like now—we trade money.

"But the point is—" I paused for emphasis, hunching earnestly toward her across the table. "The point is that it all comes down to the simple proposition that you've got no choice but to trust the policeman who's handling things. There's just no other way it can work. And if you'll just think about it a minute, you'll see that I'm right."

Again I paused, letting the silence lengthen as she frowned down at the Formica table, making up her mind. I gave her a full minute before I said:

"There's one last thing you should think about—" As I said it, I took my shield case from my pocket, flipped it open and slid my badge across the table. "That's a lieutenant's badge," I said, pointing to it. "And that badge means that you can trust me to do what I say I'm going to do. Because, for sure, you don't get to be a police lieutenant without making, literally, thousands of deals. And, every time, you've got to do your damnedest to keep your word. It's not always possible. I'd be lying to you if I said I never had to break my word. But I wouldn't be a lieutenant—or even a detective— if I didn't deliver, most of the time. It's as simple as that." I let a final beat pass before I said, "And that's all I've got to say, Carole. Now it's your turn. You can either tell me why we're here—give me a name—or else you can walk away, no questions asked. It's your choice." As I sat back in my chair and folded my arms, I could feel the packet of fifty-dollar bills in my breast pocket.

For a long moment, deciding, she studied me. Watching her, I calculated the odds less than even that she'd talk.

I was wrong.

"I live with a guy named Bruce Hoadley." She spoke in a low, mumbling monotone, now with her eyes downcast.

"We've been living together for about six months, I guess."

"What's the address?" I took out my notebook and pen.

"It's on Eddy Street, right near Leavenworth."

"What's the address, Carole?"

"It's—" She swallowed, then took the final plunge: "It's 765 Eddy. Apartment 417. It's the top floor."

"All right. Go ahead."

"Well, we—" She swallowed again, harder this time. "We've been having trouble lately. Which, if I'm honest with myself, is why I'm copping. I mean, he works for some massage parlors. And—you know—there's always some action, if you're looking for it. Which I knew, of course, all along. I mean, that's how we got together."

"You worked for a massage parlor, you mean."

"Yeah. But I never—you know—did anything except just with the hands. I mean, I'm not like some of them. I mean—" She looked at me intently, anxious that I understand. "I mean, I never *sold* it, in my whole life. Not once."

In the Tenderloin, I knew, this final shred of morality was often defended so fiercely that, among the girls, an accusation of "selling it" could be a knife-fighting matter.

So, solemnly, I nodded. "I believe you."

"Yeah. Well—" She jerked her hand, gesturing self-defensively. "Well, it's true," she said truculently.

"I know."

"Well, anyhow—" She began to shake her head. "Anyhow, the point is that everything's—you know—unraveling. I mean, it's not that he's just fooling around. That's not it. Not really. It's just that—Christ—lately, he's changed. Like, instead of being cool about it, for instance, he talks about how he's fooling around, to rub my nose in it. And he's been drinking, too, lately. And then, about two weeks ago, he hit me. I mean, he didn't just hit me once. He kept on, and on, and on. I swear to God, I thought he was going to kill me.

"So, anyhow—" Now her voice had fallen desperately low. Her gestures were slack, signifying some final surrender to the inevitable. "So, anyhow, I decided—right then—that I was going to split. Except that I wasn't going to walk away crying. I was going to take some hide with me. I mean, I been hit often enough in my life that, this time, something just snapped, you know?" As she spoke, her hard, street-wise eyes sought mine, searching for some essential sign of confirmation. And, again, I nodded solemnly in reply.

"Everyone's got a limit," I said. "If you don't have a limit —if you don't draw a line, and stick to it—then you don't have anything. You're nothing."

And, hearing myself say it, I was surprised to realize that I meant what I was saying. In this improbable place, talking to this negligible person, I'd stumbled upon a good, serviceable definition of integrity.

So, oddly pleased with myself, I smiled encouragement as she answered:

"Yeah. Well, anyhow, something snapped, like I said. So I decided that I was going to watch for my chance, and really stick it to him. And it turned out that I didn't have long to wait. I mean, pretty soon I started to get the idea that what was really on his mind—why he knocked me around, and everything—was that he was in some kind of trouble. And it was—you know—really getting to him."

"What kind of trouble?"

"Money. See, he gambles. I mean, it's the old story, down in the Tenderloin. Either you're a junkie, or else you're a gambler. So, either way, you're going to end up with nothing. And in the meantime you're going to make a lot of people suffer for your habit."

"He was in hock to someone. Is that it?"

Wearily, she nodded. "That's it. And the more he squirmed, the worse it got."

I knew what was coming. Over the years, I'd seen a hundred variations played on this same relentless theme. Which, ultimately, came down to the underworld's version of *Faust:* you get in deep enough, you either sell your soul to square the debt, or else you die.

And in the Tenderloin, you sell your soul by agreeing to kill someone on order. Trigger men aren't born. They simply run out of time and money.

"And you think that, to square his tab, he killed Rebecca Carlton." As I spoke, I was watching her face intently, searching for a reaction.

Once more, suddenly exhausted, she dumbly nodded.

She believed it.

Whether or not it was true, she believed that Bruce Hoadley had killed Rebecca Carlton.

"Who'd he owe?"

Quickly, she shook her head, involuntarily shying at the question. "That's not part of the deal. I'm giving you Bruce. No one else." As she said it, I saw fear flicker deep in her eyes. Whoever held Bruce Hoadley's marker, Carole feared him.

"All right. But where's the proof?"

She reached into a pocket and passed a ticket stub across the table. It was a ticket to last night's concert.

"You'll have to have more than that," I said quietly. "You know that, don't you?"

For a moment she didn't reply, but instead picked up the ticket and held it in her palm for a moment, staring at it. Her fingernails were painted a bright red, matching her lipstick. The fingernails were bitten to the quick.

"I'm not trying to give you a hard time," I said. "But—" I gestured to the ticket stub. "But there were sixty-five thousand of those things sold. And they all look alike." I spoke softly, apologetically.

"Yeah," she answered, drawing a last long, hopeless sigh. "Yeah, I know that."

"Well?"

"Well—" For one final moment she hesitated. Then, with infinite effort, she raised her eyes from the ticket stub. She'd come face to face with her moment of no return. Just as there were girls who sold it and girls who didn't, there were those who snitched and those who didn't.

"Was she shot with a revolver?" she asked. "A Smith and Wesson, caliber .357?"

I reached in my pocket, withdrew the fifty-dollar bills, and tucked them into the brown envelope. I folded the envelope twice and silently passed it across the red Formica table.

As her hand closed around the envelope, she said, "I wouldn't be doing this, if it wasn't for the reward, you know. I mean—" She bit her trembling lip. "I mean, it had to be a lot of money, to make me do it. You know?"

"Yes," I answered quietly. "I know."

Twelve

My meeting with Carole lasted until four P.M. By seven o'clock, back at the Hall, I'd learned a lot about Bruce Hoadley. He was thirty-three years old, a native of San Francisco. His mother had died when he was twelve. His father was unknown. He'd been made a ward of the court and had lived in three different foster homes until he was arrested at age sixteen, for car theft. Since it was his first offence, sentence was suspended. Two years later, he'd fallen for possession of stolen goods and had drawn ten years, of which he served eighteen months at Camarillo. At age twenty-five, he was arrested for pandering, but the case never came to trial because of insufficient evidence. Translation: the girl was too scared to testify.

Since his arrest for pandering, Hoadley hadn't had any more trouble with the law. The reason, according to Captain Jepson, head of the Tenderloin Detail, was Hoadley's association with a woman named Sally Grant. For years, Sally had run a string of high-priced call girls. Now, at age forty-six, Sally operated four of the biggest, most lucrative massage parlors anywhere west of New York City. Each of her parlors ran a quarter page ad in the Yellow Pages. One parlor featured exotic Oriental girls. Another featured Swedish girls. "Hot co-eds" was a third specialty, and the fourth ad simply read, "Beautiful girls, none over thirty." Hotel calls were a specialty, and all major credit cards were accepted.

At first Hoadley provided the muscle for Sally's call-girl operation. Later, he'd managed one of the massage parlors. But Hoadley apparently lacked the finesse necessary to deal with the high-rolling tourists that Sally wanted for her clientele. So Hoadley had returned to the work he did best: providing Sally's muscle. If a customer got too abusive or too demanding, Hoadley took care of the problem. If one of the girls got out of line, Hoadley handled it. If a payoff became necessary, Hoadley carried the money and set up the meeting. If competition threatened, Hoadley started a fire, or broke a window, or beat up one of the competitors. Over the years, Sally Grant had learned that she could trust Hoadley. In return, again according to Jepson, she paid him an estimated twenty thousand dollars a year straight salary.

I asked Jepson to commit all his available manpower in an effort to find Hoadley. At first Jepson objected. His squad was running over budget, he said, and he'd recently spent an entire half day in the auditor's office—followed, a week later, by a visit from an independent efficiency expert, hired by the Board of Supervisors. I let Chief Dwyer decide. A half hour later, Jepson's squad was turning the Tenderloin inside out. By eight o'clock Saturday night, no leads had developed. At eight-thirty, I decided to go home.

By nine o'clock, with my shoes off and my revolver and cuffs in my top dresser drawer, I was sitting on my sofa, staring at the phone. All day, I'd tried to find the time to phone Ann—or so I'd told myself. The truth was, though, that I'd used a tight schedule as an excuse for not making the call.

Now I was alone—just me, and the phone, and the memory of how we'd parted, last night. I'd run out of excuses.

But then I remembered that I hadn't eaten anything since I'd taken the plastic-wrapped sandwich and the Styrofoam container of coffee to my desk, more than eight hours ago. So I went into the kitchen, opened the refrigerator and made a sandwich of peanut butter and two thick slices of French bread. With the sandwich in one hand and a glass of milk in the other I went into the living room, found an old movie on TV and settled down to watch Rock Hudson fight the Battle of the Bulge.

By the time I'd finished eating, my watch read nine-thirty. In another half hour, it would be too late to call.

I sighed, got to my feet, switched off the TV and walked to the phone. For a moment I stood irresolutely, wondering whether I should check with Friedman, who was still at the Hall. If they found Hoadley, Friedman might not remember to have the suspect paraffin tested. Should I remind him?

The answer, of course, was no. Friedman would remember.

So, reluctantly, I picked up the phone and dialed.

"Hello?" It was Dan, Ann's oldest son. He'd just turned seventeen. It was because of Dan that I'd first met her almost a year ago. Dan had been a witness to murder—and briefly a suspect. Over the years, I'd told hundreds of parents that one of their children was in trouble. I'd seen countless reactions, from breast-beating lamentations to homicidal rage to utter indifference. But I'd never seen anyone react with more natural dignity than Ann.

"It's Frank," I said. "Is your mother there?"

"Yeah. Just a minute, Frank. Hey, will I see you tomorrow?"

"I'm not sure. That's why I'm calling."

"Hey—is it about Rebecca Carlton? Is that it?"

"That's it."

"Hey—great. I knew you'd be on it, Frank. Just a little while ago I was telling Sandy that I'd bet money on it."

"Who's Sandy?"

"She's—you know—a girl."

"Oh. Well, good luck, you and Sandy."

"Yeah. Thanks."

"Let me talk to your mother, will you?"

"I guess you can't say whether you know who killed her, can you, Frank?"

"No. Not now." I hesitated, then added, "Even if I knew, I couldn't say."

"Yeah, I figured. Well, here's Mom. 'Night."

"Goodnight."

A moment later I heard a click when Ann came on the line, and another click when Dan got off. She was taking the call in her bedroom.

"I was going to call you when I got home last night," I said. "But then this Rebecca Carlton thing came up."

"Yes, I heard Dan talking." There was a polite pause before she said, "How are you doing? On the case, I mean?"

"There's nothing definite yet. We might have a break, though. I should know something in an hour or so. With luck."

"I hope it works out."

"Thanks."

Another silence followed, this one at my end. Finally I said, "I—ah—felt terrible when I got home last night."

"I know," she answered quietly. "I did, too."

"Have you talked to your father today?"

"He called about noon, from the airport."

"I—ah—didn't mean to be hard on him last night."

"I know you didn't."

"I didn't mean to be hard on you, either."

"I know that, too." She spoke quietly, tonelessly, without either warmth or hostility. She could have been talking to a stranger. For a long moment we endured a helpless, hopeless silence. Then, struggling alone, I said:

"I—ah—don't think I can go with you and the boys, tomorrow. It's this case—Rebecca Carlton. It's making

116

headlines all over the country. When that happens, we get a lot of heat."

"It's all right."

"I *wanted* to go. You know that, don't you?" I searched for something more to say, but the right words weren't there. So, finally, I said, "I wanted to be with all three of you tomorrow." This time, I sensed that the silence offered more hope. But, still, the right words wouldn't come—for either of us.

"If I can manage it," I ventured, "if there's any way— maybe I can come by tomorrow night. We can talk."

She hesitated briefly, then said, "All right. But not too late. I'm breaking in a student teacher on Monday. It'll be a tough day. And the boys and I probably won't be back from dinner tomorrow until nine o'clock, at least."

"I'll call you at nine-thirty. Whether or not I can come by, I'll at least call."

"All right."

"If you're not there, I'll keep trying."

"Yes." Another silence began. Then she said, "Good luck. With the case, I mean." Once more she spoke formally, from a distance.

"With the case?" Asking the question, I tried to tease her, hopefully to end the conversation on a light, intimate note.

But she didn't—or couldn't—respond with anything but a formal-sounding: "You know what I mean."

To myself, I sighed. Answering: "I know what you mean. I'll call you tomorrow."

"Goodnight, Frank."

"Goodnight, Ann."

The phone had hardly touched the cradle when it rang. Almost gratefully—knowing it must be the Hall—I picked up the receiver. Tonight, work would be welcome.

"It's Pete, Frank. We've got Hoadley staked out."

"Where?"

"At Sally Grant's place, on Russian Hill."

117

"What's the address?"

"2445 Leavenworth. Near Greenwich."

"Who's there?"

"Canelli's on the front, and Culligan's at the rear. They've each got two G.W. men, for backup. You want me to come?" The tentative note in his voice made it plain that he'd rather go home to bed.

"No, go home. When we get him down to the Hall, if it's not too late, I'll call you."

"Right. Good luck."

"Thanks."

Thirteen

2445 Leavenworth was a Spanish-style town house that had probably cost twenty-five thousand dollars to build in the forties, and was probably worth two hundred thousand now. The house was built on a corner lot with a view from the front of the San Francisco skyline and a view from the rear of the Golden Gate Bridge. The house was two-storied, with stucco walls, hand-hewn shutters and trim, a red tile roof and a portico-style entryway leading to a massive front door, intricately carved. The property was surrounded on all four sides by a six-foot adobe wall, painted white and topped with red tiles. Tall, spiky palm trees grew in the front garden. A wood-planked, iron-studded front gate was set into the wall.

As I opened the door of Canelli's cruiser and slipped into the passenger's seat, Canelli pointed to the house. "It looks like vice still pays pretty good, Lieutenant," he said cheerfully.

"It always has, Canelli. Are you sure he's in there?"

"Pretty sure. See, Sally Grant's in Las Vegas for the weekend, and Hoadley's staying in her house. She's got about four poodles. So whenever she's out of town, Hoadley's got to take care of them. She's crazy about poodles, it turns out."

"Where'd you get your information?"

"There's a girl named Kathy, who runs one of Sally's massage parlors. And after Captain Jepson talked to her for a couple of minutes, and explained all the ways he could make life miserable for her, she suddenly got very cooperative." Admiringly, Canelli shood his head. "That Captain Jepson, he's got the Tenderloin working for him like a well-oiled machine. I mean, he plays it like a player piano, or something. Anything he wants, he gets. Instantly."

"Are you sure Hoadley's in there, though?" I asked.

"We don't have a picture of him," Canelli said, "so I can't be absolutely positive. But the description in his file fits whoever I saw through an upstairs window. That was about ten minutes ago. Now he's downstairs, I think. He's about thirty, around two hundred pounds. He's a big, broad-shouldered guy with curly blond hair and a knife scar across one cheek."

"Did you see the scar?"

"Yessir." He showed me a pair of binoculars. "I got a pretty good look at him. A lucky look, you might say."

"Then we've probably got a make." I picked up the walkie-talkie, lying on the seat beside Canelli. "Is Culligan tuned in?"

"Yessir."

I pressed the transmit button. "This is Lieutenant Hastings. What's it look like back there?"

"Tight as a drum, Lieutenant," Culligan answered. "We're in the back alley. There's one gate, that's all. And the wall goes all the way around the house, six feet high. It couldn't be better."

"Can you see the wall on either side?"

"Yessir. We're spread out."

"Have you got a shotgun?"

"I left it in the car. You want me to get it? The car's right here."

I considered, then decided to say, "Use your own judgment."

"We're pretty exposed, Lieutenant. That's why I left it in the car. We've already had people snooping around."

"Are you the only one with a radio back there?"

"Yessir."

"All right, stand by." I turned to Canelli. "Where're your two men?"

"One's there—" He pointed to a blue Plymouth sedan. "And one's over there, behind that tall privet hedge."

"Have they both got radios?"

"Yessir."

I glanced at the dial of my own radio, then pressed the transmit button and said, "Is everyone on channel eight? Sound off."

The three positions came in, loud and clear.

"All right, here we go."

Canelli and I got out of the car, quickly crossed the street, and tried the front gate. It was secured by an electrically controlled lock, as I'd suspected. Handing the radio to Canelli, I slipped a spring steel probe from my pocket and worked at the gate.

"Some of them ring an alarm when they're tripped," Canelli whispered.

"I know that," I snapped. "Just keep your eye on the door, will you?"

"Yessir." From his tone of voice, I knew Canelli's feelings were hurt. "Sorry," I muttered. "I'm short on sleep."

"It's okay, Lieutenant." Plainly, the apology pleased him.

Swearing under my breath, I stepped back from the gate. "This isn't going to work." As I spoke, I eyed the wall, six feet high. In the dim glow from a nearby streetlight, I saw a row of spikes set between the tiles at the top of the wall. Although the heavily planked gate was only five feet high, it, too, was spiked along the top. Gingerly, I tested one of the spikes. It was needle sharp.

"This place is a goddamn fortress," I said, at the same time taking the radio. "Culligan, we're stopped, in the front. How about the back gate? Can you jimmy it?"

"I might be able to jimmy it," he answered doubtfully. "But everything back here's wired. And it looks like one of those real fancy alarm systems, with backups for the backups."

"Crap." As I said it, I heard Canelli say, "Uh-oh," and felt him touch my arm. Following his pointing finger, I saw the figure of a tall man approaching. He was walking a dog—a big, dangerous-looking Doberman. With about thirty feet separating us, the man tugged at a long leather leash, pulling the dog to a stop. The man and the dog were motionless now, impassively watching us. Without doubt, they thought we were burglars.

"Talk to him," I ordered. "Get rid of him."

Slipping his shield case from his pocket, Canelli cautiously approached the pair, still standing at alert. Deep in his throat, the dog was growling. To myself, I smiled. At times like this, rank had its pleasures.

As Canelli drew closer, the growling grew deeper, more ominous. At the end of the leash, the Doberman was straining to get at Canelli. Stopping well short of the dog, Canelli held up his shield case.

Suddenly the dog snarled. Teeth bared, it lunged for Canelli.

"God—*damn.*" Canelli leaped back. "*Hold* him," he hissed.

Five furious strides took me to Canelli's side, facing the tall stranger. "If you don't get out of here right now," I grated, "I'm going to arrest you for disobeying the lawful order of an officer acting in the performance of his duty. You'll spend the night in jail, I promise you. And your goddamn dog'll be in the S.P.C.A."

"What the hell's it all about, anyhow?" the man blustered.

I raised the radio. "Are you going? Or do I call for the

goddamn wagon?" As I said it, the dog lunged again, this time at me.

Standing behind me now, Canelli scolded: "You'd better do it. He's a lieutenant. And he means it." But his voice rose to a high, uncertain note, ineffectually indignant.

"Oh, Jesus. Cops and robbers. Big deal." The man jerked at the leash. "Come on, Crusher."

Still facing us, the dog moved back one menacing, leash-straining step—then another. Even in the dim light, I could see his fangs dripping saliva.

"Hurry up," I said. *"Move* it."

And, as the man finally succeeded in hauling the Dober-man away, Canelli loudly echoed: "Yeah—move it."

"Not so loud," I said angrily, turning back to face the house. As I stood staring irresolutely at the gate, I saw a small speaker set into the gate's hand-hewn frame. A button was placed just below the speaker.

"The only way we're going to get in," I muttered, "is to ring the goddamn bell. Either that, or order an assault team."

Canelli nodded discouraged agreement. "Looks like you're right, Lieutenant."

I pressed the radio's transmit button, and told Culligan that we were going to do it by the book. When Culligan acknowledged, I pushed the bell button.

Almost immediately, a man's voice said, "Yeah? Who's there?"

"Am I speaking to Bruce Hoadley?"

A silence. Then, cautiously: "Who is this? Who's out there?"

"It's the police, Hoadley. Open up."

Another silence, longer this time. Finally: "What'd you want?"

"We want to talk to you."

"What about?"

"We've got a complaint against you," I lied. "Assault on one Frederick Shelby."

Whenever I tried the ruse I always used the same name, with a few variations. Years ago, in high school, I'd played football with Fred Shelby.

"Who the hell's Frederick Shelby? I never heard of him."

"He says you roughed him up, six weeks ago. At the Mark Hopkins Hotel. He lives in St. Louis, and he was here for a convention. The girl called you, he says. And you attacked him."

"You've got the wrong man."

"That may be. But you'll have to sign the complaint, saying that we read it to you."

I heard an aggrieved sigh. Then, resigned: "All right. Hold on a minute." The speaker clicked, and went dead.

"As soon as he opens the gate," I said, "we'll hit him hard."

"Right," Canelli breathed, slipping his revolver from its holster and holding it close to the gate, concealed.

"I'll hit him first," I said, drawing my own revolver.

A half minute passed.

A minute.

Raising the radio, I asked, "Any change back there, Culligan?"

"No."

"He could be coming your way."

"All right."

But the next moment the front door swung slowly open. Kicking four frisking, yapping miniature white poodles back into the house, Hoadley closed the door on them and came striding down a short flagstone walk. As the front door swung open, floodlights had come on, illuminating the entryway, the flagstone walk and the gate. Hoadley was wearing a light leather jacket, flared slacks and a striped sport shirt. With his curly hair, broad shoulders and slim hips, he was a handsome man who moved with the graceful economy of a natural athlete. His gait was rolling, insolent and swaggering. With the light behind him, I couldn't see his face. But he could see mine—plainly.

As he came close to the gate, he reached out with his left hand for the latch. At the same time, his right hand disappeared behind his back. He was reaching into his hip pocket.

While I tried to keep my expression noncommital, I handed the walkie-talkie to Canelli, then raised my revolver until its muzzle came just below the top of the gate.

"This won't take long, Hoadley," I said. "Not if you're really the wrong man."

"Watch his right hand, Lieutenant," Canelli whispered.

"I see it."

Now the light shone full in Hoadley's face. He showed no sign of anxiety, or anger. Instead, he wore the hood's standard expression facing arrest: puzzlement, combined with a kind of outraged innocence.

As his left hand came closer to the latch, I surreptitiously braced myself, bending my knees and planting my feet more firmly. When the latch was released, I would crash my shoulder into the gate. If the gate struck him, throwing him off balance, I'd have the split second I needed, whether or not he had a gun.

I heard the latch click, saw the gate begin to move away from its frame. Instantly I lowered my shoulder and hit the gate, hard.

But, instead of striking Hoadley, the gate swung wide as he stepped quickly back. Lunging forward, momentarily off balance as I tripped on the uneven flagstones, I fought for balance as I pivoted to face him, raising my revolver.

"Freeze," a voice screamed . . .

Hoadley's voice, not Canelli's.

I was facing an automatic, aimed squarely at my chest.

"Freeze," he screamed again. "Drop the fucking guns. Both of them. *Drop* them, or he dies."

With my revolver angled down toward the flagstones, I slowly, deliberately straightened to face him squarely. About six feet separated us. At that range, he couldn't miss. In the glare of the floodlights, the automatic's bore was enormous.

Hoadley's eyes were wild; the gun was shaking violently as he raved:

"All right, here it comes. Bite it, you bastard."

"Wait—" I raised my free hand, as if to ward off the bullet. "Don't. Here it is." Holding his eyes locked with mine, I slowly, cautiously bent my knees, laying my revolver on the flagstones. Behind me, I heard another metallic click as Canelli's gun came down.

For one desperate, incoherent moment, all I could think about was Sergeant Galt, at the police academy. *"A cop's the same as his gun,"* he'd said. *"If you give up your gun, you're no cop."*

In fourteen years, I'd never given up my gun.

"Move," Hoadley screamed suddenly, gesticulating with the automatic. "Get back, away from the goddamn gun. *Move* it."

With our hands raised to shoulder height, side by side, Canelli and I stepped off the flagstones and into ankle-high ivy.

"St. Louis, eh," Hoadley breathed viciously. "Complaints, eh? I should kill you. I should blow your goddamn heads off." He stooped, caught up our revolvers, thrust one in either pocket of his leather jacket. Now, one slow step at a time, he was moving toward the open gate. His hand was tightening around the automatic. His finger was curved on the trigger; the safety catch was off. Another ounce of pressure, and the gun would fire.

"Lie down," he hissed. "Flat on your face. Now."

"Oh, Jesus," Canelli said. It wasn't a curse, it was a prayer. I could hear terror in his voice—the same mouth-parched, throat-clenched terror I felt.

As I looked at Canelli lowering himself to all fours, I saw the walkie-talkie bulging in his jacket pocket. Was the radio on transmit? Could Culligan make out words, with the radio muffled by the thickness of a pocket?

As if I were doing push-ups, I lowered myself into the

thick, damp-smelling ivy. Turning my head away from Hoadley, I whispered, "Is the radio on?"

"No."

"Christ."

Now Hoadley advanced on us. I could see his booted feet less than a yard from my face. "Is there anyone else?" he said. "Any other cops?"

"No," I lied. "Just us. We came about a complaint. Like I told you."

"A lieutenant, eh? About a complaint, eh?" His voice was hoarse, choked by the fury that tore at his throat. He took another step toward us. Now he stood directly above me.

"A *complaint,* eh? You—you—" As his voice suddenly rose to a high, hysterical note, I felt his feet shift in the ivy beside me . . . felt his boot crash into my rib cage.

As I groaned, Hoadley's voice dropped again, trembling as he spoke close to my ear. "I'm leaving now," he breathed. "I'm going to get in my car, and leave. It's parked across the street. I can sit in my car, and still see you. And if you come after me—if you stick your fucking heads up—I'll kill you. I swear to God, I'll kill you."

"Go ahead," I gasped, struggling for breath. "Leave." With the right side of my head flat on the ground, I watched him begin moving toward the gate, one step at a time. "Go ahead. We won't stop you."

"You're goddamn right you won't stop me, you sons of bitches."

He was within fifteen feet of the open gate—ten feet—five feet. With every step, his wildly unsteady gun threatened us.

Then, in the open gateway, a silent black shape appeared.

It was the Doberman, straining against his leash.

Followed by a tall silhouette of the man, demanding: "What the hell's going—"

As Hoadley turned toward the voice, I pushed myself away from the ground, got my feet under me, lunged for Hoadley's legs. Instantly, he turned to face me, bringing up the automatic. At the same moment, a black form leaped through the darkness, straight for his throat. As my arms closed around Hoadley's thrashing legs, I felt the force of the dog's weight crashing into him. My right hand found the automatic's barrel. I released his legs, clamping both hands around the barrel. I twisted the gun, throwing all my weight against his right arm, incredibly strong. In the swearing, snarling, thrashing melee, I saw Canelli fall on Hoadley's left arm. Suddenly, a knee crashed into my chest. Still clinging to the gun, I was thrown on my back—to face the Doberman's teeth, flecked red with blood. Above the shouting and snarling, I heard Hoadley scream. "He's killing me. Get him off. He's killing me."

"Drop it," I shouted. "Drop the goddamn gun."

"Jesus. Please. Get him off."

"Then *drop* it."

And, suddenly, I felt his fingers give way. The gun was mine. Above me, the dog still raged. Then I saw the leash jerk taut.

"Come on, Crusher. *Back.*" Again, the leash jerked taut. The dog was giving ground. I found the automatic's safety catch, set it, tossed the gun carefully in a nearby flower bed and reached for my handcuffs. Beside me, holding his shoulder with bloodied fingers, Hoadley was whimpering.

Fourteen

The young, bearded intern was shaking his head doubtfully.

"I don't know, Lieutenant. I'd like to help. But I've got my duty, just like you've got yours. And the man's in shock. The lacerations aren't a problem. But shock is *always* a problem. Why don't you come back tomorrow morning?"

I drew a deep, slow breath, then said, "Are you a Rebecca Carlton fan, by any chance?"

He looked at me, then looked down the hospital corridor, where a patrolman was posted outside Hoadley's room.

"You mean—" His questioning stare was skeptically cautious.

I nodded. "According to our information, he murdered Rebecca Carlton."

"Well, I'll be damned." His bright, quick eyes shone with sudden interest. He was a teen-ager again, star-struck. But, a moment later, he countered conscientiously: "All the more reason, then, for us to take precautions, it seems to me. Don't forget Lee Harvey Oswald."

I looked at him thoughtfully, trying to decide how he'd react to pressure. Something about the aggressive set of his jaw suggested that he'd dig in his heels even harder. So I tried to sound placating as I said, "Listen, Doctor, I don't want to give you a hard time. But you've only got two choices. Either let me talk to him, or else turn me over to your supervisor. I don't like to put it like that, but I can't help myself. This man is a suspect in a homicide that's front-page news everywhere. It's the kind of publicity that a lawyer would do anything to get. *Anything.* And, to be honest with you, I want to interrogate Hoadley before word gets out that we've got someone in custody. Because, when that happens, my job immediately becomes tougher. And, believe me, it's tough enough already."

He'd stood impassively eying me as I spoke. Now he turned to look at a wall clock, which read almost midnight. Finally he turned back to face me. "If you want to call Doctor Saunders, Lieutenant, be my guest. But I can tell you that he'll be totally pissed off. He went home yesterday afternoon with a cold and fever." The intern's eyes were calm, his voice deliberate, his manner a little haughty. The jaw was set at an even more uncompromising angle. Like most doctors, he considered himself superior to mere policemen.

So I decided to try pandering to his sense of superiority. Looking him earnestly in the eye I said, "Listen, Doctor, there must be some way we can work this out. Isn't there something you can suggest? Some way around it?" I paused, assessing his reaction. Arms folded across his stethoscope, he waited for me to continue. He knew he'd won the first round. But he looked as if he might be generous in victory.

"Why don't you come in the room with me?" I asked. "Just the two of us. You can watch him. And if you're worried about him, I swear to God I'll knock it off."

"Well—" He began judiciously stroking his neatly trimmed blond beard, obviously enjoying the ease with which he'd forced me to compromise.

"Well, I suppose we could try that." Then, suddenly, he smiled. It was an unexpectedly boyish smile. "God, what a gas," he said impulsively, "hearing him confess to murdering Rebecca Carlton."

"There's no guarantees, though," I said. "Not in my business."

"Nor in my business, either, Lieutenant. Come on—" Eagerly, he led the way down the corridor. "You know," he said, "I've got every record that Rebecca Carlton ever cut. I'm a collector, as a matter of fact. I've even got her version of 'Careless Love' which was the first single she ever cut, ten years ago."

As we stopped before Hoadley's door while I identified myself to the patrolman, the intern said, "Let's really put the blocks to him. What'd you say?"

As he looked from me to the intern, the patrolman blinked.

Lying flat on his back, staring up at the ceiling, Hoadley licked his mucus-stuck lips, weakly hawked as he tried to clear his throat, and said, "All I want to know is whether that dog was yours." His voice was toneless, weak and thick. He was heavily sedated. As I watched him, I wondered whether his sedation would work for me or against me. Across the bed, the intern reached for Hoadley's wrist, glanced at his watch, counted, then nodded to me.

"It wasn't my dog, Hoadley."

"Was it the police department's?"

"No. He belongs to a man named McNie. He's an interior designer who lives three doors from Sally Grant's house."

"Jesus—" Noisily, he cleared his throat again. "Yeah. I remember now. I remember seeing him when I walked her goddamn poodles." Weakly, he smiled. His words slurred thickly together as he said, "He's a mean bastard, that dog."

"Listen, Hoadley, we don't have a lot of time, so let's get to it." I pointed to his right hand, lying beside him on the bed. "We've got a witness who'll connect you to the gun that killed Rebecca Carlton. We've got a positive paraffin test on your right wrist, proving that you fired a gun during the past forty-eight hours. And we've also got your fingerprint on one of the cartridges inside the gun's cylinder." The last statement was a lie, risky with a witness present. But I could always deny that I'd said it, and hope for the best.

"You used rubber gloves when you shot her, but not when you loaded the gun," I said.

"Bullshit," he answered blearily. "It was already loaded when she gave it—" Confused, he broke off. Then, realizing what he'd said, he laboriously turned his head on the pillow so that he could scan my face, trying to discover whether his slip of the tongue had registered—whether I knew that I had my first break.

"When who gave it to you?" I asked softly.

Quickly—desperately—he turned his head away.

Who had given him the gun? Was it Rebecca? No, not Rebecca. At least, not according to my conception of Rebecca Carlton and her life. It was a wide-open life—and yet closely proscribed. Everything Rebecca had done was on public view, even her sex life. And someone like Hoadley simply didn't fit.

I decided on one last gamble:

"It was Sally Grant," I said. "You did the job for her. She got the gun, somehow—and she gave it to you." I tried to speak in a flat, matter-of-fact voice, implying that the truth of the statement was self-evident.

Suddenly his head thrashed back and forth, denying it. The movement made him cry out in pain; his free hand flew to his wounded shoulder. The intern raised a warning hand to me.

"You owed her money, and you were working it off." But, even as I said it, I could see the fallacy in the theory. If Hoadley couldn't have gotten access to the gun, then Sally Grant probably couldn't, either.

Yet I could see fear in Hoadley's eyes. I knew that I was close to the truth—close to breaking him down. I knew that he and Sally Grant had done the job. His weak, wall-eyed protest confirmed it: "No, Jesus. You got it all wrong. You—"

"I've got it all *right,* Hoadley. I've got the whole story. Everything. All I need."

Again he turned to look at me. With great effort, speaking with a kind of exaggerated, drunken precision, he said, "All you've got is talk. Just talk."

"Wrong. I've got you tied to the murder weapon. I've got you tied to it two ways, at least. And I've got a witness who'll swear you did the job. And I've got a motive, too. Money. You owed Sally Grant a bundle. To square it, you pulled the trigger. It's an airtight case. There isn't a D.A. in the country who wouldn't jump at a chance to prosecute you, with evidence like that." As his eyes still searched my face, I let a beat pass before I said, "Whoever prosecutes you, Hoadley, he'll be famous. That's a powerful incentive. He can get a death sentence, sure as hell. He'll get his picture on the cover of *Time.*" Again I paused. Then, with delicately timed malice, I added, "You might get your picture on the cover, too. When you're executed."

Leaning suddenly across the bed, eyes shining with excitement, the intern said, "He's right, Hoadley. He's telling you the truth. You're as good as dead right now."

"But—" The injured man's tongue circled his lips as he laboriously turned on the pillow to stare at the doctor, then returned his gaze to me. "But, Jesus, you've got it all wrong. I—you—"

"The only way you can help yourself," I said, "is to take Sally with you. If she'll admit that she hired you—if you give us enough to convict her—then the D.A. will probably give you a break. If I ask him to do it, he will. If I tell him that you didn't plan the murder—that you just pulled the trigger —he'll go easy on you."

"It's a con," he whispered. "A fucking con." The words were desperately defiant. But, deep in his eyes, I saw terror beginning. No one wants to face death.

"Remember what I said about the D.A.'s reputation,

Hoadley," I said softly. "He'll be playing to the audience, all the time. He'll be a celebrity—especially if he can nail someone like Sally. He doesn't want you. You're nothing. He wants someone who'll make a big crash, falling."

"Yeah," the intern echoed. "You're a zero, Hoadley. "You're nothing but a goddamn cipher."

Frowning at the intern, surreptitiously shaking my head, I rose from my chair. The time had come for the closing bit of business: the walkaway.

"It's up to you, Hoadley," I said, shrugging. "Either way, you're going to jail. You assaulted me with a gun last night. With your record, that'll get you fifty years, minimum." I let a moment of silence pass, at the same time signaling for the intern to leave the suspect's bedside. Then, softly, I said, "Either way, you're screwed. But one way, you make it hard for yourself. The other way—" I spread my hands. "The other way, I could help you. It's your choice." I raised my arm, pointing to the door. "But if I leave here—if I walk through that door— it's your ass. You'll be inside for thirty years, at least. You'll be an old man, when you get out."

"*If* you get out," the intern put in eagerly.

Hoadley's lips twisted in a small, weak smile, shakily defiant. "There's lots of people tried to nail Sally," he whispered. "But none of them ever did. And you won't, either. And if you don't get her, you won't get me." He cleared his throat, coughed up phlegm, then said distinctly, "So fuck off."

I had no choice but to play out the walkaway. So, furious with myself for pressing him too hard, I left the room— followed by the young intern, his eyes still shining.

In the hallway outside, the patrolman said, "There's a message for you, Lieutenant. You're supposed to call Communications. Sergeant Halliday."

"Thanks." I walked down the hallway to a pay phone, and quickly dialed Communications.

"I've got an urgent message from Inspector Culligan, Lieutenant Hastings."

"What's the message?" As I spoke, I eyed the intern, excitedly pacing the hallway beside the phone booth. He was reliving the interrogation.

"Inspector Culligan says to tell you that Sally Grant just got home. He wants instructions."

"Tell him not to take any action until I get there. I'm leaving now."

"Yessir."

Fifteen

For the second time that night I checked with Culligan, in the rear alley, then pressed Sally Grant's door buzzer. The time was one-fifteen A.M., and as I leaned against the wall beside the gate, yawning, I massaged my side, where Hoadley had kicked me.

If I ever got him alone, in a windowless interrogation room, I would pay him back.

"Keep your thumb on the button, Canelli," I said wearily.

"Yessir." With his thumb obediently in place, he said, "How're you feeling, Lieutenant?"

"I wouldn't be surprised if I had a broken rib."

"Does it hurt when you take a deep breath?"

I nodded.

"Then it's probably broken, all right." Sadly, he shook his head. "He was a real tough one, you know that? If it hadn't been for the dog, I think we would've been in real trouble."

"He wasn't so tough in the hospital," I answered shortly.

"Jeeze, I thought he was going to pull the trigger, though, you know that? I thought he was going to—"

"Who the hell's there?" It was a woman's voice, coming

through the speaker beside me. I leaned toward the speaker, saying, "It's the police. Open up."

"It's one o'clock in the morning, for Christ's sake."

"If you don't talk to me now, I'll be back tomorrow with a warrant. We'll take you downtown, if we have to come back. Take your choice. I don't care, either way. I could use the sleep." As I said it, I heard Canelli groan. Working shorthanded on a weekend, we'd gone through all our reserves. So, while I slept, Canelli would be standing stakeout.

"Who's talking, anyhow?" Even though her voice was electronically distorted, I could sense caution in the question—calculation, too.

"My name is Hastings. Lieutenant Frank Hastings. Homicide."

"Homicide?" A moment of silence followed before she asked, "Is Captain Jepson with you?"

"This isn't a vice bust, Sally. I'm working on a murder."

"Who's murdered?"

"Let me in, and I'll tell you."

After a final moment of silence, the buzzer sounded and the gate swung open under my hand.

Sally Grant opened the front door, examined my badge and I.D., looked into my eyes for one long, appraising moment, then turned her back and walked through an ornate archway and into an elaborately furnished living room. As she walked, swinging her broad, bulging hips, four tiny white poodles frisked and yapped around her. When she seated herself on a brocaded silk sofa, the poodles jumped up beside her, two on each side.

At forty-six years old, without her makeup, with her long, bleached-blonde hair hanging in tumbled disarray around her shoulders, she looked exactly like what she was—a massage-parlor madame. Her eyes were as hard and unrevealing as two pale-blue marbles. The line of her mouth was as cruel as a drill sergeant's, harassing recruits. She was wearing a white satin dressing gown over a bright-red nightgown. Her figure had probably once been provocative, full-breasted and voluptuous. Now, though, she was simply fat.

Idly scratching one of the poodles, she looked at me impassively for a moment, then said, "I saw Captain Jepson four days ago. On Wednesday. He didn't say anything about any murder." Her voice, too, was almost a caricature of a madame's: harsh and brassy, gravel-throated.

Instead of replying to the implied question, I said, "I understand you just got back from Las Vegas. Is that right?"

Revealing uneven teeth and a thick pink tongue, she yawned in my face. "That's right, Lieutenant. I've been driving for twelve hours straight. And I don't mind telling you, I'm pooped. So whatever you got to say, I'd appreciate it if you'd say it quick."

"Why did you drive? Why didn't you fly?"

"Because," she answered, "I'm scared of flying. Five years ago I was in a chartered airplane—flying to Las Vegas, as a matter of fact. First one engine quit. It only had two, and one quit. Then it got lost going through the mountains. It couldn't fly over the mountains on just one engine. So it had to go through a pass. In a snowstorm." Remembering, she shook her head. "I'll never forget it. Never."

"So you haven't been in an airplane since," Canelli said. "Is that right?"

Turning to Canelli, she took a long, insolent moment to look him up and down before she said, "Who're you, anyhow?"

Grinning sheepishly, he said, "My name's Canelli. Inspector Canelli."

Obviously unimpressed, she grunted, "Well, you're right, Canelli. I haven't flown since. And I'll never fly again, either."

"When did you leave for Las Vegas?" I asked.

The hard, expressionless eyes returned to me. "I left Thursday," she said curtly. "About noon."

"Did you go on business, or pleasure?"

"I haven't had a vacation for six years. Does that answer your question?"

"Did you go with anyone?"

"One of my girls drove my car. I hate to drive, especially long distances."

"What kind of a car do you have?"

"A Cadillac."

"You don't have a garage?"

"I keep it downtown, in one of the hotel garages."

"Which hotel?"

"The Hilton."

"That must cost a bundle," Canelli said.

She didn't bother to reply. Instead, looking at me, she said, "Now, what's this all about, anyhow? Who's been murdered?"

Holding her gaze, trying to disconcert her with a long, silent stare, I didn't reply. The tactic failed. After a hard, uncompromising moment she exhaled irritably.

"Listen, Lieutenant—" As she shifted impatiently on the sofa, the dressing gown parted to reveal a thick knee and the white, lumpy flesh of her thigh. "Let's not play eye contact, eh? It's too late for games."

In spite of myself, I smiled. Sally Grant was tough. Smart, and tough. She'd seen it all, at least once.

Quietly—still watching her carefully for a reaction—I said, "Rebecca Carlton's dead, Sally. She was killed Friday night. And we think you're involved."

"How the hell could I be involved," she snapped. "I was in Las Vegas Friday night."

"I'm not saying you pulled the trigger."

"What *are* you saying, then?"

"We've got Bruce Hoadley in custody. Did you know about it?"

"What'd you mean, did I know about it?" she asked belligerently. "All I know, he wasn't here when I got back." As she spoke, she stroked one of the dogs, as if to reassure herself that it hadn't suffered during Hoadley's absence.

"Does Bruce Hoadley owe you money?" I asked.

"As a matter of fact, he does. But what's that got to do with Rebecca Carlton?"

"How much does he owe you?"

"I forget. A few thousand. But he's working it off." Still stroking the dog, she shrugged. "He's a gambler. He always owes me money. I let him go for a while, then I tighten up. You know—like fishing. You give them some slack, then you tighten up."

"It's like you want to keep him on the hook, then," Canelli put in. "So you always have someone to do your dirty work."

Once more she looked Canelli deliberately up and down before she asked, "What kind of dirty work are you talking about, anyhow?"

"Let's get back to Rebecca Carlton." I asked, "What was your connection with her?"

She looked at me for a long, calculating moment before she said, "Suppose you tell me, Lieutenant. What *was* my connection with her?"

Now it was my turn to calculate. Obviously, she was trying to determine how much I knew. If I took a chance—made a lucky guess—I might shake her composure, and therefore learn something from her reaction. But if she was as smart as she seemed, she would simply break off the interrogation, and call her lawyer.

So I must play the same game she was playing, keeping her off balance while I tried to trap her.

Sometimes the truth was the best means of disconcerting a suspect. "To be honest," I answered slowly, "I haven't been able to establish a connection. And I haven't been able to establish how the .357 magnum got from Sam Wright, to Rebecca Carlton, to you, to Hoadley—and then back again, when it was ditched at the Cow Palace, after the shooting. But I will, Sally. Believe me, I'll get it all connected. And when I do, I'll have the last piece of the puzzle. I'll have the motive, too. I don't have it now. But I'll get it." As I spoke, I got to my feet. Looking down at her, I said softly, "And when I get it all put together, Sally, then you'll fall for Murder One. You'll fall just as hard as Hoadley."

I turned, and left the house without looking back. On the sidewalk outside, I turned to Canelli. "Stake her out, front and back—tight. Now. Right now. When I get home, I'll arrange for your relief, probably at eight o'clock tomorrow morning." I stifled a yawn, and said goodnight. As I walked away, I heard Canelli sigh deeply.

Sixteen

At seven-thirty the next morning—Sunday—my bedside phone rang.

"I thought I'd let you sleep an extra hour," Friedman said. "Myself, I've been up since six A.M."

"What happened?"

"Shall I give you the build-up, or do you just want the punch line?"

"Listen, Pete, I didn't get to sleep until two-thirty."

"All right, here's the punch line. Sally Grant is dead. Murdered."

"But—Christ—her place was staked out, front and back."

"Maybe now you want the build-up."

"What is it?"

"Well, in sequence, she left her house about two A.M., by cab. The cab called for her at her back gate. Culligan followed her, with a G.W. man. She went to the Hilton, went inside, and promptly disappeared. Later it developed that she probably went downstairs to the garage, got in her Cadillac and drove off—while Culligan was waiting for her to come out of the hallway that led to the ladies' room. Culligan, needless to say, is mortified."

"Where the hell was Canelli?"

"He was guarding the front of the house, not the back. So, when Sally took off, Culligan told him to stay put. Quite properly. Why?"

"Because Canelli knew that she kept her car at the Hilton. If he'd been following her, he might not've lost her."

"What can I say? Those're the breaks."

"How'd she die?"

"A gunshot wound to the right temple was fatal, but she was also shot in the upper chest. That one probably put her out of action, and the one to the head finished the job. She was in her car, behind the wheel. Apparently she'd parked in a lovers' lane close to the top of Twin Peaks—the one called The Crescent. Anyhow, that's where she was found, at about five A.M. A black-and-white car saw her window shot out, and investigated. I got the call a half hour later."

"She went out to meet someone, sure as hell. I'll bet she made a call as soon as I left, and set up a meeting."

"Did she know her house was staked out? Did you tell her?"

"No."

"She probably saw Canelli out in front," Friedman mused. "So she tried the back. That's the only way it makes sense. Culligan said he and the G.W. man were parked at opposite ends of the alley. So she probably didn't see them."

"So what now?"

"Now," Friedman said, "we do the obvious. First, we find out where our so-called suspects were, at two this morning. Second, we see if we can connect Sally with one—or more —of them. And then, third, we see whether we can connect Sally and Rebecca."

"Why do you think there's a connection between Sally and the others?"

"I don't, necessarily. I'm just looking for a motive. I mean, if we assume that it came down like Carole said—that Sally planned the job and Hoadley pulled the trigger—then we've got to figure out a motive for Sally. And, what's more, it has to be a pretty good motive. I'll deny I ever said it, but she had Jepson tucked right inside her bulging brassiere. She had it made, in other words. She was rich, and successful in her chosen profession. So why would she risk falling for murder?"

I was sitting up in bed now, resigned to getting up and going to work. "I was hoping to take today off," I said ruefully.

"Likewise."

"Or, at least, I want to get off tonight. I've *got* to get off tonight."

"Then take it off. What's the problem?"

"The problem," I said sourly, "is that people keep getting murdered. And you know as well as I do that it's just you and me. There's no one else to supervise."

"It sounds like whatever you've got to do tonight is more important than your sworn duty."

"It is."

"Well, don't sweat it. Anything that comes up, I'll handle it."

"Thanks. I'll take you up on it."

A moment of silence followed. Then Friedman said, "Judging by the particular love-struck tone of your voice, I'd say that what you've got to do tonight involves Ann Haywood, my favorite schoolteacher."

Irritated at the ease with which he'd guessed the truth—and angry at myself for making it so easy—I didn't answer.

But Friedman, typically, didn't let it drop. "I also get the feeling," he said casually, "that you and Ann are at some kind of midlife crossroads. Am I right?"

"Listen, Pete, this isn't—"

"Let's assume I'm right," he continued blandly. "And let's also assume, just for the sake of argument, that you're scared shitless of getting married again. Which would make sense, considering how close you play your emotions to your vest. So then, let's assume that—"

"Listen. It's not even eight o'clock, for God's sake, on Sunday morning. Do I really have to listen to all this?"

"No. But, see, that's another character defect that I've been meaning to point out. You've got a tendency to—"

"*Christ.* Come *on.*"

"All right. Sorry. How's your ribs, by the way?"

I took a deep breath—and winced. "Terrible."

"You want to go back to bed? Go on sick call?"

"No. I've had cracked ribs before. I'll get them taped up, later. What'd you want me to do?"

"How about taking another shot at Hoadley?" he suggested. "If he really did pull the trigger, he probably knows more about Sally than he's telling."

"All right." I swung my legs out of bed. "Where'll you be?"

"At the Hall," Friedman said. "Sitting in the center of my spider web, feeling for vibrations."

"Oh, Jesus."

"Sally's dead?" Hoadley asked.

Drawing a chair up to his bedside, I nodded as I sat down. "That's right, Hoadley. I interrogated her early this morning, when she got home from Las Vegas. As soon as I left, she obviously called someone to arrange a meeting—quick. Whoever she met must've killed her."

"I don't believe you. It's a goddamn con."

"Listen, Hoadley," I said wearily, "I wouldn't've gotten out of bed at seven-thirty on Sunday morning just to run a con on you. Ten o'clock, maybe. But not seven-thirty. Not with four hours sleep."

I saw him swallow, saw his eyes wander away, losing focus. Finally he asked, "When'd she get killed?"

"Sometime between two A.M. and five A.M. Why?"

Slowly, he shook his head. "No reason."

"Do you know who she met? Did she have an appointment to meet someone, as soon as she got back in town?"

He didn't reply. His eyes were still unfocused, and he was frowning thoughtfully. I watched his scarred, big-knuckled brawler's hands fret absently on the counterpane. Freshly shaved, with his face washed and his hair combed, he was a remarkably good-looking man. His eyes were a clear china blue. His mouth was small, shaped like a corrupted cupid's. Hoadley was one of the baby-faced thugs—the kind that are often the most brutal, the most sadistic. At the thought, I touched my side. There'd been no reason for that final kick. He'd done it purely for pleasure.

"Who else was involved?" I asked quietly. "There were three of you, at least. Maybe more. We know that. Who were they?"

The china blue eyes finally focused on me, eyes that were so empty and expressionless that they seemed almost innocent.

"Last night, you said you had a witness," he replied carefully. "What'd you mean by that, anyhow?"

"I meant exactly what I said."

"Someone turned me. Is that what you meant?"

"That's right, Hoadley."

"It was Carole, wasn't it?"

I smiled at him—signifying that, yes, it was Carole. Then I said, "No comment." Still slightly smiling.

"It was, though," he insisted. "She said she was going to stick it to me, because I was moving out. And that's what she did. She framed me."

"How could she frame you?" I pointed to his hand. "Did she put the gun in your hand, and pull the trigger? Did she bribe us to come up with a positive paraffin test?"

"That don't make me a murderer, just because maybe I shot a gun. It could've been target practice, you know." As he said it, his cupid's mouth stirred in a small, smug smile. He was pleased with his quip.

"Don't forget your fingerprint, Hoadley."

He looked at me calmly for a moment, then slowly, deliberately shook his head. "There wasn't any fingerprint. Not on the bullets."

"You didn't even check, then, to see if the gun was loaded?"

The smug little smile was my only answer. Looking into the bland blue eyes, I realized that my single success last night—his slip of the tongue—had resulted from the sedatives he'd taken, not from my skill at interrogation. Clear-headed now, no longer in pain from the dog bites, he'd decided that he was safer with Sally dead than he'd been when she was alive.

He was probably right.

The paraffin test was circumstantial. The "fingerprint" had been a hoax. And Carole Platt's testimony was probably worthless.

My only remaining edge was last night's fight, and his attempt to escape.

I glanced over my shoulder at the door, then hitched my chair closer to the bed. Looking him straight in the eyes, I spoke in a quiet, businesslike voice.

"We may or may not have a standoff on the Carlton murder, Hoadley. You did it, all right. I know it, and you know I know it. I might not be able to prove it, though. Both of us know that, too. But, sure as hell, I *can* prove that, last night, you attacked two police officers with a gun. The charge will be assault with intent to commit murder. There'll be three witnesses, to prove it—me, my partner and McNie, the owner of the Doberman. And I promise you, Hoadley—" I hesitated for a long, ominous moment. "I promise you," I repeated solemnly, "that when they lock you up for that they'll throw away the key."

The smile faltered, then finally failed. But the eyes remained steady, defying me. He'd take his chances.

Or would he?

"It doesn't seem to bother you, taking a fall." As I said it, I watched him closely. Had he picked up on the invitation in my voice—the suggestion that he could still make a deal?

His bandaged shoulder rose and then fell as he shrugged. "Nobody wants to take a fall." He spoke tentatively, probing. Yes, he'd picked up on it.

I decided to let him begin the bargaining, and in the silence that followed, each of us tried to measure the other's intentions carefully. It was a delicate, decisive moment. Finally he said, "Last night, you said you wanted Sally. You said you'd give me a break, if I gave her to you. But now she's dead. So—" Again he shrugged. "So I can't very well give her to you. So where's my edge?"

"Things have changed since last night," I said. "Last night, we thought it was just you and Sally. Now we know that there was someone else—someone more important, probably. That's who we want."

"But what if I can't help you? What if what I've got doesn't add up to anything. Then what?"

"All you've got to do is try. I don't expect you to give me a name. I don't think you've got a name to give me. But you can tell me what you know. It might just be one piece, but someone else might have another piece."

He snorted. "You must think I'm pretty stupid. You get me to confess to murder. You got a confession. All I've got is a promise."

"I'm not asking you to confess to murder, Hoadley. I'm just asking you to cooperate. Tell me how it came down. If you're telling the truth, you'll help yourself. Otherwise—" I spread my hands. "Otherwise, you're screwed. You're screwed good. You lie to me, and I'll do everything I can—pull every string—to put you away until you're sixty years old. And I'll do it, too. I promise you."

I watched the improbably innocent eyes narrow as he thought about it. Then, as clearly as if I'd been able to eavesdrop on his thoughts, I saw him devising a plan to save himself. He'd do what they all did: mix a little truth with a few lies, and hope for the best.

148

First—elaborately resigned—he sighed, shaking his head. "I guess I got to trust you," he said. "I guess I got no choice."

Except for a slight inclination of my head, I didn't respond. I was waiting for the show to begin.

"What happened, see, was that I got pretty deep into some guys, and they told me that I didn't have much time left before they'd start breaking things like fingers and knees. And, Christ, I was desperate. See, there wasn't nobody I could go to for help. I was all tapped out. I couldn't even do a robbery. Sally, she told me a long time ago that if I ever robbed anyone, or did any breaking and entering, or anything, I was through with her. I mean, all I had to do was get *questioned,* and I was through. Because, see, Sally is—was—always inside the law. Always."

I nodded. "All right. So how did it go?"

"Well, I needed money, like I said. And I couldn't go to Sally, I knew, because I already owed her about seven thousand. I mean, I was working it down. It started out being about ten thousand, and I had it down to seven. But, still, I owed her. And she'd already told me, no more loans. Which is the reason, see, that I got into trouble, gambling. I mean, I thought, what the hell, the only chance I had to get back even was if I doubled some bets, you know. And—" This time, his piously regretful sigh was genuine. "And, for a while, it worked, too. I was almost even. But then, Christ, it all turned sour. Before I knew what happened, it seemed like, I owed some guys about twelve thousand. So then I start hearing about finger-breaking, and all that.

"So, just about the time I was thinking that I'd have to leave town, Sally told me that she wanted me to drive her over to Berkeley, where she's thinking about opening a couple of parlors, if she can get the backing. That was about ten days ago. And on the way back from Berkeley, she says she knows I'm having trouble. She says she'll be sorry to lose me, but she knows I'll have to leave town. And then she starts in about how tough it's going to be on me, giving up the deal I got with her and starting in again—and all that's supposing that some guys don't find out where I run to, and maybe do worse than break a couple of fingers, once they find me, for a lesson to anyone else who might think of splitting. That's how they do it, you know. They got to keep their reputation solid, or they're screwed."

"All right." I nodded impatiently. "I know how it goes."

"Yeah. Well, anyhow, as soon as she started talking about my troubles and everything, I knew she had something in mind. So, pretty soon, she comes up with it. She says that she'll pay off my markers, and forget about what I owe her and give me ten thousand dollars in cash, if I wanted to take a little risk. Which, I knew, wasn't no little risk. But, anyhow, I said go ahead. So we kept driving around while she gave me the rundown. We drove all the way down to Half Moon Bay and back, while she laid it out.

"She said that a friend of hers wanted this singer offed. And she said that the friend had it all set up—with a plan, and a gun, and everything, all laid out.

"Well—" He looked at me with his round, mock-guileless eyes. "Well, I don't mind admitting to you that I was tempted. I mean, she was talking about twenty-nine thousand dollars. I'd have a chance to start clean again, with a ten-thousand-dollar stake. It was tempting, all right. I don't deny it." Piously, he nodded over the fraudulent admission. "I even took the gun home, while I thought about it. Who knows—" He shrugged. "I might've even took one of the bullets out, though I don't remember doing it. But then, Jesus, it suddenly hit me. I mean, Jesus, murder—that's too heavy, no matter how much money she was talking. So finally I gave the goddamn gun back, and told her to forget it. I told her that, what the hell, if I had to leave town, that's what I'd do. So—" He paused, catching his breath. Then, as if he'd thought of some new twist to his story, he brightened almost imperceptibly. "So about that time, see, Carole starts to get pissed off. I mean, my chances of disappearing wouldn't be very good, with her hanging around my neck. So I told her to leave. Alone." He looked at me, transparently trying to calculate my reaction. "So I guess you know how it goes from there, Lieutenant." As he said it, he sighed. It was a counterfeit sigh of contentment, signifying that he felt better for having told me the truth.

Except that only the first part of his "confession" was true. According to the conventions—according to the rules of the game—he wasn't expected to confess to murder. I wanted Sally, and he'd given her to me. Or, at least, he'd told me all he knew. The rest was up to me.

"Let's get back to Sally's friend," I said finally.

"Yeah. Sure." He settled himself more comfortably on his pillow. "What'd you want to know?"

"First, was it a man, or a woman?"

He let a long, laborious beat pass before he shook his head, smiling at me with his cherubic mouth. "Christ, now that's funny. I don't think she said. I mean, I just figured—you know—that it was a man. But—" He shrugged. "But I don't think she said."

"How many times did she mention this friend?"

"Oh—two, three times, maybe. No more."

"She said the friend had a plan. Did that mean that he had everything figured out, down to the last detail?"

He nodded. "That's the way it seemed to me, yeah. Everything was cool, she said. When the time came, I'd get instructions."

"You say that you assumed that her friend was a man. What else did you assume about him?"

"Honest, Lieutenant," he said earnestly, "I can't tell you a thing about him. All I know is, she was doing it for him, she said. It was his show. He was the main man. She was just —you know—handling the details for him."

"Did you believe her?"

"How do you mean?"

151

"I mean, do you think she was doing him a favor?"

His expression cleared as he shook his head. "No. Sally never did nobody a favor in her life, unless she got something out of it."

"What'd you think she was getting out of this?"

"Money," he answered promptly. "For Sally, that's all there was. Just money."

"But she had plenty of money."

Once more, he shook his head. "Wrong, Lieutenant. Sally never had enough money. She was just like the rest of us. She always wanted more. Lots more."

Seventeen

As soon as I walked into the squad room, Canelli got to his feet and came toward me. He was slowly, sadly shaking his head.

"Jeeze, Lieutenant, I'm sure sorry about last night. If I'd only've known she was headed for the Hilton—" He let it go dolefully unfinished.

"It's not your fault, Canelli. Forget it."

"Yeah, well, it's nice of you to say it, Lieutenant. But I know she was just about all we had. And I just want you to know, I feel terrible about how she got killed, and everything." Today, Canelli was in a morose mood. It always happened, when he lost sleep. Friedman's reaction to fatigue was usually black humor. When I got tired, I got irritable. Canelli suffered.

"You did what you should've done, Canelli. You stayed at your post. For all you knew, she could've been trying to fake you out. I'd've done the same thing, in your place. And, what's more, I'd've ordered you to do exactly what you did, if you'd asked me. So don't waste time and energy stewing about it. All right?"

"Yeah, Lieutenant. All right. How're you feeling, anyhow? How's your ribs?"

I touched the bandages that bound me from my waist to my upper chest. "I just had them taped. They'll be all right."

"That's good. I'm glad to hear it. That Hoadley, he's tough. I feel like I went ten rounds with Ali. He's mean, too."

"When he's washed up, with his hair combed, he looks like a choirboy."

"No fooling?" Disbelievingly, Canelli blinked. Then, thinking about it, he said, "Sometimes those choirboys can fool you, though. Right?"

"Right. What's been happening, down here? Any developments?"

"Aw—*Jeeze.*" Ruefully, he snapped his fingers, annoyed with himself. "Jeeze, I forgot to tell you. Lieutenant Friedman wants to see you, right away. He's got someone with him."

"Thanks."

Gesturing me to a chair, Friedman said, "Do you know Ed Lewis, Frank? Napa County sheriff's office."

"No, I don't think so." I put out my hand. "I'm Frank Hastings."

"It's a pleasure," he said. "I've been hearing good things about you, lately." His voice was low-pitched and pleasant, softened by a slow, easy drawl. He was a big, muscular man, and his hand felt as if it had been carved from an oak slab. His grip was firm but gentle—noncompetitive. His grin was wide and cheerful—also noncompetitive.

"Thanks," I answered, returning his smile.

As the three of us sat down, Friedman said, "Actually, it's *Captain* Lewis." Friedman smiled owlishly at me. "We're outranked, Frank."

Lewis studied Friedman for a moment before he said, "You know, Pete, I've wondered about that." As he spoke, he turned to me, saying, "I've known Pete for years. I knew him when he first made lieutenant. I don't even think you were in Homicide then, Frank."

In reply, I nodded silent confirmation. Friedman had been a homicide lieutenant while I was still in uniform, on patrol.

"I knew Captain Kreiger, too," Lewis continued, turning back to Friedman. "And I've got to say, I've wondered what the score is here. I don't mean to pry, but—" He paused for an apologetic moment, then decided to say simply, "But I've wondered why they didn't make you captain, Pete. Everyone knows you're one of the brainiest homicide men in the country."

At the compliment, Friedman gravely inclined his head. Then, airily waving a pudgy hand, he said, "You've already put your finger on it, Ed. I'm brainy—too brainy for my own good. Which is to say that I don't bother to deny that I'm brainy. I don't know how matters are arranged in Napa County, but in San Francisco, if you're going to make captain, you've got to be liked by your superior officers. And no one likes a smart-ass, which is the way I'm viewed." He paused, ironically watching Lewis's obvious discomfort.

"Another problem," Friedman said, "is that I don't play the game."

"The game?"

"Yeah. The scratch-my-back game. See, my back never seems to itch."

Amused now, Lewis smiled broadly. "You've still got your private little war going with the brass, then. Is that what I hear you saying?"

"I guess that's what I'm saying, Ed. And I'm also saying that I don't give a damn whether I ever make captain. Frank and I have been comanaging Homicide for more than a year, now. It's a good arrangement, too. It works. Frank handles the hot pursuits and the shootouts, which means that I don't have to stay in shape. He also handles the subsequent TV appearances, which means that I don't have to worry whether my shirt's clean." Friedman spread his hands wide over his cluttered desk. "It's perfect. It suits me. As for Frank, to the untrained eye he looks like a captain should look. Sometimes he even acts like a captain, under duress. But when you know him better, you'll realize that he's too stubborn and too short-tempered to cut it for very long with the brass. Which is to say that, really, he's too virtuous."

"Listen—" I leaned forward in my chair. "I appreciate the analysis, but I thought you wanted to see me. It was something important, I thought."

"You were right." Friedman waved genially to Lewis. "Give him the run-down, Ed. From the top."

Lewis turned to face me, saying, "It's about Bernard Carlton's death. Do you know about it?"

"He died in a plane crash," I said.

Lewis nodded. "Right. Just a little more than three weeks ago. He kept his airplane at Ralston Field. Do you know where it is?"

"No."

"It's between Vallejo and Sonoma, on Route 121, in Napa County. It's not much of an airport—just one macadam runway, about twenty-five hundred feet long. But, for some reason, a lot of very affluent people keep their airplanes at Ralston. Like Bernard Carlton."

I looked at Friedman, then looked at Lewis, hard. "Was there something irregular about the accident?" I asked. "Is that it?"

"That's it exactly," he answered. "Until day before yesterday—Friday—everyone, including me, assumed that it was just another light plane accident. But then the FAA called —the Federal Aviation Administration. They investigate every crash, to try and determine cause. And it turns out that Carlton's airplane was deliberately sabotaged."

"How?"

Instead of answering, Ralston gestured to Friedman, who spoke briefly to the receptionist. A moment later, a tall, thin man entered the office. He was dressed in Western-style clothing, including high-heeled boots.

156

"This is Bill Anthony," Lewis said, waving the tall man to a chair. "He's the owner and operator of Ralston Field. The reason he's dressed like a cowboy, he owns a couple of the best cutting horses in Northern California, and he's on his way to a gymkhana, over in Concord. So he doesn't have much time." Once more, Lewis gestured to the newcomer. "Give them the run-down, Bill. Just like you told it to me. Including the background. Everything."

"Okay—" Anthony glanced at his watch. "But I'll have to make it quick. I'm due in Concord in an hour."

"The quicker the better," Friedman said, gesturing for him to begin.

"Well," Anthony said, settling himself in his chair and crossing his long legs, "Carlton didn't start taking flying lessons until two years ago—when he was fifty-seven years old. But he turned out to have natural ability, and inside six months he had his license. Of course"—Anthony smiled—"of course, he had lots of money, which doesn't hurt. And lots of time, too.

"So, anyhow, he bought himself an airplane—even before he soloed, as a matter of fact. He bought a Piper 140, which is a basic four-place airplane. And, as he got more proficient, he started to just plain fly the wings off that airplane. Every other day, it seemed, he was taking it up. And the better he got at handling the airplane, the more reckless he got. He used to take that 140 off the ground like it was a fighter plane —and he'd land it the same way.

"Then, about a year ago, he got a Piper Arrow, which has a lot more power than the 140. And then, Christ, he *really* started hot-dogging it, with that Arrow. He was warned three times, at least, by the FAA. And then, about six months ago, he had his license lifted for thirty days. That was for being drunk and disorderly around an airplane, up in Oregon."

"It sounds like it was only a matter of time before he killed himself," I said.

"True. And, after he got his license back, he got worse, not better. Plus, about that time, he got rated for night flying, which he really loved. But, naturally, there's more of a tendency for people to drink after dark. So, as you say—" He turned to me, agreeing with my point. "It was just a matter of time. And, sure enough, it happened just about like I expected it would. He got out to the field about ten that night, the way we pieced the story together. He had a woman with him. They got into the Arrow, and they took off. Even before they did the mechanical inspection, the FAA figured that he'd had a partial power failure when he was about a hundred feet from the ground—which is the worst place to have any power failure, partial or not. Assuming that he was taking off into the wind—which, with Carlton, you couldn't assume, especially when he was drinking—then it looked like he tried to turn back to the field, which is the worst thing you can do, if you don't have enough altitude. So, anyhow—" Anthony spread his hands. "He crashed. And burned."

"Was anyone at the field when it happened?" Friedman asked.

Anthony shook his head. "No. It's a very small field, as Ed probably told you. It's checked once every hour by a security patrol, but that's all."

"How about runway lights?"

"Carlton probably turned them on," Anthony said. "We have a PCL lighting system. Which means that the runway lights can be turned on by a radio signal from a plane. They go off automatically after five minutes."

"So what did the FAA find when they examined the wreckage?" Friedman asked.

"They found sugar in Carlton's gas," Anthony answered.

"And that caused the crash?" I asked.

Anthony nodded. "Definitely. No question about it."

"Didn't Carlton do a preflight?" Friedman asked.

"It's doubtful," Anthony answered. "About half the time, day or night, he never bothered about preflighting." Then, looking more closely at Friedman, he said, "Are you a flyer, by any chance?"

"I used to be. During the war."

"Oh, yeah?" Interested now, Anthony turned to face Friedman fully. "What'd you fly, anyhow?"

"B-24s. But I haven't flown for years."

"Huh—" Anthony was plainly impressed. Then, regretfully, he looked again at his watch. "Listen," he said, getting to his feet, "I've *got* to go."

"Just one more question," Friedman said, rising with Anthony and walking with the flyer to the door. "Was it generally known that Carlton didn't always preflight his airplane?"

"I suppose so," Anthony answered. "It certainly wasn't any secret. He'd do the obvious things—the run-ups, and the mag checks, things like that. But it was very rare that he'd even bother to walk around the airplane to see if everything was attached, much less go to the bother of draining off some gas from the tanks to check for water or contaminates. And, of course, he was even less likely to do a walkaround at night, since he'd have to bother with a flashlight."

"It sounds to me," I said, "like Carlton had a death wish."

Anthony nodded. "I'd say so, too, Lieutenant. Well—goodbye. Good luck." He waved, smiled amiably, and left the office.

Friedman turned to Lewis. "Is there anything more, Ed? Have you got any leads—any opinions, about who might've sabotaged the airplane?"

"I don't know whether you'd call them leads, exactly," Lewis answered. "But there's a couple of things that might add up to something. Which is why I'm here, really. Because it gets into your jurisdiction."

"What kinds of things?"

"Well, first, there was Mrs. Carlton's reaction, when I told her about the crash. I decided to tell her myself, rather than call your department. So, about midnight, I rang her doorbell. At first she didn't answer the door. I figured she was a heavy sleeper, so I kept ringing—kept my thumb on the buzzer. And finally she came to the door. She was dressed in a terrycloth robe, and it was pretty plain she didn't have anything underneath."

Obviously, Lewis didn't approve of a lady answering the door wearing only a bathrobe. So, poking perverse fun, Friedman leered broadly. Ignoring him, Lewis plodded stolidly ahead: "I started with the usual routine—said that there'd been an accident, and asked if I could come inside—mostly as an excuse to get her sitting down. We went into the living room, and I started the story. But I didn't get very far before a man wandered into the living room—also in a bathrobe."

Still leering playfully, Friedman chuckled. "Carlton was flying with a woman while his wife was shacked up with a guy. Everything comes out even."

Pointedly, Lewis didn't respond. To Lewis, extramarital sex was plainly no laughing matter.

"The guy came in and sat down," Lewis went on, "as calm as he could be. So I figured, what the hell, I'd just come out with it—which I did."

"How'd she react?" I asked.

"Very calmly," Lewis answered. "Very goddamn calmly indeed. She said that it was obvious Carlton would kill himself. The only question was when. Then the guy, if you can believe it, chimed in with some mumbo-jumbo about how he had a self-destructive karma, or some such crap."

"Who's the guy?" Friedman asked, reaching for a note pad.

"His name is Donald Fay. He said he was a sculptor." Obviously, Lewis was dubious. "He looked like he was in his early thirties, if that. And she's forty, at least."

I couldn't resist saying: "A very sexy forty, though."

Lewis shrugged his broad, muscular shoulders. "If you like the neurotic type, I guess you'd call her sexy. I wouldn't, though."

"Was that all?" Friedman asked.

"For then, that was all. Obviously, Mrs. Carlton didn't

need me—not with Donald Fay there. So I went back home, and didn't think anymore about it—not until day before yesterday, like I said, when I heard about the sugar in the gas. When I heard that, I naturally started checking around. I started at the airfield. I've known Bill Anthony for years. In fact, he used to fly for the sheriff's department, years ago. So he was very helpful. Between the two of us, we spent the last two days contacting people who might've seen someone fooling around with Carlton's airplane. Luckily, we could pinpoint the time frame, since he'd been flying the day before he was killed."

"Was the airplane hangered?" Friedman asked. "Or was it tied down?"

"It was tied down. There's only one hanger at Ralston Field. That's mostly for repairs and, especially, painting."

"Did you have any luck?" I asked.

"Nobody at the field remembered anything, and neither did the security patrol. But then, last night, we got lucky. It turned out that the night before Carlton was killed, a couple of teen-agers—friends of Bill's son—were out by the airport, parked. Necking. That's one of the favorite spots in the county, for kids. And they said that just before midnight they saw a car drive up to the gate."

"How's the field secured?" I asked.

"It's not really secured," Lewis answered. "But there's a parking lot that's separated from the airfield itself by a single section of cyclone fence. There's a pedestrian gate at the center of the fence, but there's no lock on the gate. That's because someone could simply walk around the end of the fence, to get to the field."

"So the fence is basically to keep cars from driving out onto the field?" Friedman asked. "Right?"

Lewis nodded. "Right."

"Okay," Friedman said, "we can visualize it."

"Well," Lewis said, "you've got to understand that the kids were parked beside the road that leads to the parking lot, not in the parking lot itself. So they couldn't identify the driver of the car, for instance. However, the boy—his name is Charlie Esterbrook—is a car freak, like so many kids. And he identified the car, which was a Mercedes 450SL convertible."

"It's too much to hope that he took the license number," Friedman said drily.

"It's not like the kids suspected the driver was doing anything wrong," replied Lewis. "Charlie's just interested in cars, like I said. Especially cars like the 450SL, which is pretty exotic. I checked with the computer in Sacramento, incidentally. There's only twenty-seven 450SLs registered in the whole Bay Area."

"Could the driver see the kids?" I asked.

Lewis shrugged. "If they could see the driver, then the driver could see them. Or, at least, he could see their car. They were right out in the open."

"What'd the driver do after he drove up to the gate?"

"He—or she—got out of the car, and walked through the gate," Lewis said. "He—or she—went out onto the field, to where the airplanes are tied down. Charlie saw the driver stop at one of the airplanes for a couple of minutes, and then go back to the Mercedes, and drive away."

"You say 'he or she,' " Friedman said. "Meaning that the kid wasn't sure, I gather."

Lewis agreed. "Right. The driver had sort of long hair, Charlie said, and was wearing pants and some kind of a jacket. That's all he could see. He showed me where they were parked. The distance from his car to the gate would've been about two hundred feet. And the parking lot isn't illuminated. So it's not surprising that he couldn't see much."

"Women walk differently from men," I said. "That should've given him some basis for at least guessing."

Lewis shook his head. "Not Charlie. He's one of these real serious, studious kids. If he doesn't know something, he doesn't guess."

"Did Charlie see what the driver did when he—or she—got to the airplane?" Friedman asked.

"He sort of stopped, like I said. Like he was just looking at an airplane, or maybe checking something."

"Did Charlie see which airplane he stopped beside?"

"No. Apparently there were other planes in the way. But it could've been Carlton's airplane, no question."

"The Piper is a low-winged airplane," Friedman said, thinking aloud as he doodled on a note pad with a stub of yellow pencil. "The gas tanks are in the wings. It wouldn't've taken any time at all for someone to do the job. Less than a minute, if he knew what he was doing."

"That's what Bill said."

Gazing down at his doodling, Friedman said to me, "I suppose it would be too much to hope that one of our suspects drives a convertible Mercedes 450 SL."

"Sam Wright drives a convertible Mercedes," I said. "But it's not a 450 SL. It's more like a 220."

"Hmmm." Friedman studied the doodle, then thoughtfully penciled in a small flourish. "Hmmm."

"Is Mrs. Carlton one of your suspects?" Lewis asked.

Friedman looked up. "She could be," he answered. "She's not exactly a front runner, but she's definitely a contender. Why?"

"Because, according to Bill Anthony, she drives a Mercedes like the one Charlie described."

Eighteen

As I pulled up in front of the elegant three-story Georgian town house, Friedman said, "The starving writer stereotype obviously doesn't apply to Bernard Carlton."

"Obviously." I set the parking brake, switched off the engine, leaned back in the seat and yawned. For the past two nights, totaled, I'd barely gotten eight hours sleep.

"I guess that writing is like acting," Friedman said. "For every actor who gets a million dollars a picture, there're hundreds who make zilch. And it's got nothing to do with talent, either. It's what the public pays to see—or read."

After he'd been discharged from the Air Corps following the second world war, Friedman had tried acting—briefly. I'd known him for years before I discovered, by accident, that he'd spent a year in Hollywood, making the rounds of the agents and the casting offices with a sheaf of 8 × 10 glossies under his arm. Questioned about that period of his life, he dismissed it as his "slim, darkly handsome phase."

"Have you ever read anything by Carlton?" I asked.

"No," Friedman admitted. "Have you?"

"No. But I understand that he was a kind of cross between

Thomas Wolfe and Harold Robbins—with a little Eugene O'Neill thrown in."

"That's a pretty salable-sounding combination," Friedman observed. "Did you see the movie *Enemies,* with Paul Newman and Jane Fonda?"

"Yes. Was that made from one of his books?"

"That's right," he answered. "According to my research, he'd had a total of five books made into movies."

"Jesus. No wonder he was rich. How'd you do your research, by the way?"

"Clara did it for me. She's read a couple of his books, it turns out. And, what's more, she's got a friend who's a librarian. And the librarian says that, in addition to making a lot of money writing, Carlton also inherited a bundle from his family, who had so-called 'old' San Francisco money. Incidentally, whenever we catch up on our sleep, Clara wants you and Ann to come over for dinner."

"Fine. Thanks."

Staring speculatively at the town house, Friedman said, "I wonder whether she'll answer the door in her bathrobe—without anything on underneath?"

"We could always ring the bell, and find out."

But Friedman was in a theorizing mood.

"Her husband and her stepdaughter were both killed, as it turns out," he said reflectively. "Which means that she and Justin, her idiot son, are going to split a fortune."

"According to her, Justin's not such an idiot. She seems to think he's got talent as a cult leader."

"Some talent," Friedman grunted. "How much talent does it take to collect a bunch of confused kids, and start pushing their buttons?"

"You probably didn't think Hitler had talent, either."

He raised his eyebrows, pursed his lips and finally nodded. "What do I say? Touché?"

Yawning again and massaging my closed eyes with thumb and forefinger, I didn't reply. Tonight, Ann was expecting

165

me to phone—but not before nine-thirty. After I phoned, I would probably go to her house, where we would talk.

Instead of sleeping, after two sleepless nights, I'd be talking—trying to discover what had gone wrong between us. Suddenly the prospect seemed a bleak one. Bleak, and exhausting—and wrong.

Last night, while I'd faced a gun, terrified, Ann had been at home, tucked in, sleeping.

Tonight, if I had the chance, I should be sleeping.

Not talking. Not defending myself against some unspecified, unfair charge.

". . . see the will?" Friedman was asking.

Wearily, I opened my eyes. "What?"

"I said, can we see the will?"

"No. Not until tomorrow. I couldn't get a court order yesterday."

Still staring at the Carlton town house, Friedman fell silent. His broad, swarthy moon face was expressionless; his dark, almond-shaped eyes were inscrutable. Since it was Sunday, he was wearing loafers, corduroy trousers, a sport shirt open at the neck and a green nylon windbreaker. The effect could have been casual, even sporty. But, on Friedman, sports clothes always looked at least one size too small.

Finally, speaking in a soft, speculative voice, he said, "God, can you imagine the headlines if it turns out that she offed her famous husband and also her equally famous stepdaughter? Can you imagine what Walter Cronkite would say? I can just see his eyebrows, twitching on the seven o'clock news."

"If we can tie her to Sally Grant," I answered, "it could happen." I realized that I, too, was speaking softly. The thought of arresting Cass Dangerfield for murder was awesome.

Could it happen today—in another hour? At the thought, I realized that I felt uncomfortable. For a moment I couldn't define the cause of my unpredictable discomfort. And then it came to me: Neither Friedman nor I were properly dressed for the job of taking someone like Cass Dangerfield into custody.

At the thought, I smiled—to myself—at the same time saying, "Did you have the lab crews go over Sally Grant's house, as well as her car? All it would take is Cass Dangerfield's fingerprints on Sally's coffee table, you know, to connect them."

"That's assuming that Cass doesn't preempt us by admitting that, yes, she knows Sally. For all we know, they could've been sorority sisters. But the answer to the question is that I've got a crew in her house. Since we don't have a warrant, though, it's a small crew. A *quiet* small crew."

"How'd they get in?"

"I stole Sally's key from her purse."

"How about fingerprints on the rest of them—the other suspects? Did the lab crews have any trouble getting them?"

Friedman shook his head. "No sweat. Everyone cooperated, to a man. And, in fact, to a woman. I decided, what the hell, I'd get Pam Cornelison's prints, too."

"What about David Behr? Did he object?"

"Apparently not. Or, if he did, I didn't hear about it. The only one that was a little pushed out of shape, I understand, was Justin. He seems to think he's one of us—not them."

Remembering my freewheeling conversations with Justin, I nodded ruefully. "I know what you mean."

"Come on." Friedman opened his door. "Let's see what she says."

Cass Dangerfield had shown us into a spacious living room, elegantly furnished with an eclectic collection of antiques, modern paintings, Oriental rugs and a museum-size floor-to-ceiling glass case displaying primitive Mayan sculpture and artifacts.

Wearing blue jeans and a white silk blouse, she sat in the center of a long tufted velvet sofa. Her arms were folded across her torso, accenting excitingly shaped breasts beneath the blouse. Her dark eyes were inscrutable as she stared at Friedman. Her low-pitched voice was tightly controlled as she said, "Do I understand that someone deliberately tampered with my husband's airplane?"

Friedman nodded. "That's right, Ms. Dangerfield." He spoke easily; his manner was almost casual. But I knew that, covertly, his poker-player eyes were assessing everything she said, every movement she made.

"But why? Why would they do it?"

"So he'd crash, probably," Friedman answered quietly. "So he'd die."

For a long, impassive moment she stared at him. Then, in the same low, tight voice, she said, "Do you know who did it?"

As I looked at Friedman I realized that I was holding my breath. Would he come at her head on? Or would he try to circle around behind her?

After a carefully calculated beat had passed, he said, "We have some leads. But, so far, there's nothing conclusive. We're still trying to piece it all together. When we know why the airplane was sabotaged, though, we'll probably have a pretty good idea who did it. Which is why we're here. We're—"

"Wait," she said, raising a peremptory hand. "I want to get this straight." As if she were interrogating Friedman, she looked at him narrowly for a moment before she said, "Are you saying that my husband was murdered? Deliberately murdered?"

"I'm saying that the accident that killed him was the result of deliberate sabotage," Friedman answered, still speaking in a slow, measured voice. "There's no question about that. Absolutely none. The only question is, what was the saboteur's intent?"

"But the accident was investigated by the FAA. They said the cause was probably engine failure."

"That's right. It was. But what they didn't know at the time—what they couldn't possibly have known until they examined the wreckage part by part—was that the engine failed because someone put sugar in the gas."

"But was it deliberate murder? Or was it vandalism?" This time, her question wasn't asked forcefully, demanding an answer. Instead, she spoke reflectively, musingly. Her eyes had strayed to the huge glass case, and the Mayan artifacts inside it.

"That," I said, "is the question. It could be either one—either murder, or a malicious prank. As Lieutenant Friedman said, it depends on the intent—on the perpetrator's motive for doing what he did."

She nodded slowly. She was obviously making an effort at self-control—and succeeding. But she couldn't conceal the effects of the effort. The muscles of her neck and jaw were drawn painfully taut. Her hands were knuckle-white as she clasped her folded arms at the elbows. Her dark eyes, still fixed on the glass display case, smoldered with suppressed emotion.

What was the emotion? Anger? Fear? Something else?

"The answer to the question," Friedman said, "probably depends on how much the perpetrator knows about the procedures pilots go through before they take an airplane up. And secondly, it also depends on how much the suspect knows about your husband's flying habits."

While he'd been speaking, her eyes had returned from the glass case and were now fixed fiercely on Friedman. Her moments of reflection had passed. Typically, she returned to the attack. Gesturing impatiently, she said sharply, "Never mind the preliminaries, Lieutenant. Get to the point, please."

The response amused Friedman—and obviously pleased him. Friedman liked nothing better than a battle of wits.

Mockingly deferential, Friedman inclined his head to her. Then, speaking in a flat, businesslike voice, he said, "How much do you know about flying, Ms. Dangerfield?"

"Next to nothing," she answered brusquely. "I dislike flying in small planes. And, especially, I disliked flying with Bernard."

Friedman smiled ruefully. "That I can understand." Then, in the same flat, impersonal voice, he said, "Before a pilot takes off, he preflights his airplane. The purpose of the preflight inspection is to guard against exactly the kind of accident that killed your husband. Because, in addition to making sure everything is attached, and checking the oil, and the antennas, et cetera, the pilot also uses a small plastic cylinder to drain a little gas from the airplane's tanks. Primarily, he's checking for water that could've leaked into the tanks past the filler cap, or else formed by condensation. But, also, he's checking for contaminants—sugar, for instance." He paused while he watched her. Then: "To be honest, I don't know whether sugar could actually be detected in the gas. Maybe it couldn't, especially at night. The point is, though, that perhaps the murderer didn't know either. But if he—or she—knew that your husband's preflight inspections were pretty sketchy, then he—or she—probably figured the odds were all the better that the sugar wouldn't be spotted."

For a moment Friedman and I sat in silence, watching Cass Dangerfield's eyes narrow, and her mouth tighten as she considered the possibilities. Then, speaking quietly, I said, "If the suspect knew of your husband's habits, and if he knew that, specifically, he was tampering with Mr. Carlton's plane, then he probably had murder in mind. Not vandalism."

"Murder." She said it softly, almost pensively. Was she shocked at the thought? Or was she intrigued? I watched her abstracted gaze wander again toward the Mayan statuary. Now the tip of her tongue touched her upper lip. It was a curiously sensual reaction, subtly suggesting that she found the thought of murder titillating. As I watched her, I remembered how she'd fingered the jeweled dagger yesterday, talking to me. Somehow that mannerism, too, had seemed subtly sensual.

170

Finally she blinked, collecting herself as she sat up straighter. In a crisp voice that matched Friedman's, she said, "Whoever did it must've known something about aviation."

Friedman shook his head. "Not really. Every high-school kid knows that sugar ruins an engine—in minutes, sometimes. Of course, the murderer couldn't've known that the engine failure would happen on takeoff, which is the worst time for it to happen. But he *could* be sure that the engine would fail, probably in flight."

"First Bernard," she said. "Then Rebecca."

"Exactly." Friedman let the single word settle silently for a moment before he said, "Lieutenant Hastings and I were saying the same thing, as a matter of fact."

I let the silence lengthen before I said, "Does the name Sally Grant mean anything to you, Ms. Dangerfield?"

She'd been staring hard at Friedman, as if she were trying to divine what he was thinking. But, when she heard my question, I saw her wince. During the entire interrogation, it was the first flash of spontaneous emotion she'd revealed.

"What's Sally Grant got to do with it?"

Friedman and I exchanged a quick, meaningful look. Murder investigations are mostly a matter of establishing connections between the victim and those he left behind—the guilty and the innocent.

And Cass Dangerfield's reaction clearly revealed that, yes, she knew the woman who had probably planned Rebecca Carlton's murder.

"You know Sally Grant," I said. It was a statement, not a question.

"Yes," she answered grimly. "Yes, I know Sally Grant— by reputation, anyhow." Her mouth was fixed in a harsh, uncompromising line. Her eyes were hard and bright, shining venomously.

I tried not to let her see my disappointment. Did she mean that all she knew about Sally Grant was what she read in the newspapers?

Taking a gambler's risk, Friedman said, "Your husband knew her." The statement was perfectly pitched, deftly understated—implying that, yes, we knew all about Bernard Carlton's connection with Sally Grant.

She waited until she was sure her emotions were under control, and then, speaking with malicious precision, said, "Sally Grant and Bernard went way back. They even predated Bernard's first marriage."

"They were lovers," I said.

Silently, she nodded.

"And he kept up their relationship, even while he was married. Is that it?" As I asked the question, my mind was leaping ahead, constructing a plausible scenario: For years, during both his marriages, Bernard Carlton and Sally Grant had continued their love affair—accounting for the anger that I saw burning so fiercely in Cass Dangerfield's eyes.

But she was shaking her head, denying it.

"No," she answered. "Or, rather, yes and no. He and Sally continued to see each other during most of Bernard's first marriage. He had—" She hesitated, searching for the right word. "He had a gargantuan sexual appetite. One woman was never enough for Bernard. Never. And his first wife understood that, just as I did. I gather that they had the usual quid pro quo. He could do anything he wanted on the side, just as long as he didn't talk about it. But then, later in his first marriage, I gather that Bernard developed—" She hesitated, searching for the word. "He developed bizarre tastes."

"Involving Sally Grant, you mean?"

"Involving Sally Grant and her girls," she answered.

"Do you mean he had a customer-proprietor relationship with her?" Friedman asked.

"No," she answered calmly, "it wasn't quite that simple, Lieutenant. At first—when they first knew each other—that might have been it. But Sally was always more than a prostitute to Bernard—and he was always more than a customer to her. So, when he had his first best seller—which, as it happens, coincided with a two-million-dollar inheritance—he set Sally up on a grand scale. It was one of his numerous indulgences—all of which he enjoyed in larger-than-life fashion." As she said it, she allowed contempt to register in her face and her voice. But, quickly, she made her face a mask again as she went on:

"Bernard saw himself as an epicurean of sex. He never admitted it, but I'm positive that he got some kind of very kinky satisfaction from setting up his own private whorehouse. I suppose, really, it's every man's fantasy. Most men, of course, would never gratify it—even if they could afford to. But Bernard was different. He had his art as an excuse, you see. He felt that he had to experience everything—and anything."

"Were Bernard and Sally partners when he died?" I asked.

She smiled: a cruel, mirthless twisting of her lips. "Hardly. Just about the time his first marriage was ending, he and Sally quarreled. I never knew why—and I never asked. But it probably involved another man—another business partner, so-called. About that time, you see, Bernard was becoming famous. Very rich, and very famous. And the more famous he became, the more demands he made, on everyone. Including Sally, I'm sure. So if he discovered that she had anyone else beside himself, he'd've been furious."

Friedman smiled. "Your husband wasn't kinky, Ms. Dangerfield. He was just spoiled—a middle-aged spoiled child."

Cass Dangerfield didn't return the smile. Plainly, she wasn't amused.

"What happened between Sally and Bernard?" I asked.

"I gather that Sally's business partner took her for everything she had—and then some," she answered, plainly pleased at the thought. By some accounts, the man disappeared with a half million dollars—cash."

"So what did Sally do?" Friedman asked. "Try to patch things up with Bernard?"

"No. She tried to blackmail him."

173

"How could she blackmail him?" Friedman asked. "I mean, it doesn't sound like your husband was very meticulous about his image."

Now her smile was grim. "You're right, Lieutenant. He liked the role he'd created for himself. The more excesses the public thought he indulged, the better he liked it. However, Sally was always farsighted, apparently. And she was prudent enough to take some signed checks from Bernard and endorse them over to some of the city fathers, for bribe money. She was also smart enough to photostat the checks —both sides, including the endorsement, and the official's signature. So, in the venacular, she had Bernard by the balls. She could probably have sent him to jail. She would've been jailed herself, of course, but she didn't care—or, at least, so she said."

"Did he actually pay her blackmail?" I asked.

"I don't know," she answered. "He never told me. And I never asked."

As she'd been speaking, calmly chronicling her husband's depravity, I'd mentally constructed another scenario. Sally had so hated Bernard that she'd killed him—and then had his daughter killed.

But who had killed Sally? And why?

"I take it," Friedman was saying, "that you never actually met Sally Grant face to face. Is that right?"

The question amused her. "That's right, Lieutenant. "That's absolutely right."

"Do you think it's possible that Sally Grant could have killed Bernard and Rebecca?" I asked.

She shrugged. Her gaze was cool and remote as she looked at me. Whatever had fired the secret fury that leaped in her eyes a few minutes before, it was apparently now forgotten —or else suppressed.

"That's your department, Lieutenant," she answered. "I wouldn't have the faintest idea what she'd do." As she spoke, she looked pointedly at her watch. Her desire to end the interview coincided with ours, and the three of us began the ritual shifting in our seats, preparing to rise.

But one question remained—and Friedman asked it: "You don't have any idea who could have killed your husband, then."

She shook her head. "Sorry."

"Who would have profited by his death?" I asked quietly. "Besides you and your son, that is."

Instead of flaring up, as I'd expected, she looked at me with a superciliously amused smile. "Is that why you're here, Lieutenant?" she asked. "Did you come to arrest me for Bernard's murder? Is that it?" Plainly, the idea amused her —even titillated her, perhaps.

Friedman answered for me. "We have to cover all the bases, Ms. Dangerfield," he said. "Which reminds me—" He waited until he had her attention before he said, "Would you mind telling us where you were on the night before your husband died? That would be a Tuesday. Between ten o'-clock, say, and midnight."

The supercilious smile widened playfully as she studied him. "You're serious, aren't you?" she said finally. "You're actually serious."

"I'm serious about asking the question," Friedman answered steadily. "But that's not to say that I'm serious about accusing you of your husband's murder."

Rising to her feet, she stood silently for a moment, looking down at Friedman with all the poise of an accomplished actress gathering herself before delivering her curtain line.

"I was with my lover, Lieutenant. We were in his apartment, on Telegraph Hill. His name is Donald Fay, and he's in the book. I'm sure he'll be happy to vouch for me."

Typically, Friedman's aplomb was equal to the challenge. Hoisting his two hundred forty pounds to his feet, he smiled at her, thanked her, and moved toward the door. It wasn't until he had his hand on the knob that he turned again to face her, casually asking, "Were you driving your car that night? Or Mr. Fay's car?"

"Neither," she answered. "Parking is terrible on Telegraph Hill. I took a cab." Her smile widened. "It was a Yellow cab, Lieutenant," she said silkily. "And, yes, I phoned for it—probably about five o'clock, I'd think."

Always able to appreciate a good performance, even if he was its victim, Friedman inclined his head politely, and opened the door.

Nineteen

"Why'd we come here?" I complained, pointing to the menu. "There isn't even a sandwich for less than four dollars."

Airily, Friedman waved away my objections. "The owner's a friend of mine. I sign the checks like a big shot. And, about half the time, I never get a bill. So figure two bucks, not four."

"Wait a minute. Are you going to charge me, whether or not you get a bill?"

"Don't worry about it. Trust me." He swept the table with a broad, mock-Jewish gesture. "Eat. Enjoy. Don't forget, it's Sunday, and we're working. We owe ourselves a treat. Even if he mails the bill."

Playing the percentages, I decided to order a six-dollar lunch, and hope for the best. After the smiling waitress had gone, I said, "One of us should phone in. It's been two hours, at least."

"Don't worry." He patted his bulging waistline. "I brought my pager. Even if you didn't."

"Mine's being repaired. I told you."

He shrugged. "I forgot."

"What now?" I asked.

He raised his thick eyebrows in an expression of pensive reflection, at the same time chewing thoughtfully at his lower lip. Finally he said, "Do you remember, years ago, when some senator suggested that the solution to the Vietnam war was to simply declare the war won, and then get the hell out?"

"How do you propose to do that?"

"Easy. We announce that Sally Grant murdered both of them, out of revenge. Presto, we're heroes. Walter Cronkite, here we come."

"How do we explain away Sally's death?"

Now the eyebrows bounced puckishly. "There's lots of murderers on the loose, murdering people for no good reason. Sally's luck might've just run out."

"With that theory, you go on Cronkite. I pass."

"You've got a better theory?"

"For one thing," I answered, "I think we should get Cass Dangerfield fingerprinted. Also, I think we should have a lab team go over her car."

"You're implying," Friedman said, "that I should've come down on her harder, there at the last."

I let my silence speak for itself.

"I suppose you're right," he answered amiably. "But I figured that if we put any more pressure on her, she'd either quit talking, or call her lawyer, or else throw us out. Or, more like it, all three. To me, she looks like one very tough lady. Besides which, she's got a pretty solid-sounding alibi for Tuesday night. Incidentally, someone should check on Sam Wright's alibi. In the dark, a Mercedes 220 might look like a 450SL."

"What motive would Sam Wright have for murdering Bernard Carlton, though?"

Friedman shrugged. "You never know. Maybe Carlton was sore at him for marrying his daughter."

"That sounds like a pretty thin motive for murder."

"Granted." He toyed thoughtfully with his fork for a moment, then said, "Maybe we're making a mistake, assuming that the two murders are connected. Also, we might be making a mistake if we assume, hands down, that Carlton's death was murder. Who knows, maybe some prankster put sugar in several airplanes, and Carlton was the only one who didn't check his gasoline."

"If that happened, Bill Anthony would've told us."

Friedman nodded glum agreement, and we sat silently, each of us mentally trying different combinations. Finally Friedman said, "If Carlton's death was murder, and if the two murders were connected, either Cass or her idiot son would be our most logical suspects. Theoretically, both of them have motives. Conceivably, Sally Grant had a motive, although it seems unlikely. Beyond those three, though, we really don't have a viable suspect for the double murders. But, on the other hand, we've got lots of people who could've wanted to kill Rebecca."

"I don't see what you're getting at."

"What I'm getting at," Friedman said, "is that we could be making a mistake, assuming that the two deaths are connected."

"Still, we—"

At Friedman's belt, his pager buzzed. Muttering a mild obscenity, he grimaced, and headed for a guest phone. In less than a minute, he returned to the table.

"That was Canelli in Communications," he said. "We're supposed to contact Justin Wade. I gather that he's got another vision for us. Something real hot, according to Canelli."

"Oh, Jesus, it's a waste of time, Pete. He's bonkers."

"You said that his mother doesn't agree. Besides, I'd like to see his set-up. Cults fascinate me."

"But we've got a lot more important things to do, it seems to me."

"What's the harm? Besides, there've been a lot of psychics

who've been scoring pretty high lately. Maybe we'll get lucky, if we keep an open mind." As he said it, the waitress arrived, and began serving our lunch. Friedman looked casually down the front of her dress. "Besides," he said, "Justin might be able to tell us about Bernard and Sally. Ever think of that?"

Also enjoying the view down the front of the waitress's dress, I shook my head absently.

"That must be it," Friedman said, pointing to a narrow driveway that curved through a thick-growing grove of eucalyptus trees. The concrete of the driveway was chipped and uneven, crisscrossed by an ancient network of lines and cracks. Tufts of grass sprouted from the cracks, and a brick curbing was overgrown with tangled vines and weeds. Two massive brick pillars flanked the driveway. Ornamental wrought-iron lanterns topped each pillar. But the iron was rusted, and the lantern's glass sides had been broken long ago.

As I turned into the driveway, I saw a huge black cat moving stealthily through the thick undergrowth beside the driveway stalking some unseen prey.

"This must be one of those old mansions built before the turn of the century," Friedman said. "There used to be several of them in this part of the city. This was the only place in San Francisco where it was possible to buy an acre of land and be a country squire. But I thought they'd all been condemned and sold off to the developers." As he spoke, we emerged from the trees.

Canelli had described Aztecca as something out of a Charles Addams cartoon. He hadn't exaggerated. The building was a huge Victorian monolith, three stories high, built entirely of wood, probably with five rooms on each floor. Originally, it must have been magnificent. Pillars supported a formal portico in front. The tall, narrow windows were curved at the top, framed in intricate wooden scrollwork.

The huge front door was carved oak, inset with stained glass. A widow's walk circled the squared-off mansard roof. Lacy wrought-iron railings surrounded a small octagonal cupola.

But many of the tall windows were boarded up. Only a few fragments of stained glass remained in the door; the rest was plywood. Of the six pillars that must have originally supported the portico, only four were standing, two of them slanting precariously. Most of the carved cornices were missing; the rest were about to fall away. Inside the cupola, with its broken windows, pigeons were nesting. Whole sections of the widow's walk's iron railing were gone; what remained was entirely rusted. A half dozen decrepit cars and pickups were parked at odd angles on the circular driveway.

"What a place for a Halloween party," Friedman muttered.

I parked behind a dented, lopsided panel truck that must have been twenty years old. After clearing our car with Communications, we mounted the rotting steps to the front door. Above the door I saw a large redwood plaque with the single word *Aztecca* deeply carved across the top in baroque letters with a primitive sun symbol beneath the legend. *Peace* and *Power* were incised below it.

As I was looking for a bell-button, the huge oak door swung slowly open. A young black woman stood in the doorway. She was dressed in a long, togalike robe that fell to the floor and was secured at the waist with a belt woven of hemp. A sun symbol hung on a heavy golden chain fell between her full breasts. The heavy metal medallion was identical to the one Justin Wade wore—but smaller. Her features were classically Negroid, perfectly formed. Her hair was worn short, sculpting her head so that it resembled a piece of primitive statuary. Beneath the robe, the curve of her torso was proud, almost arrogant. With her dark head held aristocratically high, she could have been a Bantu princess.

She looked at me gravely, unsmiling. "You're Lieutenant Hastings." Her voice was low, musky and melodious.

"Yes. And this is Lieutenant Friedman."

"I'm Anya." She moved grudgingly back from the doorway, reluctantly gesturing for us to come inside. Even though we'd been invited, it was obvious that she considered our presence an intrusion. Entering a huge central hallway, we might have stepped back through time to the last century. Incredibly elaborate carvings and rococo woodwork seemed to glower down on us like overbearing gargoyles. The sidewalls were paneled to plate-rail height with dark, somber wood. The oak floors were parquet, intricately patterned. Above the paneled wainscoting, the walls and ceilings were painted the brownish-red color of dried blood. Centered on an ornamental Victorian lighting medallion, a huge Mayan sun symbol had been painted in gilt on the ceiling.

Two men wearing broad leather belts and heavy boots stood guard at either end of the hallway. Their robes had been cut off at the elbow and knee, revealing massively muscled arms and legs. Watching us, their eyes were expressionless. Each man held a spear with a thick wooden shaft and a broad, gleaming blade.

"Justin is waiting for you," the woman said.

"Did you talk to Inspector Canelli when he was here?" I asked.

She nodded: one measured inclination of her head. "Yes."

"You're the—" I hesitated, searching for the phrase. "You're Justin's assistant?"

Instead of answering, she turned and motioned for us to follow her down a central hallway that led to the rear of the mansion. As we followed her down the dark, gloomy passage, we came abreast of an archway that opened on what must have once been a formal ballroom. In the center of the room's polished wooden floor a low dais had been fashioned from branches and boughs arranged around a plywood platform. A robed figure, head shaved, was crouched on the dais both arms stretched overhead. A dozen other figures, identically robed, heads shaven, crouched in similar attitudes in a

182

circle around the dais. Each of them wore the sun symbol.

We passed three smaller rooms opening off the central hallway. Each of the rooms, I noticed, had its door removed. In each room silent, white-robed figures were watching us as we passed. I remembered the times I'd walked down the corridors of county jails, feeling prisoners' eyes on me.

Anya knocked at a carved walnut door at the end of the hallway. She waited a moment, listening, then opened the tall door and gestured us inside.

Originally the room must have been a large dining room. Tall leaded bay windows looked out on the overgrown remains of what was once a formal garden. The garden had been planned around a miniature marble water temple: delicately fluted columns circling a small pool. But now, like the temples of ancient Greece, some of the pillars and cornices had fallen to the ground. Tangled vines overgrew the ruins.

With the glare of the midday sun behind them, the curve of the bay windows was blindingly bright. The rest of the room was in shadow, with the side windows heavily curtained. Wearing a long white robe identical to that worn by his followers, Justin Wade sat in a huge claw-carved armchair that could have come from a medieval castle. With his back to the bright light from the bay windows, and shadowed by the chair that rose high above his head, Justin was an indistinct shape: a mystically disembodied figure, speaking in a voice without substance:

"Do you suspect me of my sister's murder, Lieutenant Hastings?"

I hesitated, trying to decide on an answer. Standing like some penitent before an enthroned monarch, I felt awkward and silly.

Friedman, though, was ready with an instant rebuttal: "Why do you ask that?"

It was a textbook gambit. If the subject tried to take the initiative by asking a question, the officer should counter with another question.

But Justin was ready with yet another question: "You asked for my fingerprints," he said solemnly. "Why?"

"Because," Friedman answered, "we're fingerprinting everyone who could possibly have gained from Rebecca's death."

"Gained? What could I have gained?"

Instead of answering, Friedman pointed to a nearby couch, actually a mattress placed on the floor and covered with a cheap chenille bedspread. "May we sit down?" He asked the question with subtly mocking deference, poking fun at the seated cult leader.

"Yes, sit down." Still holding his own, Justin gave his permission with a regal flair.

"Thank you," Friedman intoned. A playful "your highness" could have been the next phrase.

"What could I have gained?" Justin repeated. As he spoke, he fingered the outsize medallion that hung around his neck.

"You could have gained money," Friedman answered promptly. "As I understand your stepfather's will, Rebecca's third of the estate will be divided between you and your mother."

With my eyes accustomed to the glaring backlight, I could see Justin's expression. He was looking at Friedman with a kind of benign contempt. He lifted his right hand and swept the room. "Do you see anything here that looks like I would murder for money, Lieutenant?" He spoke softly, condescendingly.

"It must cost money to run a cult," Friedman answered blandly. "Or do your people sell flowers at airports?"

Immobile in his baronial chair, with his fingers curled loosely around the lion heads carved on each of the chair's arms, Justin stared contemptuously at Friedman. Finally he said: "What's your definition of a cult, Lieutenant?"

"A cult is a group of zealots who're under the control of a bigger zealot," Friedman answered promptly. "Or, if he isn't a bigger zealot, then he's a smarter zealot. And, in that case, he's probably also a rich zealot."

184

"And what's your definition of a zealot, Lieutenant?" He spoke calmly, almost benignly. But his fingers, I noticed, had tightened on the lion heads.

"Listen, Justin, I didn't come here to play Twenty Questions," Friedman said brusquely. "My opinion of you and your operation isn't important. We're investigating a murder. And we're here because you called to say you've got some information for us. So, if you don't mind, we'll take the information and run."

Still playing at his game of one-upmanship, Justin asked, "How many people do you suspect of killing Rebecca?"

Instead of replying directly, Friedman took a moment to consider. Then, modifying his previous impatient manner, he said, "We think we know who actually fired the shot that killed her. It was a man named Hoadley. And we think we know who hired him. It was probably a woman named Sally Grant. But, still, we don't think we've gotten to the bottom of it." He spoke directly; his manner was one-to-one. On appearance, Friedman had suddenly decided to take Justin into his confidence.

"Why haven't you gotten to the bottom of it?" Justin asked.

"Because Sally Grant was murdered last night."

For a long, inscrutable moment Justin studied Friedman. Then he turned to me, saying, "It was because of Sally Grant that I called you, Lieutenant."

"How do you mean?" Again, I felt awkward and silly, asking the question.

He allowed another long, solemn silence pass before he said, "Early this morning—sometime after midnight—I awakened suddenly. I'd had a dream, a terrible, blood-spattered dream. I saw a woman's head disappear. It was—" He broke off, shaking his head and momentarily closing his eyes. His face was pale; his voice trembled as he said: "It was worse—it hurt me more—than the vision I saw of Rebecca, dying. Rebecca, at least, wasn't disfigured. But Sally Grant—" He slowly, somberly shook his

185

head. Then: "Her death was terrible. It was a monstrosity." Now his voice was almost inaudible. His eyes had lost their focus. Watching him closely, I wondered whether he'd fallen into a light trance.

"Do I understand," Friedman said, "that you think you woke up at the moment Sally Grant died? You saw her die, and the vision shocked you awake. Is that it?"

Calmly, Justin turned to face him. His voice was quiet and steady now; his eyes had come back into a kind of dreamy focus. His hands rested limply on the lion-headed chair arms. "I don't know when she died," he answered. "Do you?"

"We think it was between two and three A.M." Friedman answered matter-of-factly. He was still playing his con man's game, pandering to Justin's portrayal of the mystic.

Or was it a game? I wondered.

Did Friedman believe what he was hearing and seeing? Watching him, I couldn't be sure. His heavily lidded eyes, as always, were unrevealing.

Justin agreed. "Yes, that would be about right."

"Did you see anything else, besides what you've described?" I asked. "Anything that could help us?"

If Friedman could play the game, so could I.

If it was a game.

Justin looked at me benignly for a moment before he gravely inclined his head. "I think so. Yes." But he didn't continue.

"Well—" I gestured impatiently. "Well, what is it?"

"Before I tell you what I saw," he answered, "you must understand how shocked I was, by the blood. Because then you'll understand how confused my impressions are. It was like a movie taken by a mad cameraman. It was terrible. Ghastly. And it—" He broke off, searching for a phrase. "And it immobilized me," he said finally. "For a while, I was helpless. I couldn't even call out for help. I couldn't think of anything but the blood."

Murmuring something sympathetic-sounding, Friedman

spoke solicitously as he said, "Let's start at the beginning. Did you see anything before she was killed?"

Justin frowned at the question. Then, with his pale eyes again unfocused, as if he were searching some dim, distant vista, he said, "At first—last night—I didn't see anything. But just now—just as we talk—I think I see something. I see —" Momentarily he closed his eyes. His sparse eyebrows drew together. And then, slowly and decisively, he nodded. "Yes. I see two cars. First, I see a large dark car, with Sally Grant inside."

"Just Sally," Friedman said. "No one else?"

"No one else," Justin repeated. "I see her driving to some place high above the city. And then, almost immediately, another car drives up. It's a smaller car, and there's a man inside."

"Can you describe him?" I asked.

Justin shook his head. "No, I can't. I only know that it's a man. Not a woman."

"All right. What happened next?"

"The man gets out of his car, and walks over to the large car. He walks very slowly. He's frightened—terrified by what he's come to do. I feel his steps dragging on the gravel of the parking lot, as if someone is holding him back. But he keeps walking. Finally he comes to the large car. He opens the door and gets in. He closes the door, and turns to face the woman —Sally Grant. She begins talking. She's frightened, too. Badly frightened. Soon they're arguing—calling each other terrible names. And then—"

Suddenly Justin shuddered sharply. As he'd been talking, his voice had thickened almost to a drunken slur. His eyes had rolled up; his mouth had fallen slightly open. His head slumped against the chair back. His hands were white now, clamped hard on the lion heads.

"And then, the man reaches inside his jacket, and takes out a gun. It's a small gun—a pistol, stuck into his belt. And—" Another shudder, more violent than the first. "And

187

then, the next moment, her head exploded in blood. The blood was everywhere, inside the car."

Speaking softly, so as not to disturb his vision, I said, "Was the man spattered with blood, too?"

He nodded. "Yes. I see him with blood on his hands, and his clothing. And even—" He gagged. "Even on his face, and in his mouth. He spits out the blood. Her blood."

"What happened then?" Friedman asked softly. "What did he do next?"

"He—" Justin frowned. Now he squinted, as if to see his vision more clearly. "He—I see him falling out of the large car. Sally Grant's car. I see him on his knees, down on the gravel. And then I see him getting up, staggering. I see him running back toward his own car. He's terrified. All he can think about is getting inside his car and escaping. He's got to hide himself—hide the blood.

"But then, at his car, he stops. He's forgotten the gun. He's got to throw it away. All along, he'd planned to throw away the gun. It was part of his plan. So he turns away from the car. He's terrified now. He's more animal than man. His jaws are dripping, like an animal's. He's stumbling again on the gravel, running toward some trees to his right. As he runs, he sees a car coming. He crouches down behind some shrubbery. The car slows— then speeds up, goes away. He's on his feet, taking the gun out of his pocket. He throws the gun away from him, far out over the treetops.

"But then, even with the gun still in the air, he hears a sound. It's metal, striking the ground—tinkling. It's his keys —his car keys and his house keys. When he threw the gun away, one of the keys caught on the gun, in the trigger guard. So the keys flew out with the gun.

"He's frantic. Now he's crying like a baby. And he's on his hands and knees, too, like a baby. But he knows he can't find the keys. Not in the dark. So he gets to his feet, runs to his car, feels under the front bumper. There's a key, there—a spare key. He gets in the car, starts the engine—drives away."

Still with his eyes half closed, still resting his head against the chair, Justin sat motionless for a moment, exhausted. Finally he whispered, "He's still terrified. Right now. Right this minute, while we talk. He feels as if he'll never be able to wash the blood from his hands."

"This man—" Friedman said. "Is he young? Old? Tall? Short?"

Slowly, with great effort, Justin shook his head. "I don't know. I'm sorry. I don't know."

"What about the woman?" I said. "You say it was Sally Grant."

A slow, heavy nod.

"How did you know it was her? Did you see her? Recognize her?"

"No," he answered. "No, I didn't see her. I've never seen her. But I knew it was her."

"How?"

Again, he shook his head. "I can't tell you, Lieutenant. I can't explain it, except to say that, for years, I've known about Sally Grant. She and my stepfather were—" He hesitated, then said, "They were friends for a long time."

"Originally they were lovers," Friedman said. "Then, later, they were business partners—in a deluxe whorehouse. Then, still later, they came to hate each other. At least, so your mother says." Friedman spoke harshly, almost brutally. He was trying to shock Justin into some reaction that would either verify what Cass had said or else contradict it.

The device didn't work. Instead, Justin moved his shoulders, shrugging languidly. "As I said, I never met Sally Grant. So I can't judge her."

"If you didn't know her," I said, "then how were you so sure it was her murder that you saw in your vision?"

"I wasn't sure," he answered. "Not until now. Your presence here—your questions, have reinforced my vision. You mentioned the name Sally Grant. And, instantly, everything became clear."

"That's very interesting," Friedman said, playing the role of an impressed listener. "Very interesting indeed." After a moment he said, "How long has Aztecca been operating?"

Justin's expression was benevolently quizzical as he said gently, "You make it sound a little like a dry-cleaning plant, Lieutenant."

"A dry-cleaning plant?"

"When you say 'operating,' it sounds like a business."

"Oh. Sorry. You didn't answer the question."

"We came here two years ago," Justin replied. "Before that, most of us were wandering in the world, alone. Each of us—each single one of us—came through hell to get here. We came through hell, and we're never going back the way we came. Never. Not in this life, or in any other life. We came here just as we came into the world—naked. We came with nothing. So everything we've got, we own. Therefore, nobody owns us. So, therefore, we're free. We've made ourselves free."

As he'd spoken, his voice had slowly hardened and deepened, taking on a kind of reedy resonance. His eyes, so strangely empty following his vision, were sharply focused now, staring intently at me. But as I tried to meet his gaze I realized that he wasn't actually looking at me. He was looking beyond me—or through me.

I decided to try to bring him back to reality.

"In my office yesterday," I said, "you mentioned that you saw Rebecca frequently—that she was interested in your work. But I have to say that no one else seems to think you and Rebecca were very close, or that she was interested in Aztecca."

Speaking to me, Friedman said, "Maybe he meant to say that he was *trying* to interest her in his work." Then he gave a sly, sidelong glance at Justin, saying: "Maybe it was a fund-raising effort."

Turning to Friedman, Justin said, "You seem to be preoccupied with money, Lieutenant. I wonder why?"

"*Was* it a fund-raising effort?" Friedman prodded gently.

Justin shrugged his bony shoulders, saying diffidently, "I suppose you could put it like that."

"Did she actually give you any money?" I asked.

"No," he answered. "But she intended to. She'd promised me. And then—" He winced. "And then she died. Perhaps it was because someone intended to harm Aztecca by killing her."

"It seems," Friedman observed, "that you have lots of enemies."

Almost benignly, Justin nodded. "Yes, Lieutenant, we do. But we are ready for them, I promise you that." As he spoke, he allowed his eyes to close. His head fell back against the back of his medieval chair. Our audience had apparently ended.

Twenty

Friedman and I stood side by side on a graveled parking area that overlooked a spectacular panorama of the San Francisco skyline, the Golden Gate Bridge and the bay beyond. The sky was a bright, clear blue. The graceful orange arch of the bridge contrasted vividly with the soft green of the Marin headlands that rose behind the bridge to the north. On the bay, hundreds of tiny white sails were festive specks on the cobalt water.

Behind us, a half-dozen police vehicles blocked access to the area. Below us, a line of more than twenty-five policemen were slipping and sliding and swearing as they searched every inch of the steep, rocky slope that dropped away from the graveled crescent.

"It's incredible," I said, shaking my head as I looked around us. "He really did see it. Down to the last detail."

"He either saw it," Friedman said mildly, "or else he was listening to the radio this morning. They had the whole story. Everything. In detail."

"But what if we find the keys? And the gun?"

Watching the frustrated, sweating searchers, Friedman

nodded thoughtfully. "That might make a believer out of me. I can't say I'd like to see my kids join Aztecca. But I'd have to admit that, yes, Justin sees things. Which I never doubted. The question is, why does he see them?"

"What'd you think of him?" I asked. "How do you read him?"

"I think he believes that crap he's spouting," Friedman answered promptly. "And that makes him a little frightening —and potentially dangerous, too. People like that, they're capable of anything."

"Even murder?"

Friedman shrugged. "Why not? Obviously, he's a practicing paranoic. Plus I'm sure he's convinced himself that he's divine. Therefore, he's convinced himself that he's incapable of doing anything wrong. He'd see murder as a burnt offering, or something. I'll bet anything that if you talked to him long enough, you'd discover that he thinks he's plugged into the cosmos, maybe with his own private line to God."

I smiled. "You could be right."

"I'll also bet," he said, "that he's been on drugs."

"You think so?"

"I think so. He has that washed out, empty-eyed look. I'll bet anything he used to be an acid head. Maybe he still is. Maybe he—"

"Hey, *Lieutenant!*"

About halfway down the steep incline, a patrolman stood beside a small, wind-twisted juniper. His right hand was raised high above his head. A ring of keys dangled from his forefinger.

"If they belong to one of our suspects," Friedman said, "put me down as a Justin Carlton fan."

"I have to admit," Friedman said, "that I hope one of those hotshot reporters downstairs doesn't hear about this. I mean—" He waved his cigar in a bemused arc. "I mean,

193

here we are—two leaders of men, sitting on our respective asses while Canelli and Culligan, the mismatched pair, dutifully drive from one suspect to the other, trying out keys in the suspect's lock. I mean, Jesus—" Shaking his head, he waved the cigar again. This time, an inch-long ash dropped to the floor in front of my desk.

"For all we know," Friedman said, "those keys belong to a pimply faced teen-ager whose girl friend had leaped out of the car in a panic when she saw his—"

My phone rang.

"It's probably not David Behr, Lieutenant." In my ear, Canelli's voice sounded apologetic. "Of course, with him, maybe it'd be hard to know. I mean, I figure he's got a couple've places to live, maybe, and who knows how many cars. But, anyhow, he says they aren't his keys. And when we asked him if we could try them in his front door, and everything, to see if they'd fit, he didn't say no. And, naturally, they didn't. Fit, I mean."

I drew a note pad toward me and crossed off David Behr, the second name. The first name, also crossed off, was Cass Dangerfield. The third name was Donald Fay, Cass's lover. Fay's name had been added at Friedman's insistence, "a hunch." Ron Massey was next, followed by Sam Wright. Pam Cornelison followed, and Richard Gee. Justin Wade's name was the last on the list.

"Where're you going next, Canelli?" I asked.

"How about Ron Massey, Lieutenant? He lives just a couple of blocks from here. Right down the hill."

"All right. Try him next."

"Yessir."

As I hung up the phone, I glanced at my watch. The time was almost five o'clock. Ann and Billy would be leaving Alcatraz for Fisherman's Wharf, where they'd meet Dan. If they started eating at six-thirty, they'd be finished by eight-thirty. A half hour later, she'd be home—waiting for my call.

"By the way," Friedman said, "miracle of miracles, a dedicated lab technician volunteered to come in today and start classifying and sorting out the fingerprints inside Sally's car, and her house. He's getting double time for his trouble, of course, unlike you and me. But it's a help."

Still thinking about Ann, I didn't answer for a moment. At best, the possibility of a fingerprint match-up was remote. And even if we could connect one of the suspects to Sally by means of fingerprints, we would still be a long way from proving a conspiracy to commit murder.

If, in fact, a conspiracy had actually existed.

Lolling in my visitor's chair, Friedman blew a long, lazy curl of cigar smoke up toward the ceiling and asked, "What're you thinking?"

"I'm wondering if we aren't causing ourselves a lot of extra work for nothing."

"How do you mean?"

"I mean that Sally had a longstanding grudge against Carlton. Why're we looking any farther? When we find her murderer—if we ever do—it might turn out that he's a hood working the lovers' lanes. It's happened before."

Friedman started another plume of smoke ceilingward before he observed mildly, "That's asking a lot of coincidence, it seems to me."

I shrugged. "A lot of stranger things have happened."

"I don't dispute it. But, for openers, how do you account for Sally taking off in the middle of the night? Right after being interrogated?"

"I don't account for it," I answered. "But why do we *have* to account for it? We're—Christ—we're asking for trouble, it seems to me. Why bother?"

"There's another problem."

"What's that?"

"You're saying she killed both Carlton and his daughter because of a longstanding grudge. Which is to say that she figured, what the hell, I'll get myself some sugar and see if

I can kill Bernard. Then, when that worked, you're saying that she decides she isn't satisfied that she'd brought Bernard down in flames. She's still mad. So she decides to kill his daughter, too."

Hearing him say it, I realized how silly it sounded. Sally had been a businesswoman. She'd been vicious, and greedy, and totally immoral. But she'd probably never done anything that she didn't think would turn a profit. Sally had been shrewd and smart.

And planning two murders of revenge wasn't smart.

I felt a little like a small, grumpy boy as I said, "Well, I just hope Justin's right, then, about the keys. Because, otherwise, we're screwed. We're at a dead end."

"You're in a pessimistic mood," Friedman answered. "Don't forget, we haven't found the gun that killed Sally. Who knows, we might get lucky. Who's supervising the search team, by the way?"

"Jamison."

Friedman nodded approval. "Excellent. Jamison has the instincts of a bloodhound. And come to think about it, he looks a little like a bloodhound. Ever notice?"

"No," I answered sourly.

"Incidentally," Friedman said, shifting to a more comfortable position, "assuming that Hoadley's telling the truth, which I'm inclined to believe, have you given much thought to how the gun that killed Rebecca got from Sam Wright, to Rebecca's motor home, to Sally Grant and finally to Hoadley?"

"Sure. Let's say Sam Wright wanted her dead. Let's also say that the gun was kept in her trailer. He goes to the trailer, and gets the gun. He gives the gun to Sally, along with a bundle of money and the promise of more to come. She gives the gun to—"

"Wait." He held up a traffic cop's hand. "Why does he give it to Sally?"

"Because he wants a cut-out. He wants a hired gun, and

he wants someone between him and the killer, in case something goes wrong. It happens all the time. He—"

My phone rang.

"It's Canelli again, Lieutenant."

He was trying to speak laconically, calmly. But I could hear the excitement plain in his voice.

"What've you got?"

"Well," he said, "I'm over at Ron Massey's."

"And?"

"And one of the keys fits his front door, if you can believe it."

"Well, I'll be damned." And to Friedman I said, "They're Ron Massey's keys."

As Friedman added his incredulous exclamations to mine, I spoke into the phone: "What's your situation, Canelli? Can the suspect hear you talking?"

"No, sir. Culligan's got him in the living room. I'm calling from his den." Now his voice was lower, more guarded. "I'm almost sure he can't hear me, anyhow. And, besides, him and Culligan are talking."

"Have you questioned him—confronted him with the evidence?"

"No, sir, I haven't. See, the first couple of times, Culligan and me, we went through this big long rigamorole, see, explaining to the subjects what we were doing, and asking permission to try the keys, and everything. You know—doing it all according to the book. I mean, Ms. Dangerfield and Mr. Behr are pretty high-powered types, you know. And we didn't want to take the risk of—"

"Canelli. Please." I took a deep breath. "Get to the point, will you?"

"Oh. Yeah. Sorry. Well, anyhow, when we got to here—to Massey's—I thought, what the hell, I'd just save myself a lot of trouble, and try a key in the front door. And, Jesus, it worked. So then, naturally, the door opens right in our faces. And there's Massey, cool as a cucumber, demanding to know what we're doing, fooling around with his front door. And then, when he took it in—you know, the keys, and everything—he said, 'Oh, good. You found my keys. I've been looking for them.' He was real cool about it, like I said. Real calm."

"How much did you tell him?"

"Nothing, Lieutenant. I mean, I said that the keys were found at the scene of a crime, but that's all I said. I figured you'd want me to call you right away."

"What did he say when you told him that?"

"He pretended to be real puzzled. You know, a big frown and everything."

"What kind of a car does he drive?"

"It's a Datsun. One of those 280Zs."

"Do the keys fit the car, too?"

"Yessir."

"What's his state of mind? Does he seem to be worried?"

"No, sir, not that I can see. He's acting more puzzled than anything. Like I said."

"And you haven't mentioned the Sally Grant murder."

"No, sir. Not a word. And Culligan didn't, either. We talked about it, beforehand—how we weren't going to say anything about it."

I paused a moment, trying to decide on the best strategy. Then: "See if you can get him to come down to the Hall voluntarily, Canelli. Sweet-talk him. Tell him that you don't know the whole story but we're holding the keys as evidence. Tell him you're acting for me, and that he's got to see me."

"Shall I read him his rights?"

"Not if you can help it. Tell him he's a witness, not a suspect. That way, maybe we'll get a shot at him before he calls his lawyer. Clear?"

"Yessir," he answered doubtfully. "But you better wish me luck. He's a pretty cool customer."

198

"Good luck."

"Thanks."

As we walked slowly down the narrow corridor to Interrogation Room A Friedman shook his head. "I can't believe it. Honest to God, I just can't believe that Justin's the real goods."

"You said it yourself, just yesterday—the police are using more clairvoyants all the time. It's progress."

"I'm not questioning that. In fact, years ago, there was a crime reporter named Stephen Drake right here in San Francisco. He worked for *The Sentinel,* and he got to be a real hotshot clairvoyant, once he got the hang of interpreting his own visions, or emanations, or whatever you call them. I used him myself, several times. He wasn't a hundred percent, like I said, because his images often came in a little out of focus. But sometimes he came in right on the money. And other times he came close enough to point us in the right direction."

"If that's the case—if you believe in ESP—then what's your problem with Justin Wade?"

"My problem with Justin Wade," he answered promptly, "is that his average seems to be a hundred percent."

"That's a problem?"

"To me, that's a problem. Besides, Justin makes me nervous. I don't like the way he acts, and I don't like the way he thinks. I figure he's an opportunist. And he's probably a liar. And, furthermore, he's a little off his rocker."

At the doorway to Room A, I turned to face him. "Why do you say he's a liar?"

"I'm not sure. I just think he lies."

"You may be right. But why worry about it? We aren't taking anything he says on faith. We've got the keys. In a little while, with luck, we'll have the gun that killed Sally. If we can tie that gun to Ron Massey along with the keys, we've got a case that any D.A. in the country would take to the

199

grand jury. He had the motive, and the opportunity, and the means to kill Rebecca—and Sally Grant, too, probably." I paused for emphasis, looking at him hard as I said, "What more do you want, for God's sake?"

"How about a confession?" Friedman said, gesturing to the door of Room A. "With a confession, I'll be happy."

"Likewise." I turned the knob and pushed open the door.

Twenty-one

As I stood leaning against the wall of the interrogation room, eying the suspect as he sat across from Friedman at a small metal table, I remembered Canelli saying that Massey had insisted on changing clothes for his trip downtown. I could believe it. Massey was impeccable in a blue blazer, white turtleneck sweater, gray flannels and Gucci loafers. With his hair carefully combed, gently stroking his small silken mustache, he could have been sitting under a striped umbrella at a Hillsborough garden party.

Shifting his sizable hams on the small, uncomfortable metal chair, Friedman was affecting a puzzled frown as he said, "I'm sorry, Massey, but I can't seem to get this straight. You say that, last night, you got home about ten P.M. from a meeting with David Behr, during which you discussed funeral arrangements and, ah, related promotional matters. And then you—"

"I don't know what you mean by 'promotional matters,' Lieutenant." Massey spoke in a cold, contemptuous voice, eying Friedman with calmly calculated distaste.

"I understood that you're planning a 'tribute' in the Cow

Palace," Friedman countered smoothly. "Isn't that correct?"

Massey nodded. "That's correct. But I'd hardly call it a promotional matter."

"Oh. Sorry." Friedman waved away his own choice of words. "Well, no matter. The point is that you got home about ten o'clock. You went directly to bed, after emptying your pockets on the dresser, according to your habit. Is that right?"

Again the suspect nodded. Watching the measured inclination of his head, I wondered whether we'd ever be successful in breaking down Massey's icy composure. A half hour into the interrogation, Massey was still in perfect control of himself.

"And then you went right to sleep," Friedman said, "and you woke up about eight o'clock this morning."

"Yes."

"That's ten hours' sleep," Friedman observed.

Massey sighed: an exasperated, long-suffering exhalation. "If you'll remember, Lieutenant, I didn't get much sleep the night before."

"Of course," Friedman said. "Neither did we, as a matter of fact. But, anyhow, you got up about eight this morning, and made yourself breakfast—in your bathrobe. Is that right?"

"That's right. It's my custom, on Sunday mornings."

"Are you a creature of habit?" Friedman asked idly.

"Yes," he answered coolly, "I suppose I am."

"I suppose you read the Sunday paper while you're eating your breakfast?"

"As a matter of fact, I do. Front to back."

Friedman nodded amiably, then said, "After breakfast, you showered and then got dressed. And it was then that you noticed your keys were missing. Is that right?" As he spoke, he reached into the side pocket of his jacket.

"That's right."

"Now, before I go on," Friedman said, "I want to establish

that you needed these keys to drive your car home last night, and to get into your house." Friedman took the keys from his pocket and placed them on the table between them.

"Of course I needed them," Massey snapped, without looking at the keys. "I've already told you that."

"I know you have," Friedman said. "But, in this business, we've got to get things absolutely straight."

In response, Massey shrugged, and glanced at his watch.

"I'd also like to get it straight that you're positive you put the keys on your dresser."

"I'm almost positive," Massey answered. "I've already told you that putting them on the dresser, along with my wallet and silver, et cetera, is a habit. Which means that I do it unconsciously, not consciously."

"But if we assume that you did it," Friedman said, "then we've got to assume that the keys would still have been on the dresser this morning."

Massey didn't reply.

"But the fact is, they were gone," Friedman said quietly. "You missed them when you got dressed. Or so you say."

"I've already—"

"Yes, yes—" Friedman raised a hand. "I know. You've already told me that. But what I'm trying to establish is that, obviously, you had the keys when you entered the house at ten o'clock. Otherwise, you wouldn't've been able to get inside. And assuming that you stayed in the house all night, then those keys had to have been in the house when you got up this morning. They might not've been on the dresser. But, logically, they had to've been inside the house. Is that correct?"

"No," Massey answered, "that's *not* correct. I could've left them in the front door, when I opened it. As a matter of fact, I do that, every once in a while, especially if I'm preoccupied, as I certainly was last night. Which is what probably happened, if it's true that the keys were found at the place where this Grant woman was murdered. Someone must've taken the keys, and put them where you would find them."

"Why would they do that?" I asked.

Turning sharply to face me, he said, "Simple. They'd do it to incriminate me. Or to send you off on a false scent. Which seems to be exactly what's happened."

I shook my head. "It didn't happen that way, Massey. The keys weren't deliberately planted."

"Why not?"

"First, the keys weren't put where we would find them. They were thrown away, along with the gun."

"And second," Friedman said, "there was a detective watching your house." He let a beat pass, allowing the suspect to think about what he'd said. Then: "He'd've seen someone on your doorstep."

Now it was Massey's turn to hesitate, as he looked from Friedman to me, then back to Friedman. Except for the muted whirring of a ventilation fan, the windowless, airless interrogation room was silent. As I returned Massey's stare, I thought I could see a shadow of fear flicker deep in his clear gray eyes. When he raised his hand to smooth down his foppish mustache, his fingers moved uncertainly. Finally he turned to face Friedman. "If those keys were found at the Crescent," he said, "then someone broke into my house and took them from my dresser, and planted them there. That's the only way it could've happened. He could've gotten in the back way, without being seen by your man." The gray eyes narrowed as they moved once more between Friedman and me. His thin voice was ragged now, no longer arrogantly clipped.

Did he know that he'd given us the break we needed? Was that why he seemed suddenly uneasy, suddenly unsure of himself? I exchanged a quick glance with Friedman. Yes, he'd heard it, too.

Still leaning against the wall, arms folded, I said, "When I talked to Inspector Canelli, he said that you told him you didn't know Sally Grant was dead. You didn't know about the murder until we told you about it. Is that right?"

He first shrugged, then nodded. "Yes," he said warily. "Yes, that's right." Once more, his thin fingers strayed to his mustache—perhaps to conceal an uncertain twitching of his mouth.

"The story wasn't in the paper," I said, "and it wasn't on TV. It was on the radio, though, beginning at about nine o'clock this morning." I paused, then asked quietly, "But, still, you're sure you didn't hear about the murder before Canelli rang your doorbell. Is that right?"

Impatiently, he nodded. "Yes, that's right. How many times do I have to *tell* you?" He spoke peevishly, blinking angrily as he looked at me. His waspish composure was deserting him.

"Well, then," I said, "how did you know that she'd been murdered at the Crescent?"

"I—" He blinked again, and then lowered his eyes. With his hand once more covering his mouth, he said, "I don't remember saying that."

"But you did say it, Massey," Friedman put in softly. "You most certainly did say it."

Eyes still averted, he shook his head in a slow, stubborn arc. "It—it's something I must've heard those detectives say. Canelli, and the other one. Or maybe I might've put on a radio, and heard about it, and then forgotten that I'd heard it."

Quickly exchanging a glance, Friedman and I mutely agreed to remain silent. This was the time for us to watch—and wait.

Finally Massey raised his eyes to meet Friedman's inscrutable stare. "This—this isn't fair. I—I'm still upset, by Rebecca's death. And you—you're confusing me. You're badgering me."

"We aren't badgering you," I said. "We're just trying to find out how your keys got to the murder scene."

"And we're also trying to find out how you knew she was

murdered at the Crescent," Friedman said. "You really can't blame us, you know. After all, you had a lot to gain by Rebecca's death—a lot of tax-free insurance dollars. In fact, right from the start, Massey, we figured you were a prime suspect. And, as matters turned out, it looks like we were right."

"We think you stole Rebecca's gun from her trailer," I said, "possibly to incriminate Sam Wright. Then we think you gave the gun to Sally Grant, along with instructions to hire a trigger man. Then, when Hoadley—the trigger man—got caught, and blew the whistle on Sally, we think she panicked. We think Sally called you last night about one A.M., and told you to meet her at the Crescent. And then—"

"Jesus Christ—" Massey leaped to his feet, sending his chair crashing to the floor. His eyes were distraught, his voice a high, thin shriek: "It's all lies. *All lies.*" He stood with his legs braced wide, futilely beating the air with impotent fists. Watching him, I remembered Behr's contemptuous evaluation of Ron Massey: a tall, handsome toady. Without his male-model's counterfeit cool, Massey was a cipher.

As Friedman rose to his feet, he said, "Did you know Sally Grant, Massey? Did you ever talk to her? Ever come in contact with her during the last two months?"

"Christ, no. I mean—" Desperately, he shook his head. "I mean, I heard of her. Almost everyone's heard of her. But I've never talked to her." Shaking his head, he let it go unfinished. Now he looked down at the overturned chair. He righted it, and sat down again heavily, elbows on the table, head in his hands. "This is insane," he muttered. "This is crazy. Completely crazy. You—you've got the wrong man. Don't you see that? Maybe your facts are right. I guess they are right. But you—Christ—you've got the wrong man." He spoke indistinctly, in a voice that trembled.

"Who's the right man, then?" I asked. "Who did it, Massey?"

Slowly, hopelessly, he shook his head, still cradled in his

hands. "I want a lawyer," he muttered. "I've got to have a lawyer. You've got to let me have a lawyer."

Catching my eye, Friedman moved his head to the interrogation room's steel door. "Excuse us a minute, will you?" he said to Massey.

Still with his head bowed, the suspect didn't reply—didn't respond. I signaled for the guard to open the door, and walked down the hallway with Friedman. As I walked, I glanced at my watch. The time was ten minutes after eight. In a little more than an hour, Ann would be expecting my call.

"What'd you think?" Friedman said, bending over the drinking fountain.

"I don't know," I answered slowly. "What'd *you* think?"

"I think," Friedman said, "that if we had the gun that killed Sally Grant, and if we had it tied to him, we'd have enough to take him into custody. As it is, though, I think the most we can get is a search warrant. What'd *you* think?"

"I think," I answered, "that you're probably right. But I also think that—"

"Lieutenant Friedman." It was the hallway guard, calling from his station at the end of the corridor. He held a telephone outstretched toward us. "It's for you."

"Thanks."

I watched Friedman walk down the corridor, take the phone from the patrolman and speak briefly into the receiver. While he listened, his thick eyebrows rose slightly. His full lips drew together, pursing thoughtfully. His dark eyes widened almost imperceptibly as he stared down at the floor beside the guard's small desk. It was as much surprise as Friedman ever allowed himself to reveal.

Finally, after speaking a last time into the receiver, Friedman gave the phone to the patrolman, thanked him and came back down the hallway toward me. Despite an obvious effort to conceal it, surprise showed plainly in his eyes.

"That was Shelby," he said, "in the lab." As he said it, his gaze fixed itself absently on a point just below the "V" of my open-necked shirt.

"Well?" I demanded. "Are you going to tell me about it? Or should I guess?"

"He says that he's got a fingerprint make from Sally Grant's car."

I decided to fold my arms and stare at him until he told me the rest of it.

"It's Justin Wade's print," Friedman said finally. "It's only two partials—not enough for admission as evidence. But Shelby says he's positive it's a make. And Shelby is a very, very conscientious man. He's also very enterprising."

"Where'd he find the print?"

"It was on the inside of her car's door handle," Friedman said. "That's why I said that Shelby's enterprising. Apparently the handle had been wiped—the outside of it, but not the inside. When Shelby dusted the handle, he didn't see any prints, naturally. But, on the off chance, he used a dental mirror to look at the inside of the handle. And there they were—two good, clear partials."

"Justin—" I shook my head. "It's hard to believe he's the one."

"Why?"

"Because," I answered, "in lots of ways, when you think about it, he's exactly right for the part. Which usually means it's someone else."

"You do remember, though, that he denied ever meeting Sally Grant."

I nodded.

"Which means that he lied to us, according to the lab."

I nodded again, and for a moment we stood silently, thoughtfully staring at each other. Finally Friedman said, "If he's the one, then at least it explains one thing."

"What's that?" I asked.

"It explains those goddamn visions. They were just devices

to throw us off the goddamn track—and throw suspicion on someone else."

"And they worked, too."

"Not on me, they didn't work," Friedman said. "I was always suspicious."

"Sure you were."

Twenty-two

Ahead I saw a shopping center parking lot, almost deserted at nine o'clock on a Sunday evening.

"Pull in there," I ordered. As Canelli swung the cruiser abruptly into the driveway—striking the curb with the right rear wheel—I reached for the microphone.

"Units two and three, on tach three, this is unit one. Let's disperse in this parking lot while we go over procedures. Don't bunch up, and stay in the cars."

As we drew to a stop beside a deserted Photomat stand, I turned to watch the two unmarked cars enter the lot and find inconspicuous parking places. When they were parked, with their lights off, I reached again for the microphone.

"Let's switch to the walkie-talkies, channel five." I picked up my own walkie-talkie, tuned to channel five, pressed the transmit button and said, "Culligan, you're number two. You're in command of backup. Clear?"

"That's clear," Culligan answered laconically.

"Marsten, you're number three."

"Right." Even though his voice came through rough and scratchy, Marsten's displeasure was plain. Culligan and Marsten didn't get along.

"All right, here's the situation. There are thirty or forty people in the Aztecca house, maybe more. Supposedly, they're all devoted to Justin Wade. Which means that, if we aren't careful, we could get in over our heads. So we're going to take it slow and easy. Canelli and I will drive up to the house, and go inside. We're going to run a con—tell Justin that we'd like him to come down to the Hall, so we can verify one of his so-called visions. If it works like it should, we'll get him outside and in the car with no problems. If something goes wrong, we'll call on channel five. Clear?"

The two units responded.

"Culligan, you and Marsten can park at opposite ends of the block, on opposite sides of the street, out of sight. I didn't see any signs of lookouts when we drove past, but you never know."

"What about covering the back?" Culligan asked.

"There's no way we can do it," I answered. "Not at night. The property backs up on waste land. We'd need fifty men, to secure the perimeter. Which means that our only real chance is to take him out the front. Which is why we have to con him."

"Does Justin know he's a suspect?" Culligan asked.

"I hope not. If he does, we could have a problem. Incidentally, if it should hit the fan, and they all start running, it could be a mess. They're all look-alikes. They all wear long white robes, and they all wear medallions around their necks, depicting the sun. But remember that, as far as I know, Justin is the only one in there with long hair. The rest of them either have their heads shaved, or else their hair's cropped close. And Justin's medallion is at least twice as large as the others'. Justin is twenty-three years old. Slight build, sallow complexion. He's got sandy hair coming almost to his shoulders. He's got a beard, too."

"What about guns?" Culligan asked. "Do they have any?"

"As far as we know, there aren't any guns. There're three or four guards with spears. But that's all."

"Spears?" It was Marsten's voice, incredulous.

"Right," I answered. "Spears. Any other questions?"

There were no questions.

"All right, then. Let's do it." I clicked off the walkie-talkie, and gestured for Canelli to start the engine.

As we got out of our car and began walking slowly toward the crumbling old mansion, I checked my watch. The time was exactly nine-thirty.

Back from her Sunday outing with Dan and Billy, Ann was waiting for my call.

I'd tried to phone her an hour ago, without success. So, before leaving the Hall, I'd asked Friedman to call her, at nine-thirty.

"It sure seems quiet," Canelli said, sotto voce. "Deserted, almost."

We were about fifty feet from the portico, with its sagging overhead beams and missing pillars. A faint flicker of amber light shone through the door's beveled glass panes. Of the four tall rococo windows across the front of the house, three were completely dark; only one glowed with faintly reflected lamplight.

Except for the pale golden light flickering from behind the door and the window, nothing stirred.

Was the place deserted?

Were we too late?

Twenty-five feet from the front door, I gestured Canelli to my side.

"See anything?" I asked.

"No, sir."

I pointed to the lighted window. "I'm going to try and see inside. Here—" I gave him the radio. "Check in with Culligan. And keep your eyes open. It's too quiet."

In the darkness, I saw him nod fervently. "You said it, Lieutenant. It feels wrong. All wrong."

Not replying, I stepped off the driveway and began picking my way through the weeds and vines that grew thick and tangled between the eucalyptus trees that surrounded us. The night sky was starless, overcast by a thick fog that had come in from the ocean during the twilight hours. Overhead, a cold wind blew through the thick-growing eucalyptus foliage, rattling the leaves with a sound as dry and brittle as paper crackling high above. I hadn't gone more than a dozen steps from the driveway before the trees and undergrowth closed in around me. I was alone, separated from Canelli. Suddenly I felt a small, stomach-tilted tremor of fear. I was a pavement cop; my instincts were tuned to the sounds of urban life. I'd trained myself to calculate the odds of surviving in the city. I was a professional hunter, and I'd learned to read the signs I found in back alleys, and in dark doorways, and in the foul-smelling rooms that sheltered my prey.

But here, surrounded by trees that grew so thick that they could have been part of an ancient forest, I felt cut off from something essential. The wind in the eucalyptus leaves confused the cues that could protect me from danger. The vines and brambles clutching at my trouser legs seemed to throw me dangerously off balance as I walked.

I unbuttoned my jacket, and loosened my revolver in its holster.

The cold touch of the gun helped—but only a little.

Then, suddenly, I emerged from the undergrowth to find myself facing the lighted window. Three strides took me to the shoulder-high windowsill. Looking through a cracked pane, I saw that the soft amber glow of light came from a hallway outside the room, not from the room itself.

And then, above the sound of wind, I heard the soft, undulating murmur of voices speaking in unison. As I listened, the sound of the voices grew slowly louder, gathering momentum. From somewhere inside, I heard the same phrases repeated—once, twice, three times.

It was a ritual chanting.

Looking to my left along the side of the house, I saw the thick, awkward figure of Canelli. He was standing just short of the portico, watching me. It was a reassuring sight.

I pointed to my right, signaling that I intended to move toward the far corner of the house. The sound of the chanting came from that direction. Perhaps, around the corner, I could see more through another window.

Canelli nodded; he understood. Now he pointed to himself, then toward me. Did I want him to come along? I shook my head.

Moving slowly and cautiously, picking my way over the uneven, rubble-strewn ground, I made my way to the right. I looked back at Canelli, waved once, and stepped around the corner. On this side of the house, three windows were lighted with the same soft golden glow. The last two windows were larger than the first, which was more ornately framed. I remembered the huge ballroom I'd seen earlier in the day, opening off the hallway to the right. If the whole cult had gathered, it was probably in the ballroom.

I was right. Peering through one of the leaded panes in the first window, I saw a large group of white-robed figures clustered in the center of the ballroom, crowded close around the small plywood platform I'd seen earlier. They were speaking in unison, repeating some short, unintelligible phrase over and over. Head bowed, arms folded, a single figure stood on the platform. The scene was dimly lit by guttering, smoking flames dancing above a half-dozen huge oil-filled braziers. Except for the Victorian ballroom's elegant embellishments and the incongruous makeshift platform, I could have been watching some strange medieval rite.

The platform was still thickly banked by branches and boughs, as I'd seen it before. But, tonight, hundreds of flowers had been entwined among the branches. As I watched and listened, the sounds of the chanting diminished, fading into silence. Quickly counting heads, I estimated the group at about forty. Some of them were standing, some were kneeling on the ornate parquet floor. Others were crouched on their knees, foreheads pressed to the floor. Each of them was facing the improvised platform, waiting expectantly.

Now the single figure slowly raised his head and spread his arms wide, palms up—eloquently accepting the silent homage from those pressing around him. It was Justin Wade. He stood with his face lifted high, long hair falling back away from his face, eyes fervently raised. It was the pose of someone communing with heaven.

Now his mouth opened. He was beginning to speak.

One of the leaded panes was broken. Standing close to it, I heard Justin say:

"Tonight—now—after the ceremony of initiation and acceptance, I have a vision to share with you. The images are disturbing—dark, ominous shapes watching us from the shadows." As he spoke, he lowered his eyes, looking out over the faces of his followers, now upturned to him. The faces were rapt, already transfixed as they listened.

"But first—" he continued, speaking in a calm, melodious monotone. "First, we welcome Sister Katherine Brand among us. She comes to us from a long way—from New Canaan, Connecticut. She's been with us, sheltered while she healed, for almost three weeks. All of you know her. You know her story—or, at least, you know some of her story. You know how she went blindly toward the West, escaping. It's a path many of you took. But, like many of you, Katherine found that even at the edge of the great, cleansing Pacific, she found no peace. She was tortured by demons that raged within and without. She was pursued by men who tried to harm her—the men her parents hired to follow and capture her. She was harassed by the police. She was arrested for a vagrant, a common criminal.

"And then, finally, she found us. It was an accidental meeting. She was in Saint Francis Park, downtown. She was dirty, and she was hungry. So, bench to bench, she was begging. Then she saw Sister Amy and Brother Michael. They were begging, too. But they were begging for all of us —for Aztecca. In that moment—that one sudden, magic moment—Katherine recognized the faces of friendship. She took their outstretched hands, and came with them—here. To Aztecca. This house became her refuge and her fortress. The men who followed her came to our door, and tried to take her from us. But the guards protected her—as they protect us all. Her pursuers were defeated, and they ran away.

"After that, Katherine Brand joined us—with her spirit, not just her body. She learned the same lessons we all learned —that our only strength is the strength we have together. If they separate us—catch us unawares—then we're powerless.

"She learned, too—as we all learned—that there is no sin, so long as we're not ashamed. She learned that, together, we live in a perpetual state of innocence, released from the conventions of this world, with our psyches free to wander through the dark, vast void—the universe that I discovered, and will help you to enter with me. She learned to cleanse her body and her mind. She learned how to liberate her spirit from the restraints of society's taboos. She learned that the body is a temple, a place for celebration. She learned that certain substances can help us in the ceremonies of liberation and celebration.

"And lastly, she learned how to render these substances from the fruit and the plants of the earth, as our ancient spiritual forefathers did, to free us for travel beyond the restraints of this earth, seeking ultimate truth for us all."

As he spoke of his forefathers, Justin used both hands to lift the big sun symbol away from his chest, extending it out toward his followers. Then, still holding the symbol suspended on its golden chain, he turned to face the entrance to the ballroom. At the same time, the audience parted before him, making a pathway to the door.

Carrying gleaming, broad-bladed spears, two of the cult's guards appeared in the doorway. Tonight, the guards wore Mayan-style helmets, painted a gleaming gold. They stood motionless in the doorway, at rigid attention, eyes front.

216

"As a symbol of her trust," Justin intoned, "Katherine comes to this ceremony pure in mind and body, as innocent as the day of her birth."

With the words, a naked girl came out of the hallway and stood between the guards. At the same moment, the crowd began the same chant I'd heard before. This time, I could make out the words:

> My—ah My—ah
> In—Tu—Tami

As the guards and the girl came toward the platform, the chanting became louder, repeating the same incantation over and over. With my vision adjusted to the guttering light, I could see more clearly into the faces of the cult members closest to the window.

Even in the uncertain light, I could clearly recognize the drug addict's fixed, blank-eyed stare.

They were an assembly of white-robed, shaven-headed zombies, mindlessly repeating their meaningless chant.

In front of the platform, the guards stopped. Moving like a robot, the naked girl mounted the short flight of three stairs to the platform. Physically she was unattractive, with broad, flat hips, sharply tapering shoulders, thick thighs and long, sagging breasts. Her face was narrow, with a small, sullen mouth and eyes set too close together. Her head was shaven.

Her eyes were as empty as a sleepwalker's.

On the platform now, she faced Justin. The two stood barely a foot apart, staring deep into each others' eyes. Justin reached into the folds of his robe and withdrew a small sun symbol. He ceremoniously placed the chain around the girl's neck, and held the medallion out for her to kiss. Then, his hands on her shoulders, he turned to face the gathering. Raising his widespread hands high above her head, Justin spoke in a clear, ringing voice:

"From this moment, Katherine Brand no longer exists.

From this body, on which I now place my hands"—he lowered his hands again to touch her shoulders—"the woman Franchesca is born, known to all those here as Sister Franchesca, one of us."

The hands were raised in final benediction. "Now, with Sister Franchesca, we number forty-three." As he spoke, the girl descended the three steps and stood with head fervently bowed while two women covered her with a robe. When the sun symbol fell in place between her breasts, the cultists began chanting:

My—ah My—ah
In—Tu—Tami

Justin stood with his head bowed, arms at his sides, utterly motionless. Slowly, inexorably, the voices grew louder, more fervent. As the chanting gathered intensity, the lifeless, masklike faces surrounding the platform began to change. Deep in the blank, dead eyes, sparks of passion kindled. A note of hysteria crept into the litany. Soon the eyes were blazing fanatically. Repeating the meaningless words, the formless mouths drew tight and cruel. All heads were turned toward the figure on the platform. In moments, the dull, passive group had become a mob.

My—ah My—ah
In—Tu—Tami

Through it all, Justin still stood motionless, head still bowed, arms still rigid at his sides.

Then, as if the chanting had generated some strange energy that pulsated through his body, he began to tremble. He was shuddering visibly as he raised his head, struggling against the strange force that possessed him. His eyes were tightly closed. His jaw was clenched. His face glistened in the dancing light, streaming perspiration. Now, suddenly, he

218

raised his outstretched hands. Instantly, the crowd fell silent. Eyes still closed, Justin began speaking in a low, strangely disembodied voice:

"I have just been away from you. I have just journeyed far from this time and place, across the great, empty mists that separate this world from the one farther out, beyond infinity.

"And it has been a terrible journey. Because it has shown me the faces of our enemies." As he said it, Justin's eyes came open. The blaze in his eyes matched the manic light dancing in his followers' eyes, all around him. His voice was deeper, suddenly more compelling:

"My pathway was lined with their faces," he said. "Each turn I took, they pressed closer. I saw their arms raised, ready to strike at me. At first, the faces were strange to me. But then, as they came closer, I could recognize them.

"I saw them for who they are—those same monsters who have followed us all through all our lives . . . who followed us here, to Aztecca . . .

"And who . . ."

He paused, traversing the crowd with his zealot's stare as he used both hands to lift his sun symbol away from his chest, holding it high.

"And who"—he repeated, dropping his voice to a low, vengeful note and pacing the words with slow, dramatic emphasis—"are preparing to attack us here, at Aztecca."

On cue, the protesting voices swelled to an ominous chorus of deadly, purposeful anger.

At that moment, something hard and sharp was jammed into the small of my back.

"Don't turn around," a voice said. "Just step back from the window. Two steps. Slow."

I sighed. "Listen, you've—"

This time, pain shot up my back. "Put up your hands. *Move.*" Once more, he jabbed me.

"All right. Take it easy." I stepped back two slow, careful steps, holding my hands shoulder high. Then, without waiting for another command, I pivoted to face one of the thick-shouldered, flat-eyed guards. He was holding a short spear against my stomach, pressed just above the naval.

"I saw you today," I said. "Earlier. I'm a police lieutenant. Put the spear down, or it's your ass."

In response, I saw his fists tighten on the spear's shaft. Even in the dim light from the tall leaded window, I could see a bright, dangerous light glinting in his eyes.

"What're you doing here?" His voice was low and hoarse, roughened by suppressed rage.

"I came to talk with Justin. He's been helping us with his stepsister's murder. We need him downtown."

"How many more are there?"

"One more. At the front door." I tried to speak steadily, reassuringly. As I spoke, I slowly lowered my hands.

"Put your hands up."

But this time he didn't jab with the spear.

Once more, I sighed. Trying to pitch my voice to a casual note of patronizing boredom, I said, "Listen, friend, I'd like to remind you that I'm a police officer, acting in the line of duty. Now—" I nodded at the spear, an inch from my stomach. "Now, I'm not going to come down on you for that. You're acting as a guard, and I looked like an intruder. There's no problem. However, that was two minutes ago. Now I've identified myself. And if you continue to threaten me, as I said, it's your ass. If you're not careful, you'll spend the night in jail."

He'd shifted into the shadow I cast, so that I couldn't see his eyes. But I saw the point of the spear drop slightly.

Irrationally, I thought that, at the very moment Ann and Pete were probably talking amiably on the phone, I was facing a shaven-headed, blank-eyed fanatic who was threatening me with a homemade spear.

"I'm going to give you exactly ten seconds," I said. "And then I'm going to—"

"Drop the goddamn spear. *Now.*" It was Canelli's voice.

He'd stepped out of the trees directly behind the guard. As the guard whirled instinctively, I grabbed the spear with both hands, stepped close and swung my knee into his crotch. He grunted and bent double. Then, holding himself, he sank to his knees and knelt in the darkness, rocking silently from side to side.

Instantly, Canelli holstered his revolver, reached for his handcuffs and grabbed the subject's arm, ready to clamp on a hammerlock.

"No. Wait. Don't." I stooped, picked up the spear and threw it deep into the trees. Then, drawing a deep breath, I stepped back from the suspect, signaling for Canelli to do the same. Still kneeling, the guard was rocking from side to side, groaning softly through tightly clenched teeth.

I moved again to the window, and looked inside. The cultists were quieter now, listening intently to Justin, who had dropped to his knees on the platform, eyes cast upward. I could see his mouth working, but I couldn't make out his words.

Should I stay with my original plan—try to con him into a car and then down to the Hall?

Or should I call for reserves, and take him out by force?

As I stood irresolutely in the shadows of the trees, listening to the murmuring of Justin's voice mingling with the sound of crickets, I again felt displaced, time-warped into an alien land where hostile forces were controlling me.

I heard Canelli clearing his throat, and saw him looking at me obliquely. The message: we should make a move. He was right. Win or lose, I had to make a decision.

I jerked my head toward the guard as I spoke to Canelli: "Let's go inside and do it, just like we planned. Bring him." And to the guard I said, "If you give me any more crap, I'll cuff you and take you downtown and book you for assaulting a police officer. But if you wise up and cooperate with us, I'll forget the charge. It's your choice. Do you understand what I'm telling you?"

221

Staring up at me blankly from his kneeling position, he didn't respond. His eyes were clearer now, unblurred by pain.

"The lieutenant's giving you a break, asshole," Canelli said, jerking the cultist to his feet. "If you had any brains, you'd say thanks. That's if." He shoved the guard toward the corner of the building. "Go on—move it. And no noise, either."

Under the portico, I took the walkie-talkie and advised Culligan that we were entering the premises. Then, mentally crossing my fingers, I tried the front door. It opened to my touch. I swung it wide, and stepped into the dimly lit entry-way.

Two booted, belted, Mayan-helmeted guards stood with arms folded across muscular chests, staring impassively at me. They stood on either side of the entrance to the long, dim corridor that led to the back of the house. The black woman, Anya, stood between the two guards. Each of the guards had propped his spear against the wall beside him. Overhead, an old-fashioned hanging oil lamp guttered softly. No one spoke, no one moved.

Then, from the ballroom, I heard the chanting begin again:

> My—ah My—ah
> In—Tu—Tami

I turned to Canelli, standing watchfully beside the disarmed guard, close beside the door. "You can go," I told the guard. "Remember what I said."

Moving with his legs close together, he walked across the foyer; without looking at the helmeted guards or the black woman, he disappeared into the darkness of the long, empty hallway. At the same time, the sound of the chanting was rising . . . rising . . .

. . . then falling, finally fading into silence.

Anya stepped forward, meeting me in the center of the foyer. Her face was impassive as she said, "What did you tell him, Lieutenant, that he should remember?"

I took a moment to consider before I said, "He thought we were prowlers, outside. He gave me a little jab with his spear. It was understandable, under the circumstances. I told him that I wouldn't press charges, if he didn't give me any more trouble."

Listening to me, staring thoughtfully straight into my eyes, she gestured to a far corner of the entry hall. "I want to ask you something," she said, walking away from me and sitting on a Victorian bench built into a small alcove. Signaling for Canelli to remain at the front door, facing the two implacable guards across the foyer, I followed her into the alcove and sat beside her.

"Why're you here, Lieutenant?" she asked. "This is the second time today. Why? What's happening, anyhow?"

Asking the question, her voice had slipped into the soft, liquid patois of the ghetto. Her cool, haughty stare had suddenly hardened, become street-corner-savvy.

Picking up the cue, I countered, "Why're you asking?"

"Because Justin's not normal. And I think it's got something to do with you."

"How do you mean, 'not normal'?"

"I mean that, ever since his stepsister got murdered, he's been a different person. That's understandable. But today, he's been—" She frowned, searching for the phrase. "He's been unreachable, almost. Way, way out."

Studying her, I tried to decide about Anya. Was she a true believer, like the rest? Or was she in it for what she could get? Counterpointing the question, the sound of chanting began again. If the disciples were inside, chanting, why was she in the lobby?

If Justin's hair was long, and the heads of the faithful shaven, why was Anya's hair worn natural, close to her head?

Finally I decided to say, "What are you—his manager? Is that it?"

Her answer was a small, knowing smile—our little secret.

Suddenly I decided that I liked her, and could probably trust her.

As if to confirm it, she said, "That's about it."

Smiling in return, I said, "You're worried about your meal ticket, then."

She thought about it for a moment before she said, "There's nothing wrong with being a manager. People like Justin—talented people—they need managers. Someone once said that if you want to succeed, you should find a need and fill it. Which is what I did." As she spoke, she turned to face the entrance to the hallway. "It's over," she said. "The meeting's over. He'll be out in a minute, probably." Then, softly, she said, "Remember, Lieutenant, Justin is—fragile. So be gentle with him."

"If I can," I promised, "I will."

She was on her feet now, moving to stand expectantly at the entrance to the dim, empty hallway. Moments later, the hallway suddenly filled with robed figures, each moving silently away from us, along the corridor. Each of the figures moved with downcast eyes, hands folded. At each doorway, a few figures turned off until, finally, the corridor was once more deserted. Except for the faint sound of shuffling feet, they could have been phantasms from the mythological netherworld of Hades: creations of the imagination, not flesh and blood.

Behind me, I could hear Canelli muttering something unintelligible.

And still the guards stood like figures carved in stone, utterly motionless. A moment later, Justin appeared in the hallway. He was turned away from us, following his wraith-like followers down the hallway.

I cleared my throat, ready to call to him, when he suddenly turned to face us. His features were completely composed as he walked slowly closer. Passing the guards, he said something I couldn't hear. One guard turned and disappeared into the hallway darkness. Listening carefully, I heard the guard's footfalls grow fainter, finally silenced by the closing of a door.

At the entrance to the corridor, the other guard now held his spear with the butt planted beside his booted foot. The broad, gleaming blade was angled forward, toward us. I saw Justin exchange a long, intent look with Anya, who was to my right. I couldn't see the woman's expression—and I couldn't read Justin's.

Moving to stand directly beneath the oil lamp hung from the ceiling, Justin spoke in the same vibrant, compelling voice that he'd used earlier, exhorting his followers:

"Is this your last trip here, Lieutenant?"

Uncertain how to answer—uncertain what he meant—I decided to counter with a question:

"Is it convenient for you to come down to the Hall of Justice with us? There've been new developments in your stepsister's murder. We think you can help us."

It was a speech that I'd mentally rehearsed a dozen times during the past hours. And probably precisely because I'd rehearsed it, the words sounded false and stilted.

"You've found out who murdered Rebecca." It was a statement, not a question.

"We're not sure," I answered. "But the information you gave us—your vision of how Sally Grant was murdered—helped very much. But we need something more from you. A statement." It was a spur-of-the-moment improvisation. Was it convincing? I couldn't decide.

Justin stood with his arms folded, head slightly averted. With the lamp directly above him, his face was in shadow, his features unreadable.

"I'm glad I could help," he said finally. He let a long, deliberate moment pass before he said, "But we can talk here." He gestured toward the dark hallway. "In my study."

I shook my head. "No. Not here."

"Why not here, Lieutenant?" I could hear an ironic, patronizing note in his voice. Suddenly I felt ineffectual, vulnerable.

And just as suddenly, I realized that, together, Friedman and I had made a tactical mistake. We should have sent a patrol car for Justin, casually requesting him to come down to the Hall, ostensibly to help us.

A Sunday night visit by a lieutenant conveyed a different, more ominous signal.

As if he could read my thoughts, he asked, "Are there just the two of you? Or are there more?"

"Just us."

And, immediately, I knew that I'd answered too quickly. Even to my own ears, the reply sounded unconvincing.

"Just you," he repeated. Then: "Yesterday, you had me fingerprinted. And now, today, you ask me to go downtown, but you won't tell me why. And when you ask me to come downtown, I feel that you're lying to me. I feel that once I go there, it's your will that I never come back to Aztecca." He said it softly, almost dreamily.

As he spoke, two helmeted guards emerged from the darkness of the hallway, taking up positions on either side of Justin with their spear butts planted on the floor next to their boots. One of the guards whispered to Justin, who glanced quickly out a window. I sensed Anya moving quietly away from my side.

Three spears, two revolvers.

At close quarters, the odds favored the spears. As if to confirm it, the third guard moved closer—and Anya moved another step away.

Had they discovered our backup team?

Did Justin know—sense—that he was a suspect?

I couldn't afford to guess at the answers.

Speaking softly aside to Canelli, I said, "Call in the backup."

As he nodded and reached for his walkie-talkie, I unbuttoned my jacket, loosened my revolver in its holster and stepped purposefully toward Justin. I would take him into custody, give him his rights and take my chances getting out.

226

As I took the first step, I felt a draft on the back of my neck. Instinctively dropping to a crouch and drawing the revolver, I pivoted to face the door.

Two guards advanced on us from the open doorway. Each man crouched over a leveled spear. I raised my revolver, aiming at the closest man. "Hold it right there," I yelled. *"Freeze."*

I saw the two spear points falter. At the same moment, behind me, I heard a short, stifled cry of pain, followed by a half-strangled obscenity. Wheeling to my right, I saw Canelli slumping to his knees. His face was strangely blank; his mouth was a prim, purse-lipped circle, innocently surprised. His eyes were glazed by shock. Blood covered the right side of his chest, and one of the helmeted guards stood with his blood-smeared spear angled down, poised for a second thrust.

I aimed at the guard's medallion and fired. He dropped his spear, staggered, fell to his knees beside Canelli.

Canelli's gun and walkie-talkie lay on the floor between them. As if they were reacting to an unspoken command, both Canelli and the guard began groping for the gun with awkward, halting fingers. Ten feet separated me from the gun. Shouting incoherently, I lunged for it. It was a deadly, desperate dance for three, executed in maddening slow motion. But I would be the winner. My free hand was sweeping across the floor, inches away from the gun butt . . .

. . . when my head exploded in a blinding burst of pain as I began falling . . .

. . . falling,
crashing spreadeagled on the parquet floor.

Twenty-three

I felt fingers prying at my right hand.

Why?

Why was I struggling against the prying fingers?

It was the gun—my service revolver, a lump of steel, pressing into my chest as I lay face down on the hard wooden floor. My fingers had wrapped themselves around the gun.

But other fingers were struggling against mine—clawing, tearing, ripping.

Inside my head, the roar of pain was a fierce, howling demon.

Desperately, I fought the ripping fingers, feebly thrashing my body from side to side. I could have been an animal—a wounded animal, futilely struggling against claws and teeth, slashing at me.

I needed help.

Officer needs help

Code Twelve. Please God, someone send out a Code Twelve.

But nobody would help me.

Sandaled feet and robes that touched the parquet floor surrounded me, but no one would help.

Braced for the effort, I gathered myself—heaved—teetered on my right shoulder . . .

. . . then fell heavily on my back, still holding the gun, now clutched in both hands. Instinctively, I'd aimed the gun at whoever had tried to wrest it from me. Blinking, I focused on the face hovering disembodied above me, haloed by light from the hanging oil lamp.

Justin's face. Eyes wild. Mouth raging. Screaming: "Shoot him, Anya. *Shoot* him."

Anya . . .

Moments before, I'd liked her.

So why would she shoot me?

Why?

I heard her voice answering, but I couldn't comprehend the words. With my revolver still trained on Justin, I turned toward the sound of her voice.

I was staring into the muzzle of another revolver. It was a service revolver: a 2-inch .38.

Canelli's gun.

From somewhere close beside me, I heard a soft, low moan. It was Canelli. Unmistakably, it was Canelli. I'd forgotten him. Bloody, wounded, I'd forgotten Canelli.

Gritting my teeth, I drew my left elbow close to my body while I held the gun still aimed at Justin. Instantly, the room tilted, began to fall away. Inside my head, the roar of demons returned.

But I couldn't close my eyes.

I would die, if I closed my eyes.

And Canelli, too.

So, panting with the effort, I rolled to my left, centering the weight of my body over the braced elbow. Now, slowly, I drew my right leg up.

I was ready.

Do or die, I was ready.

Was it a joke? A bad joke?

No.

I pushed with the leg, heaved with the arm. While the room whirled wildly, I felt myself rising—rising—

Suddenly, miraculously, I was sitting up. Splay-legged. Exhausted. But, still, sitting up. The room was tilting again, tipping, turning in a wobbly, sickening circle. But I was sitting up.

Glad, and proud.

No infant could have been more proud. Or no beetle, either, who'd managed to turn from his back to his belly. We were a team, the three of us: me, the baby, the beetle. Together, we would win. We would *live.*

Momentarily, I closed my eyes. When I opened them, the room had steadied. I could look for Canelli.

He was lying full-length beside me. His eyes were closed. His face was pale, glazed with sweat. But his chest was rhythmically rising and falling. He was alive. For a while, at least—for now—he was alive.

The walkie-talkie lay close beside him. Smashed.

The guard lay behind Canelli, to the left. Also with his eyes closed. Also with blood glistening on his chest.

But also alive. Thank God. I'd killed too many men already. At night, in dreams, they raged around me.

Close beside me, Justin and Anya were whispering. Justin's voice was shaking, near hysteria. The black woman's voice was cold, calculating.

As I listened to them, I realized that my head was clearing. The howling demons had quieted, grumbling now.

Still with my revolver trained on Justin's medallion, I threw a quick glance around the foyer. The scene resembled the staging of some ancient Greek play. The actors—Justin, Anya, Canelli, me and the wounded guard—were surrounded by the white-robed chorus, standing silent as ghosts in a graveyard. On either side of the lobby door, spears raised, the two guards stood like costumed sentinels, guarding the gates to Hades.

I returned my gaze to the black woman, still holding the revolver aimed at my chest. It was in her eyes that I would find the answers I must have. They were snapping black eyes, fixed on mine with fierce intensity. I'd seen those eyes before. On every ghetto street corner, in every dark doorway. They were the eyes of the enemy.

So I was staring into the face of the enemy—looking for help.

I knew I must speak quietly, without fear. With authority. "You won't pull that trigger."

"You won't either," she said softly.

"Not if I can help it." As I spoke, a sudden sharp pain sliced at the base of my skull. Involuntarily, I put a hand to my head. My hair was wet and sticky. My fingers were bloody. Absently, I wiped my fingers across the parquet floor beside me.

"What the hell is this all about?" she asked.

"We're going to arrest him for last night's murder of Sally Grant.

As I said it, a quick, electric murmur swept the figures crowded together in the foyer. But a moment later, they fell silent. Their faces were frozen, unreadable. Their eyes were fixed on Justin.

Were they waiting for a sign from him—a signal to attack?

I turned to face Anya squarely. I saw her eyes flicker aside toward Justin, then come back to me. "Who's Sally Grant?"

"The woman he hired to have Rebecca Carlton killed. We'd found out about Sally's connection to the murder, and would've arrested her. When he discovered that we knew about her, he killed her. He couldn't afford to risk her talking."

"When was Sally Grant killed?" she asked. "What time, last night?"

"Between one and two A.M. This morning, really."

231

This time, her ghetto-smart eyes were narrowed as she looked at Justin. "One o'clock—" She said it thoughtfully, speculatively.

I turned to look at Justin, who stood above me like an avenging angel. His eyes were wide and wild; the muscles of his throat were drawn tight as twisted rope. His arms were half raised, so that his white-knuckled fists rested against his breastbone. Around his mouth, the sparse sandy hair of his beard was quivering.

Was he trembling from rage? Or from fear?

Suddenly he turned on the woman. His voice was hardly more than a whisper as he hissed, "He's lying, Anya. You *know* he's lying."

She didn't answer. Instead, she simply looked at him, deciding. But now the muzzle of Canelli's .38 was lowered, pointing down at the floor.

Still whispering fiercely, Justin said, "They're out there, Anya. Two cars of them. Maybe more. They're going to attack us. We've got to escape. Now. Right now."

"They heard that shot," I said. "By now, there're a hundred men. More than a hundred."

Justin turned on me. "You're lying. *Lying.*" Suddenly, from inside his robe, he withdrew a small radio—a walkie-talkie. "This is proof," he said, holding the radio in a trembling hand. "Proof that you're lying. I have guards outside. And they report to me."

"Where did you go, last night?" Anya asked quietly. "You left about one-fifteen. A car came down the driveway—a Cadillac, without lights. I saw a woman get out and knock at your window. Then I saw you get in the car and drive away."

Now Justin whirled to face her. Standing in a crouch, he lashed her with a voice filled with fury: "Are you accusing me, you black whore?" Crooked into claws now, his hands moved spasmodically, as if he would strangle her.

Anya's whole face contracted as she stepped away from

him. Deliberately, she raised the revolver. Now her gun, too, was aimed at Justin's huge sunburst medallion.

"I already been in jail, Justin," she said softly. "I spent six months in jail, when I was eighteen. And I didn't like it. So, sure as hell, I'm not going back. Not for you. Not for anybody."

"Guards," he shouted. *"Here. Come here."*

Silently, the white-robed figures parted to make a corridor for the two guards who stood in front of the closed front door. Facing the guards, I said, "Stay there. Right there. You're not involved. Keep it that way. Justin's committed murder. He's going to jail. If you help him, you're as guilty as he is. Anya isn't going to jail for him. You don't have to go, either."

"Kill her," Justin screamed. "Kill her, the enemy among us. You've taken an oath. You've sworn to obey me. *Me.*"

I saw one of the guards advance a step, two steps. Then he stopped, looking back over his shoulder. He was waiting for his companion to join him.

The second guard didn't move. He simply stood at attention, eyes straight ahead. But, beneath the chin strap of his ceremonial helmet, I saw his Adam's apple bobbing uneasily.

Slowly the path between Justin and the guards closed. As if they were obeying some silent command, the white-robed figures turned toward Justin, watching him with their empty eyes.

First Anya had defied him. And now the guards.

Before the impassive figures, Justin's authority was threatened. He was on trial.

Justin screamed.

It was a primitive, incoherent sound, expressing an agony so pure that it was almost exquisite. He threw up his head, threw his arms wide and spoke directly to whatever gods he worshipped:

"I did it for them," he raged. "For *them*—" He lowered one arm, pointing at the silent circle that surrounded us.

"With the money, I'll start a march that will sweep the world. And they will march with me—beside me. In exchange for three evil, corrupted lives—for three who deserved to die—I gave them everything we needed. Everything—"

Still with his face upraised, arms spread wide, eyes on fire, panting for breath, he broke off. For a moment he stood silently, lips parted, as if he were intently listening for some distant voice that only he could hear.

Then, suddenly, he turned to the silent circle.

"I did it for you," he said solemnly. "Everything I've done, I've done for you. I've shown you the way to reclaim your lost souls. I've shown you how to conquer the world. With my visions, I've shown you the way. I've saved you.

"And now—" His voice dropped dramatically as he swept them with his zealot's gaze. "And now, you must save me. I am in your hands. My life is in your hands. Only you can save me from those outside, waiting to kill me."

As if his neck had snapped, his chin fell on his chest. His arms fell to his sides, inert. As he shook his head in one final gesture of submission, his hair fell free, covering his face.

From a rear rank, someone began chanting.

My—ah My—ah
In—Tu—Tami.

One by one, other voices took up the chant. The circle shifted and heaved, tightening around us. Instinctively, Anya and I moved closer together, standing over Canelli and the wounded guard.

"He did it for himself," I shouted. "He didn't do it for you. He—Christ—he killed his stepfather and his stepsister because he hated them. Because he's insane. He's a murderer. He could die for what he did. And you could, too, if you help him."

The chanting was louder now, more ominously purposeful. Standing in front of me, Justin remained motionless, head hanging, body slack: the Messiah, betrayed and resigned. Waiting for Judgment Day. By abandoning his fate to them, he'd made them a mob. Looking into the cultists' faces, I saw the empty eyes come alive, focusing purposefully on us. As the circle drew closer around us, hands were raised, fingers were flexing.

Beside me, Anya said, "Do something, for God's sake. *Do* something, or we've had it."

"Give me the gun."

Instantly, she obeyed.

I raised Canelli's revolver and fired at the ceiling.

Momentarily, the chanting broke off, then began again, on a higher, more hysterical note. Beside me, Anya screamed. A cultist was clutching her medallion; the chain was cutting into her neck, pulling her forward. I saw her set herself, and kick for the cultist's crotch. Instantly, the figure went down.

I fired in the air again—and again. The chanting was louder, hysterical now. With a gun in each hand, Western style, I crossed a leg over Canelli, standing astride him.

But the guns were useless. Each shot had made the mindless chanting more frantic—made the faceless figures more frenzied.

I felt a hand clutching at my shoulder. I slashed backward with a revolver, felt metal strike flesh, heard a grunt of pain.

"Shoot them," Anya shouted. "You've got to shoot someone."

Was she right?

Or wrong?

I couldn't decide.

Shrieking some unintelligible obscenity, she threw herself on Justin, still standing motionless, head bowed. With one hand she clutched his hair, forcing his head back. With the other hand she gripped the chain of his medallion, twisting it tight around his scrawny neck. One of her dark-brown legs crooked itself around his ankles as she tripped him, threw him to the floor. Still with her hand tangled in his hair, still clutching the chain, both legs around him now, she was trying to kill him.

Instantly, white-robed figures threw themselves on her. Arms thrashing, fingers crooked like savage talons, they were a pack of murderous savages. The rhythm of the chanting suddenly broke; the incoherent voice of a mob filled the room, screaming.

The figures thrashed in the center of the foyer, below the big oil lamp. Instinctively—without thought—I aimed at the lamp, and fired. The lamp exploded in a burst of burning oil, cascading down like a fountain on fire. Instantly, the writhing figures turned to flames. A grotesque dance erupted as arms flailed at flaming white cloth. The odor of burning oil and cloth and flesh was thick and acrid.

Something struck me in the back, hard. As I whirled, gun raised, finger on the trigger, I felt my legs buckle as a body struck my knees. A fist clubbed the side of my head, turning the demons of pain loose inside. Suddenly the room tilted as darkness closed in around me.

As I began to fall, a calm, cool corner of my mind rendered a judgment: the time had come to kill someone. Anyone. The shot should go to the head. An exploding skull, spattering brains and blood on clean white robes, might be my only hope for survival—and Canelli's, too.

As I fell across Canelli, I tried to steady my revolver on the nearest target: a shaved skull, close beside me.

Was it a woman's skull?

I couldn't be sure.

But, in nightmare slow-motion, I realized that I hadn't time to choose. Deliberately—regretfully—I tightened my finger on the trigger . . .

. . . when the upper part of the tall oak door and the two windows set high in the outer wall exploded, showering glass and wood and plaster down inside as the sound of submachine-gun fire crashed above us like hailstones from hell. The door swung open, revealing the figure of one riot-clad police-man—two policemen—three policemen. At the same instant, searchlights turned the night outside a bright, blazing white.

I relaxed my finger on the trigger and tucked both guns under me as I fell on Canelli. Then, gratefully, I closed my eyes and let the darkness come.

Twenty-four

Someone was in the room. Even with my eyes closed, I could sense someone near me.

So, slowly, I opened my eyes.

With his full lips curved in his standard impish, owlish smile, Friedman sat beside my bed. I had a fleeting impression of his round body overflowing a small chair: Humpty Dumpty, precariously balanced on a metal hospital chair.

"You've got a concussion," Friedman announced, "and also a hairline fracture of the skull. You're not supposed to talk, just listen. And, according to the doctor, you aren't even supposed to listen too much. However, I persuaded him that you'd recover faster if you were brought up-to-date. Which is why I'm here—to bring you up-to-date in as few words as possible. To which end"—he withdrew a crumpled slip of paper from the pocket of his nylon jacket—"to which end, I've made some notes." He held the paper close to a pale cone of light that came from a lamp somewhere behind my head.

"First," he said, "there's you. You're in the police ward of County Hospital, as you've probably figured out. The time

238

is six o'clock Monday morning—in other words, approximately eight hours after you and Canelli hit Aztecca—or Aztecca hit you, depending on how you look at it. As I said, you've got a medium-grade concussion and a negligible fracture of the skull. You'll be flat on your back for at least two days, and you'll be in the hospital for a week. After that, you'll be home for about a week, and then you'll start working four hours a day. In a month, the doctor guarantees that you'll be good as new. So much for you.

"Canelli, too, will be all right. The spear was deflected by his rib cage on the right side, but it tore some muscles under the arm—badly. Canelli is very, very sore, and he was in shock. But he'll probably be out of the hospital before you will. He says thanks for saving his life, which apparently you did. So much for Canelli.

"Anya, the black girl, has lots of contusions, and two broken fingers and a badly dislocated shoulder. One of her legs is severely burned. Canelli thinks she's on our side—that she helped you. I want you to nod once if she helped you a little, twice if she helped you a lot."

I nodded twice—then twice more.

"All right. Good. I'll tell the D.A.," Friedman said. "Now we come to Justin Wade. Justin is just down the hallway, under observation. The doctor is mystified about his condition. There doesn't seem to be anything physically wrong with him, except for minor burns and some of the symptoms associated with shock. Anyhow, for whatever reason, he seems to be out of his head a little. Which turned out to be a real break for us. Because he started to ramble, or else rave, depending on your point of view. Culligan thought he was in one of his patented trances, which is probably a pretty good guess.

"Anyhow, by the time I got out to Aztecca, the situation was stabilized, more or less. So, after they put you and Canelli in the ambulance, I took Justin in my car, with Culligan and a driver in front, and me in the back, with

Justin—and unmarked cars in front and back of us, with machine guns. I told the driver to take the long way around to the Hall, hoping to get a confession before the lawyers arrived. But immediately, it was obvious that Justin was pretty much out of it. So, thinking fast, I decided that his spaced-out condition was a good excuse for not taking him to the Hall at all. So I took him right here, to the hospital, and sneaked him in while the two reporters on duty were following you and Canelli—which was a stroke of luck.

"And then I got another break—a doctor who turned out to be a real cop buff. He said he helped you interrogate Hoadley, which I must say surprised me a little. Anyhow, he didn't object to me interrogating Justin, and taping the interrogation, which I did. Whether or not the tape will stand up as evidence is doubtful, since a lawyer could probably maintain that the subject wasn't in possession of his faculties.

"However, admissible or not, it all came out—everything. And, Jesus, it was fascinating. Eerie, and fascinating. He talked for at least an hour, nonstop. It was like I pushed the on button, and he started talking, like a wind-up toy.

"He started where all good stories start—with what happened to him when he was a child. Apparently his mother really screwed him up. Maybe she screwed him, too, for all I know. I kind of think she did. But, anyhow, by the time he was a teen-ager, he was obviously pretty kinky. He was a total misfit—one of those ugly, pimple-faced kids all the other kids torment. That's when his visions started, I guess.

"When his mother married Carlton, it apparently tipped Justin over the edge into his own world, and that's where he's been ever since. He obviously hated Bernard and Rebecca. He focused all his frustrations on them. If I had to guess, I'd say that, really, he lusted after Rebecca—but that love turned into hate, as the saying goes. Or maybe he really lusted after Cass, and that turned into lust for Rebecca, et cetera, et cetera. However it happened, though, he was also pretty mad at Cass, too—probably because she was screwing her husband, and assorted other men.

"So Justin apparently decided to tie it all up into one neat bundle. He waited until Cass was off for her weekly roll in the hay with Donald Fay. He took her car, and went to the airport, and jinxed the airplane. He didn't think it was wrong, not at all. He was doing it for Aztecca. That's how it all started, apparently—that's what focused everything for him. See, he'd tried to get money from Bernard, for Aztecca. Bernard declined. So, naturally, he had to die. Rebecca also declined—and died for the same reason. Or maybe the survivorship clause in Bernard's will sealed Rebecca's fate. It's hard to tell. Anyhow, Justin contacted Sally with a straight business proposition. He gave Sally some on account, with more to come when he got his hands on Bernard's estate.

"Actually," Friedman said, "he was pretty damn clever. His so-called efforts to help us were nothing more than a device for throwing us off the track—and throwing suspicion on Sam Wright, who he also considered evil, probably because he'd screwed Rebecca. Ron Massey suffered the same fate, of course, but only after Justin realized that he couldn't get into Sam Wright's house, to steal something of his. He was able to get into Massey's house through the rear door, undetected—just as Massey thought. In fact, talk about your cool customer, he took a cab to Massey's house, after he'd killed Sally—and even had the cabbie wait for him, and then take him back to the Crescent. There's an outdoor phone booth less than a block away from the Crescent, so calling the cab wasn't a problem. He told the cabbie that he'd lost his keys and couldn't find a spare set at home, so he had to go back to the Crescent. Then he called another cab and got back to Aztecca. His total cab fare was more than thirty dollars—which he took from Sally's purse, if you can believe it. And, yes, the gun's still out there somewhere below the Crescent. He got the gun at a pawnshop, a month ago.

"So we've got a full and complete confession," Friedman said, for whatever it's worth after a good lawyer has his innings. And, already, it's shaping up as one of the trials of the decade, with media coverage like you wouldn't believe.

Cityside reporters and a couple of local TV cameramen came with the reinforcements Culligan ordered, so the whole show at Aztecca is on film. Incidentally, Culligan did a damn good job. He heard your first shot and responded immediately. But he was smart enough to go through the trees, instead of up the driveway, so he didn't get spotted. And, as soon as he looked in through the windows and saw the situation, he knew it was more than he could handle. So he called for help before he made his move.

"He also had some luck," Friedman admitted. "Justin's troops were inside, it develops. Not outside. But, anyhow, Culligan did a good job. With your approval, I'm putting him in for a departmental commendation. Nod once, please."

I nodded.

"Good," Friedman said, rising briskly to his feet. "That's settled. Now I'm going home. I'll look in on you later today. I'm glad you weren't badly hurt. When I saw them loading you into the ambulance, I have to admit that I thought maybe you had your brains scrambled." He dropped a hand on my shoulder and smiled. It was a curiously self-conscious gesture, and his smile was almost shy: a small boy's smile, embarrassed to show emotion.

I watched him leave the room, then let my eyes close slowly. The bed was warm and the sheets smelled fresh and clean, recalling sickroom scenes from my childhood. Once, when I'd been six years old, I'd had the flu. I'd had a high fever, and sometimes it seemed that I could hear faraway music. When the fever was highest, I'd thought that the music might have come from heaven. But when the fever dropped, I realized that the music had been an illusion—and heaven, too.

"Frank?"

Was it my mother calling?

No. She'd died four years ago. I'd been with her when she died, shrunken by cancer, asking for my father, who'd left her when I was fourteen, and gone off with his secretary.

But the touch was hers: a soft, cool hand, light on my forehead.

Why? How?

I opened my eyes.

Ann was standing close beside my bed, bending over me, kissing me on the lips. It was a lover's kiss, quick and fierce, promising passion. Then, gently, she kissed me on the forehead. It was a mother's kiss, promising warmth and protection.

And—yes—I heard her murmur: "When you leave here, you're coming to my house. I'm going to take care of you, Frank."

"Yes," I whispered. "Please."

About the Author

COLLIN WILCOX was born in Detroit and educated at Antioch College. Since 1950 he has lived in San Francisco, where he operated a small business before becoming a full-time mystery/suspense novelist. Mr. Wilcox writes that "the most important things in my life are my two sons, my Victorian house, my typewriter, my pilot's license, my books and my ten-speed bike."